A Dark Holme Publication

Ethereal Nightmares

An Anthology of Twisted Tales

A Publication by
Dark Holme Publishing
Edited by Kerry Holmes
Cover design by Lena Ashford

Copyright © 2024 Dark Holme Publishing All rights reserved

2nd Edition

Paperback ISBN 978-1-0686164-4-0
Hardback ISBN 978-1-0686164-1-9

The characters and events portrayed in this book are fictitious. Any similarity to real persons, living or dead, is coincidental and not intended by the author.

No part of this book may be reproduced, or stored in a retrieval system, or transmitted in any form or by any means, electronic, mechanical, photocopying, recording, or otherwise, without express written permission of the publisher.

www.darkholmepublishing.uk

Contents

A word by our Founder

Alright folks, buckle up and get ready for a rollercoaster ride through the realms of darkness and fantasy! But before we dive into the shadows, let's take a moment to give credit where credit's due.

First and foremost, a massive shout-out to the one and only Dr. Rob O'Connor. Without his guidance and inspiration, Dark Holme Publishing wouldn't even be a flicker in the literary world. So, let's raise our metaphorical hats to Dr. Rob O'Connor!

Next, a heartfelt thank you to each and every one of you wonderful souls out there. Whether you submitted your spine-chilling tales, shared our posts like wildfire, or simply followed along with eager anticipation, you are the lifeblood of Dark Holme's debut anthology, *Ethereal Nightmares: An Anthology of Twisted Tales*.

Gather close, fellow adventurers, for we embark on a descent into the labyrinthine depths of our imaginations. Here, we've assembled a macabre collection of stories that will set your hearts pounding, your spines tingling, and your minds adrift in landscapes laced with both dread and dark wonder.

From bone-chilling horror to mind-bending dark fantasy, we've got it all lined up for you. So, whether you prefer a cup of steaming hot tea, a cold beer, or a classy glass of wine, grab your beverage of choice, kick back, and let's dive headfirst into *Ethereal Nightmares*!

Get ready for a wild ride, my friends. The shadows await, and they're calling your name! Let's dive in and lose ourselves in the darkness together.

Kerry Holmes
Dark Holme Publishing

The Babies

J.M. Faulkner

Jack dropped from the windowsill, slipped on the bathroom tiles, and caught the sink with his elbow—crack. He sucked in a lungful of brisk air, held it, and waited for the tramping of feet and snap of light switches.

Nothing. A sluggish drip came from the corner shower basin. Jack gave his throbbing elbow a rub and puffed through the hole in his balaclava.

Behind him, the ground-floor window was raised to the top of the frame, the sash panel beside the lock smashed out. A hand reached over the debris glistening on the sill, and Jack lifted Michelle inside.

'We go straight for the jewellery,' he said, dragging his snowy boots on a bathmat. The age-old habit of stomping his feet clean before entering a neighbour's house had kicked in, just beneath his level of acknowledgement.

'I'm not thick, Jack, you don't need to repeat yourself. No reason to believe the old lady has much cash lying around.'

'Old ladies *always* hoard cash. Don't trust the banks.'

They edged their way through the hallway in the dark, feeding the cornice of the half-panelled wall through their hands, their shoulders bumping portraits. Once they reached the living room, Jack flicked on the ceiling light.

Michelle bounded back into the hall, avoiding the glow. Her eyes were bright and incredulous in her balaclava. 'What are you doing?'

'Relax, Shell, I watched the house for two to three days. Old bird has to be staying with family.'

But could she have slipped in without his noticing? Three weeks on the trot, Thursday through Monday, the doddering homeowner at number 27 had left her sizable, detached house empty. When last Thursday rolled around, Jack had reversed his Fiat 500 into the gloom of an alley nearby and shut off the engine. He wasn't drumming the steering wheel long before a taxi pulled into 27's driveway. The routine was playing out as expected, with one exception—

Michelle shook an envelope at him, but it was easy enough to pick out the addressee written on the front: *Mrs. Gretchen Jones.*

'Can't believe you talked me into this.' A howl threatened to break through her whisper. The envelope scrunched in her fingers. 'Imagine Daryl found out his parents were a couple of common crooks. Thieves!'

'Sorry I didn't get furloughed, Shell.' He sighed and massaged his brow with a balled fist. 'Look, this place is an absolute mansion. We get in, we get out. Whatever we sell will tide us over until I find a job.' Michelle held his gaze, and Jack added, 'Don't think I'm proud of this. We get out and never mention it again.'

Something on the coffee table caught his attention. A bell with a brass head and wooden shaft.

'Here.' He walked over and raised the bell high toward the

ceiling. Before Michelle could so much as inhale, he snapped his arm straight.

It must have been a six or seven-bedroom house, but at that moment, with the bell clanging inside their skulls, it felt like the building had shrunk to the size of a closet with the two of them locked inside.

The clamour dissipated, and Jack dropped the bell into the plush carpet. He wasn't in the habit of scaring people, so the thick lipped grin that etched across his mouth took him as much by surprise as it did unease. 'See, we get out of this unscathed, be the parents that brought the bread home during the downturn.'

'And what about the guilt of doing it, Jack?'

Despite the unbroken harmony throughout the house following the bell ring, Jack crept upstairs with the lights switched off. Playing the big man while Michelle did an impression of Bambi in headlights was one thing, quite another was leading them into the unknown.

A creak on the landing stifled his step. His eyelids dropped like the blade of a guillotine, the voluntary darkness protecting him from whatever lurked in the involuntary. He shifted and heard the cry of his own stupid foot.

Michelle's groan on the stairs was soon in his wake. She couldn't disguise the triumph in her voice. 'After you.'

Jack edged one way in the corridor, and Michelle another. He heard the squeak of door hinges and thumping of drawers as she committed to business, room by room, like an old hand.

He found less than three digits in notes and a bunch of costume jewellery in a dresser in the master bedroom. He stuffed his rucksack full. The weight on his back, he thought about Daryl peering up at him from his pushchair, a picture of innocent adoration.

What would Daryl think of them if he ever found out about the burglary? Because that's what it was, right? Burglary? No, the word had a severity to it that sat uncomfortably. This was a…

Jack sucked his teeth. Why did Michelle have to say that thing about guilt for?

And all this trouble for what? They were three months late on rent and the loot here wouldn't cover half of it. To tempt Sleepy Steve into babysitting Daryl for an hour tonight, they had surrendered the last supermarket brand pizza in their freezer. They couldn't peel back their mattress and hand him stashed change because there wasn't any.

Last week, with the landlord banging on their front window and threatening to make them homeless—Daryl along with them—robbing the old lady felt like the only option. Damn, it felt like the reasonable option.

But the only thing Jack had accomplished was stealing a heavy conscience.

He was thinking he couldn't let Michelle rattle him, that Daryl hadn't started teething yet, when he slid open the wardrobe door and spotted the safe.

It squatted in the gloom, a hulking, dusk-green box that stretched the width of the wardrobe and came to his hip. It reminded him more of a treasure chest than a safe, something better discovered buried in sand than in the back of an old lady's wardrobe. No dial. Floral and decorative feet. A rusted, brass keyhole that winked at him.

Jack pictured himself wrapping Daryl a Hornby train set for Christmas, a gift he wouldn't feel ashamed of sharing. He'd get a job eventually, and if his colleagues were inclined to ask, he'd say: I bought my Daryl a Hornby train set for under the tree.

Now, if only he had—

'What's that?'

He twisted around. Michelle's silhouette blocked the doorway, pointing to the bedside table. A baby monitor.

Amazingly, she hadn't noticed the safe.

She crossed the room and examined the screen. 'Why would an old lady own—'

The screen illuminated in her hands, blinding them both. Jack heard the monitor clatter between her feet, but he didn't find out why until his sight adjusted.

A baby was beaming into the camera lens.

Neither of them was fond of baby monitors, from an aesthetic point of view. There was something uncanny about seeing your normally pink-skinned child through a night vision filter, like a criminal caught on CCTV. Using one meant they could cuddle up in front of the television of an evening, but they spent as much time staring into the monitor watching for the rise and fall of Daryl's chest, attentive to the tin quality of his respiration, as they did enjoying themselves.

When their son slept, neither of them had to look hard to imagine the blanket inside the cot looked like the white interior of a coffin.

'I checked every room,' Michelle said. 'I...'

'Could be connected to where she's staying. You know, with family.' Jack swallowed, finding himself too quick to supply an answer. Unless her relatives lived next door, wouldn't the signal have been too far away?

Whatever. What mattered now was finding the key to that safe.

'Right. Yeah.' She put the monitor down carefully, like doing otherwise might have disturbed the baby. 'You can connect anywhere with the internet these days.'

'Totally... Here, guess what I fou—'

'Look, a tablet.'

Caught off guard by the baby monitor and mesmerised by the safe, Jack had forgotten why they were here. Torches, lockpicks, tools—they didn't have any of that. They had come with a camping rucksack, winter gloves, and hats they could roll down their faces with eye level circles cut out the front. This was strictly a smash n grab crime, not professional. A one-off.

But for a moment there, Jack had fallen into the illusion they were bank robbers on a heist, Bonnie and Clyde with a safe to bust. Picking up a tablet, though, that was the kind of light-fingered tomfoolery on par with his experience level.

'Nice catch. Let's bag it and get out.'

Michelle crawled across the foot of the mattress. She swooped up the tablet on the second bedside table, and Jack unzipped the rucksack, ready.

The tablet lit up in her hands. She stiffened, gasped in the dark.

'What? Shell?'

A stifled sounding squeak escaped her throat.

When Jack was a child, his mother used to read to him until he drifted to sleep. If that failed, or if she couldn't stay any longer because of a planned phone call with Aunt Mary Jane, he resisted sleep with the utmost intensity. A navy bathrobe hung from the bedroom door hanger, slack and completely still. In the dark, though, when the door was shut and the curtains were closed, the thing looked positively alive. The edges blurred and snaked. Jack would squint into the foggy corner, trying to chase the illusion away before it became a nightmare, and would discover it was really a bathrobe after all. Lifeless again until his eyelids came over heavy.

Michelle reminded him of that bathrobe, stirring at the edges while at the same time being completely inanimate. But if he could focus enough, squint, then maybe he would be able to make head and tail of her, see her take a breath.

'Shell?' Sweat broke out on his forehead. 'Say something.'

Her eyes shone like torches on the screen.

'Dammit, Michelle. Shell!'

Her lips fluttered, carrying out a voiceless conversation.

'Do I have to come over there?'

'It's dead.' It came out muffled. Her mouth sounded wet and trembly. 'Purple skin, bulging eyes—Jack, it's looking right at me.'

He made his way around the bed and slapped the tablet out of her hands. It padded on the duvet. 'Don't be stupid. Let's get...'

He saw it.

'C-can't be real.' His tongue lumped up in his throat. The baby was leering right into the camera, right at him. Utterly lifeless. 'It's fake.'

She started reaching down, and Jack wanted to launch the device across the room, but he found he could neither move nor speak under the baby's glare. Something otherworldly held him in a ridged tangle.

'Could be a static image,' Michelle said, turning it over in her hands. 'A picture. Do you think so, Jack? It could be a picture, right?'

'What's that?'

A crude message was scratched into the tablet's back, as if by the point of a knitting needle through the plastic. It ran straight through the logo:

Don't upset the babies.

The tablet slipped through Michelle's fingers. She tried to catch it with her knee, but that only made things worse. It cartwheeled over her prying arms and whacked something in the corner of the room, hard.

And at that moment the ceiling light in the corridor snapped on and poured into the master bedroom at their feet.

Both retreated a step.

'Jack, what the hell? Get me out of here. I don't want to be here anymore. I don't want to do this.'

He pinned a forefinger to his lips and shushed her, gently patted her arm. He hadn't heard the front door open, nor was there any sound coming from the staircase. No keys jangling or scraping shoes.

'Stay here. I need to check it out.'

A cinch from Michelle's fingers on his underarm prevented his escape.

'No, no, that's how morons get…' She appeared to be searching for the right word, and settled on, 'in trouble.'

Trouble? He had staked out the house for days and not so much as a curtain had stirred within. A leaflet flapped in the letterbox, no one signed for the parcel that came and went back to the van, and no doting neighbours popped by to water old Gretchen's houseplants. If ever there was a friendless hermit, Monday through Thursday she holed up in number 27. From the moment she went doddering down the path, the house had been empty. Jack was certain of it.

But he couldn't help but recall the gust that stopped her short of the taxi's passenger door, as though to whisper, *you've forgotten your purse*. Leaves barrelled and scraped over the asphalt. The hem of her shawl buffeted a shadow on her face.

She locked eyes with Jack through the Fiat's windshield.

Then she was in the taxi and out of sight.

'We'll be fine,' he told Michelle, although the hair on his neck pricked up, remembering how his trainers had been propped up on the dashboard, and how the old woman had taken the wind out of him—but she couldn't have seen him. The alleyway had been as black as Hades that night. 'She's not due back until tomorrow evening.'

'And if you're wrong?'

He broke away from her and stuck his neck out the door, first left and then right. Nothing appeared out of the ordinary, except for an opulence that struck him as Victorian. Oak coloured wainscotting occupied the lower portion of the walls from the landing, down the staircase and through to the lobby visible through the banister.

Perhaps his mistake was scanning for a shawled, crone like figure. A nose bulbous with rosacea.

Only after he gave up searching for her did he realise the chandelier suspended from the ceiling hung like a black cobweb. Not a glimmer of light burned in its crystals. What's more, the picture frames cramming the walls were empty. No, not empty. They were occupied with flat, reflective screens.

Baby monitors covered every inch of wall space, obscuring the sallow wallpaper peaking beneath. Feeling their way through the dark earlier, they had been unwittingly bumping and touching them.

Now they bleached the lobby and landing in light.

Jack rubbed his sweating, dirty palms on his jeans.

Michelle was pleading with him from the bedroom, but he couldn't make out a word. Whether she was whispering, or if he had compartmentalised and mentally packaged her away somewhere, he couldn't tell.

There was a knotty, sangria coloured smear about a foot wide in the cream carpet runner. It stretched the length of the entire landing.

Michelle's fingers bit into his underarm. 'Anyone there?'

He returned a weak shake of his head, not really seeing anything but the spectacle before them. The monitors hadn't turned themselves on, that was for sure.

She pushed into the doorway so that they shared the frame and peered around, and Jack deferred completely to her reaction. Her eyes were slits, looking for a figure lurking in a corner somewhere, as he had been. When she stepped into the light, Jack determined to delegate all responsibility to her. If she couldn't see anything, then neither could he.

The ground appeared to drop beneath her; such was the force that launched her into the wall beside him. A monitor fell loose and tumbled onto the carpet runner. It came to a standstill and switched on, a forked split in the screen illuminating like a bolt of lightning.

A baby peered up at them through the cracks.

One by one, the monitors pulsed an electric white, racing toward them.

Michelle retreated into the doorway. 'What the fuck?' Her chest was heaving up, up, down; up, up, down. She clutched at her heart. 'They're everywhere. Jack? Jack—'

'Shhh.' He caught her lapel and pressed her into the door frame, resisting the urge to clap a hand over her mouth. 'Let's not freak out, eh? We go straight down those stairs, slowly, and out the way we came in. With me?'

'... Can't.'

'Only thing scarier than going out there is staying put.'

She closed her eyes, apparently clearing her head, and Jack smoothed her lapel with a feathery touch. His bid to keep her quiet had been rougher than intended, but she accepted his tactile apology without complaint, if she was conscious of it at all.

'Right.' Michelle exhaled through her nostrils. She peered into the landing through the doorway, where the house made not so much as a creak. 'Slowly. Right. But don't let go of my hand. *Slow.*'

Attached, they stepped over the stained runner and edged their way to the head of the staircase, where they paused to look over the handrail.

The front door—

Closed.

Shoes—

Neatly lined up.

The rug—

Spotless, without snow.

Jack puffed through his lips. If Gretchen had caught them red-handed, he didn't know what they would have done. But he couldn't have brought himself to hurt her. He knew that much.

Michelle squeezed his hand.

Softly, she said, 'The babies are watching.'

'I know.'

'Some of them are blue, Jack. They're…'

'I know.' He didn't look up—he didn't need to. He could *feel* their gaze pouring over him like cold milk down the back of his shirt. 'Ready?'

He took a step and the topmost stair groaned. A thousand eyes were on him, and he found himself thinking, *don't upset the babies.*

'J-Jack…' Her fingers were wire in his palm, grounding his jitters. He could be brave for her, if not himself. 'That blood on the c-carpet runner?'

'Ask me later,' he whispered.

When they reached the ground floor, the winter air leaking through the broken bathroom window stretched out to greet them. It took everything Jack had to keep from bolting. Every shadow had the potential to explode into a shrieking hag.

The old homeowner—Gretchen—had seemed short sighted, wooden, and arthritic in her movements. Vulnerable. But not now.

In the living room the bell remained on the carpet, skirt facing up, clapper poking out like a tongue. Jack doubled over and inhaled a whooping, bellyful of breath. Stress left his lungs in a quivering rush.

Michelle nudged him, her eyes kinetic with urgency.

Jack gave a tired shake of his head. 'Minute. There's no monitors.' He pointed around the room in an arc. He couldn't catch his breath, so inhaled sharply through his nostrils and let it all out. 'If we can make noise anywhere, it's here.'

'You sure?'

'Rang that bell, didn't I?'

'But what about Steve?' she creaked. 'We said we'd be back in an hour, tops. Uh-uh, he told us he ain't a babysitter, Jack.'

'Relax, Sleepy ain't selfish. Daryl's good until we get back,' he panted. 'Moment. Please.'

Once Jack had composed himself, Michelle insisted they move on, having gathered some of the courage Jack had burned through. They crept through the hall while keeping a shoulder width's distance from the walls on either side. A frigid breeze rushed from the bathroom ahead, and the sweat festering beneath Jack's clothes nipped at his skin.

In the kitchen next to the bathroom Jack saw a key rack above an unwashed pile of frying pans. Burned oil and animal fat mingled with the cold. On the left was a set of twinkling yale keys; to the right, a thick skeleton type key—something for a garden gate or chest, with an off green colour and several rust gold keychains. All of them bells.

And then Jack felt a tug on his arm. Michelle led him into the bathroom. The glacial air made him shiver, set his nose to trickling on his upper lip.

'Careful,' she said, 'the floor's wet from our boots.' She swiped the glass debris from the sill, and it sprinkled and clinked on the floor. She mounted the sill, tottered, and landed outside with a soft pluff in the snow.

She scrubbed her coat down, then held out her arms to catch the rucksack.

But Jack didn't budge. Her face grew blurry and distant. The key in the kitchen, that thing was big enough to be a paperweight. It had to be for the safe.

'Jack?'

'We went through all this trouble for nothing.'

'What?'

'So, we pay our bills for another month, whoopee. Before we know it, the landlord is sticking his nose through the letterbox while we cringe behind the sofa again, playing like we're not at home.'

'Fuck money. Daryl is waiting for us. Come home.'

He dropped his chin and gripped the window frame. 'I can't.'

Michelle was speechless, open-mouthed. A copper skinned innocent with a snowy backdrop. He should have kept the burglary to himself.

'Sorry I talked you into this.'

Jack shoved away from the window, and a half-scream, half-whisper chased him inside. Gritting his teeth, he hurried into the kitchen, distancing himself from his inner voice crying, *The kitchen door hadn't been open when you came in.* No bother, he yanked the jingling key from the rack and came to a halt in the living room.

The bell in the carpet. Brass body, wooden handle.

Some part of his brain said, *Dinner bell.* Then it adopted his mother's lethargic tones: *You can't have the Hornby train set—put that down. You're greedy, Jacky, that's your problem. Oh, it's fine now while Mother's minding your pennies. But you wait until you're all grow'd up like me. Greed will get the better of you, and you'll be sorry you ever asked me for a Hornby train set.*

Ahead, the hallway's baby monitors emitted a radiant path. The hair on Jack's neck pricked up. He thought, Last chance.

He put his head down and strode into the glow. The monitors at his flanks blinked in recognition, the babies tracking his disturbance with beady, vacant eyes.

The foot of the staircase came into view. December air from the bathroom followed and stirred up the adrenalin coursing through his veins. It proved impossible to suppress the vibrations that whipped at his solar plexus, shortened his breath.

Growing up, his mother never had enough money, either. He suspected meth and marijuana were the problem, because sometimes when she ducked behind the sofa, the landlord's silhouette was visible through the curtain. Other times it was a branch from a maple at the end of the driveway.

And despite what his mother said, he didn't have an Aunt Mary Jane.

Jack didn't want that future for Daryl, one tainted by poverty, paranoia and uncompassionate landlords.

The cycle had to break.

Like ripping a band-aid off, he thought, as he spread his weight on the first step. A third step followed a second, and up and up he climbed. He kept on walking and walking…

And walking?

He peered up from the wainscoting. The staircase—an obtusely lit tunnel—stretched ahead of him. He had ascended all of three steps.

Floaters flickered in his field of vision, and he came over dizzy. He pounded for the top, but the landing fled from him. The stair runner strung out like a piece of gum, and he felt himself becoming unmoored from the ground, tumbling freefall towards the ceiling.

His boot snagged the lip of the top step. The wood groaned and Jack caught the handrail, both feet striking solid ground.

Somewhere, a baby chuckled. His bladder twinged.

Outside the master bedroom, he bent at the waist and sucked in a breath. His mind was unravelling. Sure, the baby monitors could have been an elaborate setup, a prank, but not what he experienced on the stairs.

A figure tramped across the lobby, visible through the banister.

Jack's eyelids vaulted open. He planted his fist in the carpet to keep from passing out. Heart lurching, he ducked into the master bedroom, put an ear to the wooden door, and pushed until he heard a quiet click. His legs gave out and he slumped into the wall.

The figure's build was too slight to be Michelle—Michelle hadn't been able to climb through the window without his help, ruling her out. Which left who, exactly? His imagination, of course. How else could he have floated upstairs? How else could reality contort the stair runner like superheated plastic?

Fear, plain and simple. Without Michelle to protect he was a coward, because in reality she was his anchor. He was nothing before they met, and he was nothing without her now.

He kneeled in front of the safe and retrieved the key from his pocket. Same design, all right, but he fought to penetrate the lock. The bell keychains jingle jangled. Testing left and right, eventually the safe door audibly popped and yawned under its own weight.

Not a penny in sight. The safe was empty except for a propped-up baby monitor, a glowing supernova in the black of space.

Little Daryl was reading his father with round, curious eyes. He cooed and kicked his feet, one bare and without a sock.

Behind Daryl, a shadow loomed in an inky corner by the wardrobe, just in the periphery of view.

Jack's diaphragm kicked for oxygen—no luck. When he took a breath, a sensation not unlike a pair of fists reached inside him, kneaded around, and groped his lungs. He pulled the balaclava from his head and wiped the snot collecting on his upper lip with it.

'Steven?'

He squinted into the monitor, trying to form a face out of the jet-black background. The shadow was too short to be his friend, far too reminiscent of the figure that had tramped across the lobby moments earlier—and why couldn't it be the same figure?

No, that was his mother's paranoia talking.

But if the staircase could transform seamlessly under his boots, then why couldn't the entity in the lobby and Daryl's bedroom be one and the same, jumping between locations just to taunt him?

… To punish him.

The entity trod stiffly toward the cot. The floor creaked, and Daryl craned his neck, perhaps thinking his mother had come to feed him.

The darkness inside the room created a fuzzy illusion not unlike the bathrobe from Jack's childhood. The entity's arms hung low at its knees, were as thin as broom handles and finished with a bristle of claws.

Daryl sniffled.

'Stop.' Jack whacked the safe.

The key and spiralling keychains vaulted from his grip and splashed on the wooden floor by his knee.

The baby monitors in the hallway fluttered white hot rays, but Jack hardly noticed. He gnawed the inside of his cheek and tasted blood.

Daryl let out a bray and turned back to the camera. A tear ballooned from the corner of one eye.

Jack took the monitor in hand, stood, and screamed Daryl's name at the top of his lungs.

The baby monitors around the house emitted a speaker breaking shrill. Jack cupped his ears and shrank to his knees. Gritting his teeth, he attempted to oust the hiss from his brain with a wail of his own. The volume surged to a zenith, scratched, and cut off.

The intruder in Daryl's bedroom evaporated into the floor. Everything fell into a profound quiet.

Jack panted and wiped his leaky nose. He wiped the fringe and damp stuck to his forehead. In the monitor between his feet, Daryl stuck out a trembling bottom lip.

And although his son couldn't see or hear him, Jack crouched and found himself speaking in soothing tones:

'It's okay, Daryl. When you're poor… You know, I got

greedy. I shouldn't have. But Daddy's here now. There you go, deep breaths. Good boy. Gooood boy.'

Michelle burst through Daryl's bedroom door and swooped him into her arms. Sleepy Steve came blundering behind, doubling over to breathe. Jack took the monitor in hand; he couldn't help but weep.

The mattress squeaked behind him. A spring. Something shuffled out of bed and two feet, one after the other, nailed the bedside rug.

Jack stiffened. His tongue engorged in his throat. He knew the voice was coming before he heard it, before the knife-like bristles lay on his shoulders, before the breath disturbed the hair on his crown—a whisper burning with hostility:

'*You upset the babies.*'

Ashur Kang vs the Army of the Undead

Caleb James K

I

'In times of war, we wait for peace. In times of peace, we wait for the next war.'

—Herroclese The Elder

*T*he crisp night air kept the stench of death at bay. Ice crystals blanketed the field and buried the bodies in a sea of white that sparkled like tiny diamonds beneath the moonlit sky. All was quiet except for the howling winds of winter tearing across the solemn plains. The only victor of this battle was Obidion the Ferryman, who was eager to transport the souls of the dead from this world to the next.

In the mountain Kingdom of Sansylgate, King Emmerick Wulfbrok sat alone in his library when a knocking upon the chamber door roused him from his reading.

'Who disturbs me at this hour,' the King said with enmity in his voice.

'It is I, Your Grace. Gilliam Chasetree.' His words—though spoken with great urgency—were softened by the solid chamber door. 'I come with news from the battlefield.'

'Enter.'

Chasetree, a stout man with tree trunk legs, a wide torso, and short arms hardened with muscle, rushed into the library.

'Permission to speak, Your Grace.'

'Go on.' King Wulfbrok set the book he was reading on a small table and folded his hands in his lap. 'Where do we stand?' he said, slowly encircling his wrinkled thumbs around one another.

'Well,' Chasetree started, dropping to one knee in front of his King. 'It is not good, Your Grace.' He took in a deep breath and exhaled slowly. 'There were no survivors.'

King Wulfbrok turned to his right and gazed out the window. The flames from the nearby fireplace danced in his clear black pupils, but his irises—grey like the sea after a storm—betrayed the fear he felt in his heart.

'So, all is lost then?'

Chasetree rose to his feet and stood with defiant confidence. 'No, Sire. As I said, there were no survivors. Not on our side nor theirs.'

The King pulled his attention away from the window and looked back at Chasetree. 'You mean to tell me, not a single soul left the battlefield alive?'

'That is correct.'

'How can that be?'

Chasetree steadied his nerves the best he could. 'It is most peculiar but not unheard of. I can only surmise to say that every man fought to the bitter end.'

'And the scouts' findings?'

'They have not reported back yet.' Chasetree bit his lip. The King was not known for holding back his temper. 'It was a Garnarian Sheepsman who reported the outcome of the battle to us.'

'A Sheepsman!' The King exploded. 'We have the fastest riders of the Five Kingdoms, and you tell me a filthy Garnarian Sheepsman learned of the outcome before our own scouts?'

'Your Grace, the weather conditions have not been favourable to—'

'To Hell with the weather conditions! This news should have been brought to my attention this morning.' He struggled to his feet. Chasetree attempted to help but King Wulfbrok smacked his hands away. 'I need to meet with the Oracle. It is the only hope we have for salvaging what remains of our land.'

Chasetree cast his eyes toward the ground and King Wulfbrok watched as the man tried to conceal the worry spreading over his rugged face.

'The Oracle is available for counsel, yes?'

'Sire. No one has seen…' Chasetree paused. He knew any lie that passed through his lips could very well send him to the gallows. It would be best to tell the truth and face the King's wrath. 'The Oracle has made it known that She does not wish to speak with you.'

'What!' The King's voice thundered with renewed anger. 'How can she deny me my right to counsel? I am of Datretian blood spanning back 13 generations.' He slammed his balled-up fist on the wooden table next to him. 'There would be no Sansylgate if it were not for the sacrifices made by my family. Their blood is one with the soil of this very land!'

'Yes, Sire. But there is nothing we can do. The Oracle's word is Divine Law.'

The King's white beard shook imperceptibly as the deep well of rage inside of him bubbled to the surface. 'Why does she refuse me?'

Chasetree knelt on one knee again. This time he bowed his head before the King. 'Forgive me. She said the blood spilt upon the Holy Plains was the ultimate insult to the Gods.' He raised his head and met the King's concerned eye. 'The blood on your hands can no longer be washed clean, so says the Divine Law of the Five Kingdoms and beyond.'

'So that is how it is?' The King spoke softly as if all the fight had left his spirit. 'I am no longer pure enough to speak with the Divine?' He looked down at his hands, scarred and misshapen from many years of battle. 'Like all great men before me, the time has come.'

King Wulfbrok extended a hand to Chasetree. The commander took it, and the King pulled him to his feet.

The King embraced Chasetree. 'May death be kind to me, my son,' he whispered in the commander's ear. 'May it come swiftly.' His words grew louder. 'And if I have truly lived a righteous life, I pray the Gods to grant me one honour. In death, I pray that in their great mercy, I shall finally know peace.'

With that, the King dismissed Chasetree and resumed his reading. Only, the words no longer held any importance to him. His mind was elsewhere; it was with the thousands of dead in the frozen field of Thodornia. And with any luck, he too would soon meet the Ferryman and be allowed to dine with his ancestors for all eternity.

If only the Gods so allowed it.

II

'Beauty can be found in any nightmare if you dare to search for it.'

—Doma of Medd

The morning sun warmed the ice-crusted field and revealed the horror of the previous day's battle. Bodies—strewn about as far as the eye could see—groaned and twitched as the gases of decay escaped the corpses. But it was a different sound, the collective murmurings of bewildered souls, that disrupted the morning peace.

High above the land in a remote mountain cave, the Oracle gazed upon the scene by using the sacred Orb of Medd. Normally inaudible to the living, the ethereal voices of the dead cried out from the mystical Orb.

Using the Orb to communicate with the Gods, the Oracle learned that when the death toll rises too quickly—such as when the Goddess of the Earth realm unleashes her vengeance upon man, or as with a massacre such as that of the Battle of Thodornia—Obidion is unable to clear the land of souls adequately; he is unable to ferry them all to the Netherworld before the portal between worlds closes.

The Gods further explained that in death, when the soul is without a body for too long, it becomes restless and will wander the Earth. When this happens, the barrier between the two worlds—the world of the living and the world of the dead—breaks down and the harmony of nature becomes unbalanced. But what troubled the Oracle most was the revelation that when the lost souls belong to that of fallen soldiers, they might return to their bodies and wander the Earth as the Draugr: the undead warriors of legend who are impervious to pain and kill the living with their superhuman strength.

Through her milky-white eyes, the Oracle watched this terrible image materialize in the Orb and then bowed her head in prayer. If these many lost souls interact with the living, a plague unlike any the world has ever known will decimate the Five Kingdoms.

'To thy great and benevolent Gods of the Five Kingdoms and beyond, please hear me now. The portal between worlds closes while souls numbered in the thousands remain in the world of the living. Honourable Obidion is unable to ferry every soul on his own, for the task is too large. I must ask of you now great ones, what are we to do? How can we rectify the insult that man has bestowed upon you by allowing such death to take place upon the Holy Plains of Thodornia?'

The cave was still, and it would remain so until the Gods responded, or the Five Kingdoms crumbled.

All the Oracle could do was wait. Her prayers were as strong as ever, but her body had grown weak with age. When she was young, she could communicate with the Gods whenever it was required of her. Her mind and body had been extraordinary and her abilities unparalleled in the Five Kingdoms. But now, her only working tools were patience and her unwavering faith in the Gods she worshipped so resolutely—with her faith being the reason for choosing such a secluded location where she could pray in peace.

The stillness of the cave was a comfort to her—it always had been—but an unexpected sound disrupted its tranquillity. The Oracle turned around, but it was too late. Evil was already upon her.

***

Among the heaps of the dead, one shape began to stir. A moan of pain rose from beneath the grey sky as the figure—

struggling against a mound of frozen corpses—rolled a Zuthunian soldier to the side. With a powerful thrust, a tall man with dark skin caked in gore emerged from a pile of severed limbs and bloody torsos. He breathed ice and shivered fiercely, but he was alive. If he were to search for whom to thank for his life being spared—whether in the form of God or man—he would need to look no farther than the dead who shielded his unconscious body from the unforgiving elements throughout the night.

The man got to his feet and braced himself on unsteady legs. He scanned the battlefield in every direction and a wave of despair washed over him. Other than the wind, hardly a sound broke the eerie silence of the all-encompassing dead.

He tried to yell out but had no voice. An intense numbness made it almost impossible to ascertain the severity of his injuries—which were no doubt numerous.

Bringing his hands to his throat, he came upon a rope pulled taut around his neck. And while he had no feeling in his fingers, raised edges of skin flapped loosely below the rope. The flesh was likely torn and raw.

With this discovery, brief flashes of memory returned to form a gruesome picture: the sound of galloping horse hooves cracked the frozen Earth, the burning pain of the jagged terrain stripped the skin from his back, and flickers of the grey sky faded in and out as the rope tightened around his neck. These fragmented images were like a bad dream reflected in the broken pieces of ice that surrounded him.

Who had dragged him through the battlefield? He did not know. Equally as mysterious was how he had managed to survive the attack, but those were things he would have to contemplate later. For now, escaping this frozen wasteland of death was all that mattered.

The man tried stepping over a body and almost fell. Prolonged exposure to the cold had rendered his legs stiff and unresponsive. He knew he had to find shelter soon or he would succumb to the frigid temperatures.

With slow and deliberate steps, he managed to get to a small clearing in the field, an icy patch of yellowed grass undisturbed by the previous day's battle. Standing in the open space, he checked his legs and arms for physical damage. He had on wool-lined fur pants, but the backside of the pants had been torn asunder and hung loosely from his bare legs underneath. Much to his surprise, his legs were undamaged, said for a few minor nicks and scratches.

His arms fared a bit worse, but the damage was minimal compared to what he had anticipated.

'Oh great Sebu, I shall not take this second chance at life for granted,' the man said to himself in a low, dry rasp.

With the frenzied desperation of a wolf facing starvation, he went about scouring the bodies for anything he could use, clothing, weapons, water, and food rations. A Zuthunian dagger—chipped but still functional—proved useful in cutting the rope from his neck. Clutched in the bloodied hand of a soldier, he pulled loose a delicate piece of fabric. Lightly perfumed, it was no doubt a gift from the soldier's wife or lover. Now it was repurposed as a head and face wrap to protect his exposed skin from the elements.

***

After some time, the wind regained its power and roared over the plains with an unbridled ferocity. Fortunately, the man had been able to cover his body head to toe with the garments and armour he had scavenged from the dead. Even so, he still reeled back with each icy gust. It was time to leave this God-forsaken land before death took him as well.

Each step took great effort as a heavy snowfall soon accompanied the wind. Regardless of nature's relentless wrath, the man managed to get free of the battlefield. He looked back only once to see an endless stretch of lily-white snow. All signs of the bloody battle had been buried and purified by the fresh powder; it appeared as if no battle had occurred at all.

If the man had been more observant, he would have noticed the slight tremor that rippled across the snow-covered field. He may have also hurried his pace once having seen the horror of what was rising from beneath the snow. Instead, he walked blindly forward, having no idea of the nightmare trailing not far behind.

III

'Pray for life or pray for death, it does not matter. In the end, only one outcome is inevitable.'

—Garnarian proverb

That night, King Wulfbrok addressed the remaining men of his army at a banquet held in honour of their fallen brethren.

'With great bravery, comes great sacrifice. And it is with heavy hearts that we honour the sacrifices made by the greatest warriors in all the Five Kingdoms. We shall never forget the names of those who fought and died so bravely upon the Holy Plains of Thodornia.' A roar of cheers erupted throughout the Grand Hall. Once the noise subsided, the King began again. 'If it be the way of the Gods, may we one day dine with them in the afterlife. And be it the way of man, may we relish their victory now. Tonight, we feast in honour of our great warriors. May the Gods bless us once more.'

With that, another eruption of cheers rang out, and the merriment continued long into the night. But the King wasn't among the revellers. He had more pressing matters to attend to. He had to prepare for his upcoming death.

**

A soft orange glow flickered on a distant hill, playing against the purple backdrop of the night sky. The snow had ceased but the wind sliced through the man like the blades of a thousand daggers. His body weary and weather-beaten, he was mere moments from collapse. But when all seemed hopeless, his warrior spirit rose from within and pushed him forward through the pain and exhaustion.

Laboured step after laboured step, he climbed the hill toward the light until an oval hut came into view. A gentle crackling escaped through the open doorway of the hut and the promise of a warm fire reinvigorated him.

Upon reaching the entrance, a squat old man with a bushy beard and bushier eyebrows greeted him.

'Say, 'tis not the time of year to be traveling through these parts,' the old man said in a strange accent.

'Where am I?' The warrior could barely raise his voice above the ripping wind.

'Quickly, come inside 'fore you catch a case of death. That's one ailment you shan't recover from,' the old man said with a chuckle.

Once inside, the bearded man gave the warrior a wool blanket and told him to sit on the floor and warm himself in front of the fire. After pinning a curtain across the entrance of the hut, he joined his new companion.

'Name is Olvin of Kurmits. That be where you are as well.'

'Kurmits?'

'Do not blame ye for never hearing of it. Not many folks live in these hills nowadays. Kurmits is a part of Thodornia.' Olvin pulled a wooden jug from a box and fixed two mugs of wine. 'Weather be too harsh for most.' He handed a mug to the man who downed the bitter wine in two long slugs.

'I am sorry to have bothered you. My name is Ashur Kang. I am a soldier of Sansylgate.' His voice still retained the painful rasp induced by the noose.

'Well tickle me with a goose feather. Ye be a long ways from Sansylgate.' Olvin took a sip of wine that stained half of his grey moustache red. 'What kind of name is Kang, if ye care to tell?' He gazed curiously at his guest's partially covered face. 'That be a northern name, no?'

The warrior, Ashur Kang, explained how during his teenage years, the chief of his village in the country of Cangro sent him to a noble family in Sansylgate. It was the head of the family who had changed his last name to Kang so the boy could one day enlist in the Northern Army.

'Back then, they did not allow tribal warriors from the south to fight with northerners.' Ashur accepted another mug of wine. 'They believed we were not educated enough for organized battle. But by giving me the surname of their noble family, my education never came into question.'

Olvin raised a bushy eyebrow. 'Ye means to tell me ye battled with the best of the Five Kingdoms?'

'Aye,' Ashur grunted.

'How old when ye first took up the sword for the family Kang?'

Ashur took a sip from his mug while he thought in silence. Not being much of a wine drinker, his head had already succumbed to a slow spin.

'My people do not keep track of the years like they do in the north. When I first experienced battle in these lands, I was no longer a boy, nor was I yet a man.' He set his mug aside and removed his head wrap, revealing in full a rugged black beard and a head of hair that was braided into a tight, intricate pattern of rows. 'That was many winters ago. Many battles waged and many men since passed.'

'Aye.' Olvin raised his mug skyward and began to speak in a singsong rhythm, 'A drink to the fight, to the man and his might, may he forever be blessed, for this, we drink on the night.'

The two men tapped their mugs and downed their wine. Ashur had managed to shake the chill from his bones and felt the warm embrace of sleep edging its way into his consciousness.

'Ye welcome to rest here 'til the morn.'

Ashur did not hear the old man's words; the world of dreams had already taken hold. In his dreams, a thundering army of the undead marched through the snow-covered hills. Their shadowy figures pushed forward beneath the pale radiance of the full moon.

Ceaseless was their pursuit—only hampered by the grotesque injuries their frozen bodies donned. All they knew was rage. The relentless fury of battle filled their non-beating hearts. There was more blood to be shed, for even in death their battle was far from over. They were the Draugr. A legend born in Hell.

***

The rhythmic clacking of wooden wheels and horse hooves echoed throughout the still streets of Sansylgate.

During the grand banquet, King Wulfbrok had finally received news of the battle from two of his scouts. While he had already learned of the outcome from the Garnarian, he had nearly choked on ale when he had heard that many of the bodies had vanished from the battlefield. He had pressed the scouts for more information, but they had nothing else to tell. It was as if all the corpses with intact legs had simply gotten up and walked off into the wilderness. There were many indents of boot-crushed ice corroborating this impossible theory, but the wind and snow had erased all other evidence.

'We must hurry,' the King said to the carriage driver.

The driver nodded in acknowledgment and whipped the horses to quicken their pace. The moon hung high above the world, and they hoped it would illuminate their way as they rushed to see the Oracle at the Caves of Divinity. If they did not reach the Oracle before daybreak, the Five Kingdoms would be no more.

IV

'Only light may vanquish the terrible night.'

—Akesian Book of Mourning

Ashur awoke to the sound of whistling air. The fire had cooled to dull embers and darkness filled the hut. He could make out the faint outline of the entrance curtain flapping loosely in the night as the freezing air forced its way inside. The homely hut had taken on the quality of a tomb.

As he slumbered, Olvin snored like a wild boar, oblivious to the world around him. Ashur got up and began to stir the embers—adding small chunks of wood until the fire began to come alive once more. Its warm radiance slowly pushed out the cold and restored the hut's welcoming ambiance.

Ashur got up and walked to the entrance. Part of the curtain had slipped from its hook and fluttered soundlessly in the wind. As he went to reattach it, a dreadful quake caught his attention.

Off in the distance—approaching from the base of the hill—was what sounded like an avalanche; a uniform rumbling of ice and snow moving all at once. It made no sense to him.

'By Sebu's might, what horrors come to me now?' Ashur said to himself as he peeked through the curtain, staring off into the desolate night.

At this, Olvin roused from his sleep and noticed Ashur standing at the hut's entrance. The orange glow of the fire sent shadows dancing upon the warrior's broad back.

'Aye, what is it that captivates ye so?' Olvin said with a sleepy husk in his voice.

Ashur replied, 'My friend, I fear I have invited death to your home.' He did not dare to look away from the scene unfolding along the snowy countryside. 'Something evil comes this way, and I think not even the Gods shall protect us this night.'

The short mountain man cleared the sleep from his eyes and got to his feet with no real urgency. 'Ye sure? That be a very bold statement.'

'Come look for yourself.'

Olvin walked over and Ashur stepped aside, allowing the man an unobstructed view of the great hills.

After several moments, Olvin said, 'I see nothing but the Goddess Moon and the white mountains she watches over.'

'Listen.'

Few men if none possess senses as sharpened as Ashur's. His instincts were more that of a lion than a man, and his hearing was unmatched. Olvin, on the other hand, had begun to succumb to age. His senses were dull and often failed him.

'I hear nothin' but wind.'

'Here, give me your hand.'

With a hint of caution, Olvin extended his open hand. Ashur placed the man's palm on the wooden frame of the entrance.

'Close your eyes.'

Olvin did as he was told.

'Don't think. Only focus on what you feel.'

At first, all the old man could feel was the icy wind on his face. But after some time, he noticed a mild tremor vibrating through his hand and arm.

With a start, he blurted out, 'To the heavens and beyond! Either the Earth is tearing itself in two or an army marches this way!'

'Is there any place to go?'

Olvin shook his head with a solemn frown. ''fraid not. The closest village be nearly a day's walk from here.' His frown deepened. 'And that be in the best weather conditions.'

With an understanding nod, Ashur went to work putting on his armour. A zen calm washed over his face while he examined his weapons: he had the Zuthunian dagger with the chipped blade—which he tied to his outer thigh—one metal-plated glove that he slipped over his left hand, a knobbed club made from the root of the poisonous killstrum tree that fit snugly in his waistband, and the Bogon Slasher from his home country of Cangro.

The slasher had always been his preferred weapon. With its sturdy blackwood handle and razor-sharp curved blade, he found it to be the perfect tool for severing his enemies' heads from their bodies.

'What kind of blade ye have there? Never seen one like that 'round these parts?'

'This is the weapon of my people,' Ashur answered without looking up.

'Not much of a reach there.' Olvin stepped closer and examined the half-crescent curve of the blade. 'Perhaps a sword would be of more use to ye, no?'

'Why do you say this?' His tone carried with it a venomous bite.

Olvin took a nervous step backward. Until now, he had not noticed what a fierce presence this man possessed. 'Well, I only mean that in battle, a longer blade would serve ye better, I think. Ye would have to get real close to a man to cut him with a blade curved like such.'

Ashur began working on his headwrap, circling it first around his injured neck, then over his face and forehead leaving only his eyes uncovered. The fire's orange and red flames flittered in his black, fathomless eyes.

Olvin started again, 'Ye would have to possess the quickness of a God to get close enough to kill a man with—'

With a sudden rush, the warrior twisted his body and sprang forward with the incredible speed of a panther. His arm shot out in a looping arc and stopped with the blade hovering mere centimetres from Olvin's corpulent neck. A few strands of the old man's wiry grey beard floated down past the slasher's hilt and settled upon the soot-covered floorboards.

'Well,' Olvin gulped, 'that be mighty close, I say.'

'Aye.' Ashur pulled back and sheathed his weapon into a unique holder that was slung crossbody over his back and torso. 'We have little time to make our escape.'

'Should we go take a look at what comes this way?'

'We have no choice in the matter. If we don't go, we may find ourselves standing in front of the flames of Hell before dawn.'

'So that is how it be, eh?'

The two men spoke no further. It was now time for action.

V

'Through the blackness of eternity, he marched on—never to see the rays of the sun again.'

—The Tale of Yetomese of Nunic

Darkness surrounded King Wulfbrok as he navigated the labyrinth of tunnels in the Caves of Divinity. He had been walking for some time—having left the carriage driver at the cave's entrance. An ethereal blue glow guided him through the never-ending night. It seemed no matter how far or how long he trudged forward, he could not catch up to the glowing light.

When his old legs grew weary and his breath laboured, he stopped and rested against the cool cavern wall. A trickle of moisture running down the surface dampened his back and sent a shiver through his body. He could advance no farther.

'Oracle, please.' The King dropped to a knee and bowed his head in a solemn show of respect. 'I give the sincerest of apologies for my transgressions. I shan't return without seeking your great wisdom.' His words echoed deep into the void.

An all-enveloping silence took hold and the King buckled under its deafening power. The sound of his heartbeat resounded through the silent caverns and beads of perspiration dotted his brow.

'What can I do,' his voice trembled, 'for you to bestow upon me your great wisdom?'

The answer came in the form of a deeper silence. Failure seemed inevitable. Death, even more so.

'So Chasetree spoke the truth? You refuse me and there is nothing I can do to sway your decision?'

The blue glow began to dim and darkness—the kind known solely by the dead or blind—crept into its place.

Facing the threat of being confined deep beneath the Earth, King Wulfbrok tried once more to persuade the unseen Oracle. 'What if I offer my life?' The blue glow blinked out of existence and left him sightless in a world of absolute black. 'What is the blood of royal lineage worth to the Gods? Because I shall offer every last drop in my veins for a single moment of your time.'

The cave began to rumble as if the tunnels were rotating like the gears inside of Sansylgate's majestic clock tower.

'You may enter.'

The voice sounded near and distant simultaneously. King Wulfbrok thought it came from two persons: one hidden in the darkness next to him and one way off within the deep cave. He was told to enter but had no idea where or what he was entering into.

'I'm afraid I cannot see even my hand before my eyes.'

A low hum accompanied by a whoosh of hot hair blew past the king. This was followed by the return of the blue glow.

It first started as a glimmer—a lone firefly flickering in the unknown depths of the underworld—but quickly illumined the entire cave with its supernatural radiance. The King in all the long years of his life had never observed anything like it.

'This way,' the voice echoed, drifting to and fro like a guiding spirit.

King Wulfbrok moved forward. His legs quaked with fatigue, but he pushed on. Stopping numerous times along the way to catch his breath, he refused to quit and always continued back on his silent descent into the Earth.

Many hours passed this way and eventually, the blue glow gave way to soft white light. The cave was not as it was before; its walls now had an ochreous hue and the cold air had become stifling hot.

Each step zapped more of his energy. His arms became heavy. His head lulled forward as he walked. Sweat slicked his white hair down and his tunic stuck to his body. He walked until he could go no more.

Exhaustion won out and he dropped to the hot ground. The old King's pulse slowed, and his breath grew faint.

'I have failed Sansylgate,' he whispered to himself.

As he closed his eyes and prepared for the death he knew would always come, a cool hand gently caressed his weathered face.

'It is time to make good on your offer, King.'

VI

'Old or young, life and death, all is forgotten when one enters the fray.'

—Cromish Proverb

The wind had picked up considerably, and with it came jagged shards of ice lifted and pulled from the hillsides.

'At this rate, we shall perish before we learn who it is that comes for us,' Olvin shouted through the howling winds.

The old man looked up at Ashur, and even though most of his face was covered, Olvin was sure the warrior was smiling.

'No, fate shall not be so kind to us on this night.' Ashur extended his long muscular arm and pointed to a nearby ridge. 'They will be upon us soon.'

The hills moved like the sluggish waves of an arctic ocean.

'Is there no hope then?' Olvin asked.

Ashur did not hear the old man's words. Nor could he feel the biting wind beating upon his body. His warrior mentality, the primitive beast that lurks within few men, had already taken over. In his ears roared the silent call of battle that only he could hear.

Death was coming for him, and it was coming fast.

'I thank you greatly for your hospitality. If Sebu grants me a life beyond this night, I shall one day repay your kindness. This, you have my word.' Ashur eased the slasher from its sheath and watched for a moment as flecks of clear ice landed and sparkled along its curved blade. 'It is now that we must part.'

'My word! Ye shan't tell me ye intend on fighting the whole army alone?' The old man raised an arm to cover his face as an icy blast whipped through. 'Aye! 'Tis madness, I say.' Olvin lowered his arm and realized he was talking to the open sky.

With the grace of a nimble lynx, Ashur had already taken down the frozen slope with noiseless footfalls. So incredible was his speed, the ice barely cracked beneath his feet.

While the army marched forward in unison, Ashur Kang made it to the hill's base and began crossing the frozen plain with the near-invisible movements of a winter phantom.

Death meant little to the rugged warrior for his people relished in the glory of battle; win or lose, live or die. As the army of the undead grew closer, a kind of jubilation rose within him. A single thought brought this jubilation to near ecstasy: how fortunate the warrior who gets the chance to revisit the same battle—how lucky to have the opportunity to send an army of men to Hell for a second time!

Old Olvin watched from the safety of his home as the silent figure charged toward the oncoming army. Why an entire army would brave the deadly elements for a single man, he could not understand. More perplexing, how could such a man exist who would so eagerly rush headlong toward his death?

The horrid details of the army came into focus as they finally made it to the open plain. These were no ordinary men; missing limbs and gaping wounds marred each member of the bloody horde. Of course, Ashur had known these men in death. He had sent many of them to meet Obidion the Ferryman. Why or how they had come to return to the world of the living, he did not know, nor did he care. The only thing that was important to him as he dashed across the ice, was to make sure that this time, the dead stayed dead.

VII

'In the mirror, it looks like I, but staring back, is but a lie.'

'Open your eyes, King Wulfbrok.'

The blue glow surrounding the Oracle pushed out the darkness and revealed a vision few have ever beheld. King Wulfbrok opened his eyes and found himself lying inside an ivory palace.

There were no visible walls and countless pure white pillars stretched to the heavens—pushing up, up, up into an unknown sky without cloud or colour. The King could not fathom what he was seeing. No mortal could begin to understand this place.

'Where are we?' the King said with a shaky voice.

The Oracle was standing in the middle of four great pillars with her back to him. 'Where? There is no 'where', foolish man.' She was gazing at a small gold sphere that she held in her hands. 'Of course, I would not expect someone of your breed to understand.'

The King stifled his rage. He had little experience dealing with such indignation but did his best to hold his tongue. He wasn't the ruler of this realm, and he knew the fact well.

'You offered your blood? Your royal blood for my time?'

A chill passed through the King's body as he stepped forward. 'I… Yes. Yes, I did,' King Wulfbrok said, holding his head high in a proud display of his royal lineage.

The Oracle turned with a sudden burst of blue light. 'What makes you think I, let alone the Gods, care about your pitiful blood?' The gold sphere she had been holding was now floating behind her without any support.

Knowing he had nothing else to bargain with, King Wulfbrok stammered, 'I, I, I know little of what the Gods desire.'

In its infinite size, the room reverberated with the Oracle's maniacal laughter. 'Fool!' Her voice boomed like thunder. 'Of course, you know nothing of what the Gods desire. You, humans, do not possess the intellect.'

'You, humans,' the king repeated silently to himself.

It subsequently dawned on him that he had been tricked. The Oracle, with her magic and great wisdom, was still a human. She was still made of flesh and blood just like him. No, this being before him was not the Oracle. It was an imposter!

'What is this cursed place,' the King demanded.

'Oh, you shall find out, King.' The blue glow surrounding the Oracle turned blood-red. 'You shall spend an eternity finding out.'

***

Ashur Kang rushed into the fray with madness in his eyes. His trusted slasher made fine work of the first group of undead soldiers.

Severed limbs fell free and heads rolled across the ice. Congealed blood oozed slowly from the Draugr warriors' wounds and made the ground sticky with clotted gore. Still, they kept coming.

Hundreds surrounded Ashur and he fought them off valiantly. To his advantage, they moved slowly with their stiff, half-frozen bodies. But their numbers were vast and the fallen continued to rise or crawl or strike out in any way they could manage. No matter how many he slew, the living dead kept coming. Headless, armless, legless, they kept coming. If Hell was full, it was now springing anew on Earth.

A headless, legless corpse crawled blindly toward the warrior and lashed out with its sword from behind.

'Fiend!' Ashur screamed after the corpse sliced his calf diagonally.

With newfound rage, Ashur used the dagger in his left hand to cut off the headless corpse's sword-wielding arm. It used its remaining forelimb to pull itself forward, so he stripped it of that as well leaving it no more than a writing torso. All the while, he swung the slasher in his right hand, felling any foe near him.

'You devils must try harder to kill a Cangrolese warrior!' he roared.

From behind struck another undead soldier. Its broken broadsword just missed its mark and instead shorn off Ashur's right sleeve. Sweat glistened on his exposed arm and his cannonball-bicep flexed powerfully as he turned, swinging the slasher downward and braining the Draugr demon. The curved blade split the Draugr's head clean in two but got embedded in the base of its skull.

The undead man waved his sword wildly as Ashur worked to pull the slasher free. Squeezing the handle with an iron grip, he kicked the Draugr's chest with the power of a warhorse, sending the undead man flying backward. The slasher broke free from the Draugr's skull, but the brief delay was long enough for the horde to descend upon the Cangrolese warrior.

He fought with all his might, but the numbers proved too great. Countless cuts stripped the flesh from his arms, legs, and torso. Ashur Kang dropped to a knee and the brilliant moonlight disappeared from his sight as a black shadow enveloped him.

He prepared for death.

***

King Wulfbrok hardly managed to jump out of the way as the Oracle's imposter rushed him. No mortal being could possess such speed, thought the King.

'No use in prolonging the inevitable,' the imposter said in a newly demonic voice.

The imposter spun around as if skating on ice. The King scrambled to his feet in time to evade another onslaught.

This time he kept to his feet and was able to move out of the way without diving to the ground.

'What type of sorcery is this?' the King bellowed.

'Fool. My kind would never have a need for human alchemy.' The imposter whirled around once more and for a brief moment, its robe fluttered, exposing its feet levitating above the floor. 'We would never degrade ourselves with your race's cheap magic.'

It rushed the King again, but this time it feinted to the left and clipped his knee. He crashed to the hard ivory floor with a heavy thud.

King Wulfbrok grimaced as he struggled but failed to stand. 'What is it you want from me?'

'Want? What makes you think I could ever want anything from a pathetic creature such as yourself?'

The imposter floated toward the King. It stretched its arms out in front revealing bone-white talons protruding from the tips of its skeletal fingers.

'Then it is for sick pleasure you brought me to this wicked place?'

The King hoped his words would delay the attack and allow him to regain his position, but the imposter looked intent on ending the skirmish without further discourse.

'Pleasure? No. Necessity.'

A great burst of hot wind blew past the King. He shielded his head with his arms as he lay on his stomach. The presence of the imposter loomed over him, but he refused to move for instinct told him that in doing so would mean certain death.

'Face me, coward,' the imposter shrieked in a hideous, guttural voice.

Like the fires of Hell, the air around the King was scorching. Sweat started dripping from his head creating a clear sheen on the ivory floor. He would not move. He could not move.

'Coward! I said face me!'

With an abrupt shift, the temperature plummeted. King Wulfbrok had no choice but to push himself up before the sweat-slick froze his skin to the ground.

'Look upon me so I may feast on your fear.'

The imposter's voice no longer held any resemblance to that of the Oracle. Only a demon straight from the endless depths of Hell could speak in such acid-laced tones, thought the King.

'I said look upon me.' The imposter erupted with another fiery gale. 'Now, pathetic mortal!'

King Wulfbrok managed to rise to his feet. He kept his head down and eyes closed, but the furious wind nearly knocked him back down. Fortunately, the hot air had melted the ice and evaporated the sweat that had pooled on the floor. This allowed the old King to maintain his footing.

'Look at me!' screamed the imposter.

'You can kill me, but I shall never do as you command!' the King roared back.

With a screech of fury, the imposter manifested a mini cyclone that encircled King Wulfbrok and launched him through the air. He hit the ground with a bone-crunching snap and slid across the ivory floor. The smooth surface did little to ease the rough friction burn against his skin.

For a moment, the King blinked in and out of the dark confines of unconsciousness, and when he came to, the palace was eerily quiet. The imposter was nowhere in sight.

The King sat up—with his head spinning and eyes unfocused—he breathed in deeply and exhaled slowly. Once his senses returned to normal, he peered out into the dark recesses of the vast palace, but not a single soul stirred. Immense loneliness washed over him.

A glint of light snatched the King's attention, and he moved his gaze upward where the gold orb was floating directly above his head. Gingerly, he stood up to study the orb.

A gentle, calming warmth radiated from the mysterious

sphere. It was impossibly smooth and crafted from a metal unlike any he had ever seen. Though he was hesitant, his instinct directed him once more. This time it told him to take hold of the golden marvel.

With the delicate touch of a master potter, the King reached out and laid a hand on each side of the orb. As soon as his skin made contact with the otherworldly metal, a blinding gold light filled the palace. He had no choice but to shut his eyes, and as soon as he did an image appeared. It was the Oracle. The true Oracle.

'You do not belong in this realm, my King,' the Oracle said in a voice that came from all directions.

'I was tricked. I thought it was you who led me to this place.'

The Oracle's image fazed in and out of existence while the brilliant gold light framed her flickering face.

'You were led astray by the shapeshifter known as Alakabaz. He used the power of the dark arts to entrap me in the Orb of Medd.'

'Was it he who refused my request for counsel?'

'Yes.'

'I see.' A wave of warm energy pulsed through the King, revitalizing his aging body. 'What is this place? Why did he bring me here?'

The Oracle's image grew more vibrant. 'This is the Hall of Yedimiah, the God of knowledge.' The lines of her face softened as if time itself was reversing. 'I know not why Alakabaz brought you here. Perhaps when he stole my body and trapped me in the Orb of Medd, he was unaware that his powers would greatly diminish. Without your fear to feed upon, he is weak. I assume he could no longer maintain his form and had to return to where he came from.' The Oracle's image finally steadied and revealed a young, beautiful woman staring back at the King. 'The Hall of Knowledge is the halfway point between worlds. Alakabaz in his weakened state was unable to take you to his castle in the Outer-Realm.'

'Are you aware of what has taken place on the lands of Thordornia?'

'I am. I was seeking guidance from the Gods when Alakabaz attacked me.

'Most of my army has been vanquished. How is Sansylgate to continue without my mightiest warriors protecting it?

The Oracle's face dropped as if her age had suddenly returned all at once. 'You ask the wrong question. It's more like, how can Sansylgate continue while those men still fight.'

'What do you mean, 'still fight'?' the King asked in disbelief. 'We have gotten word straight from the battlefield. All lives were lost'.

'Lost, yes. But their souls are not at rest. They have been blocked from crossing over.'

The King furrowed his brows. 'I don't understand. How can this be?'

'You sent your men to fight on the Holy Plains of Thordornia. The Gods forbade the spilling of blood on its sacred soil, and you disobeyed. Because of this, they instructed Obidion to leave the souls of the dead in the Earth realm until a sacrifice is made to appease them.'

'A sacrifice?'

'Yes. They demand the blood of the one responsible for the battle.'

The King swallowed hard. 'You mean my blood?'

The Oracle nodded. Her true age had returned, and her image was beginning to dissipate.

'What shall I do?'

'When you thought Alakabaz was I, you offered your royal blood, but it is to the Gods your blood must be given.' The Oracle's voice was hollow, and her words seemed to float away as she spoke. 'The only way to end this is for you to die with your men and lead their souls to the other side, but you cannot end your own life nor can a lost soul end it for you.'

The golden light had become unbearable and blinded the King to the Oracle's image.

'The sacred soil must taste your blood, and there is a warrior who now fights on the holy land that is worthy enough to kill a king.'

'But how am I to get there if I'm stuck in this place?'

An icy rush of wind blew through King Wulfbrok's hair and the golden light relaxed to a white glow.

'All you must do, my King, is open your eyes,' the Oracle said with the softness of a phantom. Her words danced upon the night air and disappeared as if they had never been spoken at all.

King Wulfbrok opened his eyes to see the world spread out beneath the moonlit sky with gleaming hills that were as white as pearls. But he had little time to admire the country's beauty because directly ahead of him, a tall warrior in the throes of battle raged against an army of the undead, and it looked as if the army was about to claim victory.

VII

To the death
A warrior shall battle
And with his final breath
Our world will rattle
As the Gods require blood.

—Old Cangrolese poem

A cacophony of clanging metal vibrated through the frozen

hills. Clouds of ice and broken permafrost billowed around the battle and cased Ashur Kang's exposed, blood-covered skin until it gave the appearance of polished armour.

Many reanimated soldiers had swarmed the warrior, but he fought back with all his might. On the defensive, he dropped low and spun 360 degrees with the slasher's blade angled out in front of him. Four soldiers fell back as the blade severed their legs at the knee, leaving them crawling through the ice on stumps that left behind clumps of semi-coagulated blood. A fifth soldier, weapon less and only sporting one arm, lunged forward.

Ashur met the soldier with an upward thrust of the dagger in his left hand. His aim was true and connected with a revolting squelch.

'To Hell with you, demon,' he growled through gritted teeth as he yanked downward to free the dagger from the soldier's skull.

Barely a second passed and six more of the Draugr soldiers were upon him. He swung the slasher in a looping arc but one of the Draugr grabbed his elbow mid-strike. With brute strength, Ashur powered through and caught his target, the fleshy neck of a charging barbarian. Due to the interference, he wasn't able to decapitate the behemoth of a man and the undead barbarian collapsed, pinning Ashur to the ground under its immense mass.

A dog pile ensued with five soldiers clamouring to rip the proud warrior apart. Three of the undead soldiers brandished swords and struck down with rabid intensity, but through the chaos, they were unable to hit Ashur. Instead, they sliced and stabbed and cut the barbarian Draugr who lay on top of the Cangrolese warrior.

King Wulfbrok, watching this unfold from a close distance, knew there was precious little time to act. Looking about with the manic drive of a much younger man, he spotted a sword on the ground.

The King hurried over and picked up the weapon. Its heft warned him of his age, but the thought fell away as soon as he charged the fight.

One of the smaller Draugr soldiers looked up in time to greet the King with the slash of its cutlass. Many years since last wielding a broadsword, King Wulfbrok's arms had grown weak and were unprepared for battle. At the last possible second, the old King's instinct kicked in and he parried the attack. He nearly dropped the sword due to the impact but regained control right as the soldier advanced again.

'You shan't kill me that easy,' he said with a liveliness he had not felt in a long time.

The Draugr soldier struck out and the King easily deflected the blow. He noticed the undead brute was unable to lift its arm higher than chest level. A broken limb or dislocated shoulder thought the King.

Parrying another strike, King Wulfbrok sidestepped the unbalanced Draugr and plunged his sword into its chest—running it through to the hilt.

With terror in his eyes, the King watched helplessly as the Draugr torqued its rigid body sideways and broke free of the King's hold, then continued to attack with the broad sword still pierced through its un-beating heart.

'You, you,' the King stammered. 'You are a monster.'

The Draugr soldier pushed forward with its unblinking, lifeless eyes fixated on the King. A wild swing sent the King falling backward to the ground. Unarmed and overmatched, all he could do was ready himself for the death blow.

Standing over the fallen King, the undead soldier lifted its sword as high as it could. Once a living, breathing person—one who may have fought for the very man he was about to kill—the Draugr soldier stared emotionless at the old King. With all the power its stiff muscles could manage, it brought down the cutlass.

CLANG

THWUNK

King Wulfbrok blinked several times. Lying next to him, staring up with those dead, milky-white eyes, was the Draugr soldier's severed head. Its teeth were gnashing as it tried and failed to bite him.

'A little too old for this, aye?'

King Wulfbrok looked up to see a hulking statue of a man towering over him. Beneath the starlight, Ashur Kang's body glistened with fresh gore.

'Battle makes old men of us all,' the King said.

'That it does.'

Ashur extended a hand to the King.

'They are relentless,' King Wulfbrok said, taking Ashur's hand in his own.

The Cangrolese warrior pulled the King to his feet. 'I do not know what sorcery has brought this upon the world, but I fear that these men—' Ashur looked over his shoulder to see another wave of soldiers closing in. '—these creatures, shall never stop.'

Ashur offered his dagger to King Wulfbrok, but the King waved it away. 'No, there is a way to put an end to this madness. But the end shall only come with my death.'

'What do you mean—'

A battle-axe howled like the winter wind as it cut through the air. Ashur jumped out of the way, but the blade ripped through the flesh on his back. As he fell, he whipped his arm upward and hooked a Draugr soldier in the eye with the tip of the slasher. The blade tore loose the eyeball from its socket.

'Run!' Ashur screamed to the King. 'You must escape while you still can.'

With one eye dangling halfway down its pallid face, the undead soldier lifted the battle-axe overhead and hammered it down. Ashur barely rolled out of the way when the axe smashed the ground with a splintering of ice and dirt.

Like an agile tiger, Ashur sprung to his feet and beheaded the soldier in one swift movement.

'Come, we have no time,' Ashur said, urging the King to leave.

'Kill me,' the King replied gravely.

Ashur's eyes widened. 'I do not… why would you…' his words trailed off in the twilight of early morning.

'You said it yourself. We have no time.' King Wulfbrok bowed his head. 'The Gods demand my royal blood to end this nightmare. Please, for the future of Sansylgate, kill me.'

It finally dawned on Ashur who was standing before him. 'King Wulfbrok,' he whispered to himself.

'Do it now. My death cannot come by my own hands.'

Even though the temperature was frigid, beads of sweat trickled down Ashur's face. He lifted the slasher into the air and held it over the King's bowed head, but he did something he had never done before in battle. He hesitated.

It was for only a moment, and as he began the swooping arc that had beheaded countless foes before, a white flash shot across his vision.

When Ashur came to, there was a terrible ringing in his head and a warm liquid flowing from his ear. A sea of white eyes stared at him. He had not fallen but his equilibrium was now off a great deal.

Ashur whirled around—almost tripping in the process—and was surprised to see a dagger-wielding King Wulfbrok felling the Draugr soldier who must have clubbed him on the head.

'Finish it,' demanded the King.

A gust of wind kicked up the metallic scent of blood as the horde of undead Draugr soldiers circled the two men. It was now or never. The fate of Sansylgate was held in Ashur Kang's mighty hand.

Without the fear of death holding them back, the horde charged. Ashur fought to keep his balance as he swung the slasher. Right as the slasher's blade made contact with the back of King Wulfbrok's neck, the horde tackled the Cangrolese warrior and pulled him down. The slasher fell to the ground as the Draugr soldiers wrapped him up in their cold arms. One of the undead soldiers picked up the dagger the King had been using.

Ashur stared into the dead man's eyes, but he could do nothing more. He was trapped.

Holding the dagger over Ashur, the soldier paused. He tilted his head slightly and without warning, snatched the tattered cloth that was still wrapped around Ashur's neck. A strange look came over the Draugr soldier's face. It was as if a memory, some faint image of his past life came to him. Then the look was gone.

The Draugr soldier drove the dagger downward toward Ashur's heart. The fierce Cangrolese warrior tensed his body in anticipation, but before he knew what was happening, he was free.

The whistling wind roared across the ice-covered hills, but all else was silent. Ashur looked around and was astonished to see that all at once, the entire army had fallen motionless to the ground. Once the shock wore off, his eyes settled on the head of King Wulfbrok lying beside his still body.

There was a slight smile on the King's face. Beneath him, through the melted ice and soaked into the sacred soil, was a pool of the King's royal blood. He had kept his word and given his blood for Sansylgate. Just as his ancestors had done.

***

All at once, the weight of the world fell upon Ashur's broad shoulders. Even the skin of his teeth hurt. The only thing he wanted to do was rest, but he knew if he did not get to shelter soon, he would freeze to death. Or bleed out. He looked around but was disoriented. The vibrant moon had dropped, and the morning sun would soon rise, but a black shadow was still currently stretched over the land. Off in the distance on top of a hill, a faint orange glow danced in the darkness.

'Olvin, my friend. I pray you have plenty of wine left.'

Ashur began the long trek across the ice.

The Breaking

R. P. Serin

The car juddered over the cattle grid and on to the single-track road. Loose gravel crunched satisfyingly under rotating tires.

The last hour of their journey had been dominated by claustrophobic woodlands, which had now given way to sweeping hills, well grazed fields, rugged heathland, and waves of pine forests that spread out across the sprawling valley below. It was a clear evening, and the peaks of Snowdonia were just visible in the distance.

The cottage, this year's setting for their annual "weekend away", was a venue set back on a craggy plateau; its white sunlit walls gleamed against the backdrop of soaring rocks and shadowy trees.

Ranjit pulled onto an area of cracked, overgrown tarmac.

'We made it,' she remarked stepping out, savouring the chance to stretch her aching legs.

'No thanks to Jo's crusty old sat nav,' Mel was leaning against the side of the car taking long pulls from her vape. 'Thank God for Google Maps.'

Jo, still sat in the front passenger seat, looked up from the bag she was sifting through. 'You know they spy on you?'

'I don't care as long as they get me where I want to go and not to Granny Afron, or wherever the hell we were heading to.'

'It's Glan-yr-afon, which is only a few miles away from here.'

Mel fell about laughing as she attempted to repeat the name back.

'Anyway,' Ranjit interrupted. 'We're here now. Just *look* at this view.' Mel folded her arms in mock annoyance as Ranjit turns around with a smile. 'Come on, that more than makes up for the drive, doesn't it?'

Karen, who'd wisely stayed out of the whole dispute, nodded in agreement, and turned towards the cottage. 'And check this out,' she said. 'The pictures don't do it justice.'

The interior was a stylised patchwork, nostalgic modernity carefully melded with antiquated farmhouse chic. Original wooden beams that looked centuries old interrupted the crisp white ceiling; quirky unmatched chairs surrounded a large oak dining table.

As Mel tried to figure out the AGA, the others argued over who was getting the ensuite. She popped open a slightly warm bottle of Prosecco before reheating the curry which she had prepared the night before.

'That took longer than I'd expected,' Mel said, placing the large casserole dish in the centre of the table. The comforting aroma of ginger, cumin, and garlic filled the room, claiming it as its own. Karen inhaled and let out a satisfied hum of approval, the three glasses of fizz showing on her face. Her usually neat and precise ponytail was already looking somewhat dishevelled.

Jo stood up, ladle in hand.

'Bloody hell, give me a chance,' Mel said, taking the lid off the pan. 'And save me a bit.' She headed back to the kitchen to grab the naans. 'The breads are a bit on the crispy side…'

'You always burn the naan's, hun,' Ranjit called back. 'Even when you use your own oven.'

Jo smiled. 'Shut your face, or I won't bother in the future.'

Suddenly, something hit the kitchen window. The old windowpane rattled fiercely but didn't break.

Mel let out an instinctive cry, nearly dropping the plate. *'Fuckin' hell!'*

Ranjit popped her head round the door. 'You okay?'

'Something hit the damn window, it sounded heavy.'

Ranjit moved in for a closer look. A red smear glinted against the dark night outside.

'What's going on?' Karen asked, holding out a bottle, ready to fill up any glass that made itself available.

'My glass is there,' Mel pointed across the kitchen. 'Check this out.'

Jo followed Karen into the kitchen. 'Looks like a bird hit it.'

'An owl?' Karen handed Mel her replenished glass. 'Ranjit?'

'I'll have a beer thanks. Don't owls have good eyesight?'

'Okay, smarty-pants,' Karen said, passing Ranjit a can from the fridge. It gave a satisfying hiss as she opened it.

Jo unhooked a torch from the wall. 'One way to find out.'

She walked to the back door and slipped her trainers on; the others followed.

Outside, they walked round to the kitchen window, its soft yellow glow illuminating the edge of the forest.

'There.' Mel pointed to the floor.

'I don't see anything.' Jo replied.

'On the floor. It's moving.'

'I see it,' Ranjit said with a twinge of nervousness. 'Shine the torch on it, Jo.'

'That might be useful,' Mel chipped in, 'or you could keep pointing it at your feet.'

Jo pointed the torch forward.

The pigeon was lying on the floor, its whole-body convulsing. One wing was extended upwards at an awkward angle, the other flapped uselessly.

Karen made a vomit sound. 'I can't look!'

'What's the stupid thing doing, flying round in the bloody dark?' Jo said.

Ranjit turned to Mel. 'We can't leave it.'

'What you lookin' at me for?'

'You're used to picking up disgusting things.'

'I drag wheelie bins to and from a truck. I don't usually deal with dying animals.'

'Come off it, you're always going on about the nasty things that fall onto the road,' Jo said. 'Didn't you find a finger once?'

'The tip of a finger, I had to pick it off the street.' Mel said. Karen made another vomit sound. 'Turned out the bloke who lived there chopped it off slicing parsnips. He threw it in the bin and bandaged what was left.'

'Exactly, nasty. So, you should deal with the pigeon. You've got the skills.'

Mel picked up the wounded bird, muttering obscenities beneath her breath.

'What should I do? The wings are well broken.' It pecked ferociously at her fingers; fighting for life even as all hope seemed to be lost.

'We could put it in a box and take it to the vets in the morning.' Karen suggested, still averting her gaze.

'It'll probably die from shock,' Jo said. 'And if it doesn't then the vet will only put it down. We can't leave it to suffer all night.'

'I picked the bloody thing up. I'm not killing it, no way!'

The four of them stood in silence.

Ranjit stepped forward, grabbed the pigeon from Mel and twisted its neck in a sharp upwards movement. It fell limp.

Mel and Jo gasped; Karen let out a small shriek. They stared at Ranjit with wide, unbelieving eyes.

'Someone had to do something,' she protested, still holding the dead bird. 'We can't stay out here all night, arguing about an F'ing pigeon. I'll just chuck it in the woods there, then we can go and eat some curry.'

'Sure, whatever you say, Ranj. You won't get any arguments from us, you mercenary psychopath.'

'I've got my eye on you, Mel.' Ranjit chuckled as she threw the carcass into the dimly lit trees.

'Dee–licious,' Jo said, placing her knife and fork triumphantly onto her empty plate.

'Mmmm, lovely. Shame about the naans.' Karen said.

'What was wrong with the naans, Kazza?' Mel said.

'Oh, Mel. They were a bit cold, that's all – it couldn't be helped.'

'I'm teasing,' Mel responded, 'they were bloody crispy too.' Karen giggled, feeling embarrassed. 'Anyway, it's your turn tomorrow.'

'What? Me?'

'You're not getting out of it this year,' Mel interrupted. 'Not now that you're a professional…What was it again?'

Karen knew what she was being set up for.

'…Sandwich Artist.' The others began laughing, drowning out further explanation.

Karen got up to clear the table.

'Don't do that now,' Ranjit said. 'It's just a silly name for someone who works in a Deli, that's all. Mel says she's a 'Refuse Collector' when we all know she's a Bin Lady.'

'Oi!' Mel said.

'At least you've got a job,' Ranjit said. The laughing stopped. She hadn't meant to sound as serious as she had.

Jo got up and put her arms around her.

'Don't be nice to me or I'll cry. I did enough of that last week.'

'It was a shit job anyway Ranj, that boss was a grade A wanker.' Mel always found a way to lighten the mood. Ranjit had always thought of it as a defence mechanism but was glad of it now.

'Racist prick.' Jo banged the table with her fist as she said it.

'He *is* a grade A wanker, but racist? He never really mentioned race.' Ranjit looked off to the side and pursed her lips. 'Well, not until he said I was using the "race" card. So come to think of it, yeah, he's a racist prick.' She frowned and looked away from the group, deep in thought. 'I loved the job though – just me, the old hotel, and the odd guest, keeping each other company through the night.'

'If that's your bag there'll be plenty of other hotels that could do with an overqualified woman who loves nothing more than helping drunks find their room.'

'Perhaps it is time for something new?'

'Top–up?' Jo held out the fourth bottle of prosecco.

No one saw the face as it stared through the kitchen window and into the dining room beyond. Only Karen and Ranjit were visible to the pale eyes. Dark wet hair stuck to a gaunt face. A forceful wind had begun howling through the valley, carrying with it the low moan of a fathomless mouth.

The four friends sat and drank for several hours more, telling the same old stories they did each year. Stories such as the time when Karen discovered a pile of pornographic magazines in Mr. Peters'–the Year 10 English teachers store cupboard, earning him the nickname Porno Peters.

It was well past midnight when they decided to call it a night. Mel was asleep at the table, and the others weren't far behind.

'We'll decide on what to do in the morning,' Jo said as she helped Ranjit escort Mel to her bed.

***

It was past eleven by the time they got up.

'Christ, I need some coffee,' Mel said, throwing back a couple of paracetamols.

'Okay, it's a bit later than we'd planned, and the weather's shit.' Jo bit into her toast as she looked out the window, to where the valley had been the day before. Now a thick fog writhed around piercing sheets of rain, folded by the wind that still raged over the hills. 'But we should still do something.'

'Whitewater rafting is out,' Ranjit said. 'Maybe we could drive down to the village.'

'I'm game, so long as it's pub–grub for lunch.' Mel had already started to look better.

'Sounds like a plan,' Ranjit replied. 'Let's get our shit together and hit the road.'

Mel drove with Karen sat beside her in the passenger seat. Rain filled the windscreen as quickly as the wipers could sweep it away. Heavy gusts of wind rocked the car as it crawled along the narrow, flooded roads.

'Nice to see you've brought the weather with you Jo,' Mel teased.

'I'm not saying it doesn't rain a lot in Manchester, but this is something else.'

'Sonny would love it,' Ranjit said. 'He never stops talking

about that big storm we had last year'.

'Noah hated them,' Jo replied. 'He used to hide under the table with the dog. I still tease him about it now.'

'You cruel bitch.' Mel closed her eyes as she laughed. The car swerved taking them towards the cliff that fell away from the roadside. Karen screamed.

'For God's sake, watch what you're doing.'

'Sorry. When's Noah back from Uni, Jo?'

'Next week. We didn't see him at all over Christmas. I can't wait.'

'Ah, that's better.' Mel switched the windscreen wipers to a slower setting. 'The trees are blocking the rain a bit.'

'I preferred it when we couldn't see.' Karen was looking up at the trees as they lurched back and forth. 'I don't fancy being in the way if one of them comes down.'

'Just sit back will ya, we'll be back on some proper roads soon.'

Suddenly the car was jolted by a powerful gust of wind. Mel struggled to keep control as the car pitched sideways. The trees leaned in, roots straining to hold them in place.

'*Oh shit,* watch that branch, it's gonna go.' Jo pointed towards a sprawling beech tree that marked an upcoming turn. It looked like it had spent centuries repelling storms such as this, but one colossal branch, thrust some fifteen feet above the road, looked as though it was giving up the ghost.

Mel squeezed the brake, but the car continued forward. The branch splintered, crashing onto the road ahead. *Better that than the cliff* she thought, easing off the brake, turning into the corner.

They braced themselves for the collision but a pothole, submerged beneath cascades of churning mud, jolted them sideways.

Over the precipice.

The front of the car smashed into the sharply descending

cliffside causing it to roll. Piercing screams cut through a background of guttural cries, the final movement of a monstrous quartet. All sense of awareness was engulfed by violence; the sickening turn of the earth and the immense sound of metal as it crashed against rock became all.

***

Ranjit didn't know how long she'd been there, but even with her eyes closed she knew what had happened, that the seatbelt was still holding her in place, that she was upside down.

Everything seemed calm. Birds chattered busily, a panoramic soundscape that spoke of early summer and fine weather. The gentle patter of water told tales of the storm now passed.

She opened her eyes: the mangled car, the broken glass, the blood. Nothing she saw corresponded with the tranquil sounds outside. She looked over. Jo's eyes were open, but they looked dull. She was silent. Ranjit touched her shoulder. The skin felt cold. Her head lolled back and forth.

Ranjit scanned her own body and exhaled with relief upon finding no obvious injuries. She released her seat belt then, having slumped to the ground, crawled through the window.

The driver's side had collapsed entirely, the wheels twisted out of shape. The ground was still sodden.

Leaves rustled gently in the breeze; the birds still sang. The sun shone through a gap in the trees in a dreaded spotlight, illuminating a theatre of carnage.

Crack.

Ranjit turned instinctively, nothing but a thick wall of trees.

She moved to the driver's side. Mel was trapped between the steering wheel and the body of the car. There was no way she could have survived with the unnaturalness of her position, the amount of blood. Ranjit was surprised by how calm she felt, how focused.

She ran around to the passenger side.

'*Karen!*'

Karen let out a small groan. Her face twitched.

Ranjit's voice shook. 'We've been in an accident. You're still in the car but I'm going to get you out.' If she could hear, she didn't respond. The seatbelt wouldn't budge.

She opened the glove compartment; the contents fell to the floor. A packet of opened tissues, a half-eaten bag of Jelly Babies, some old CD's, and a cheap looking gadget. The bright orange handle had a hammer on one side for smashing car windows and a hooked blade on the other for slicing through seatbelts.

Yes!

They'd teased Mel when she'd first shown it to them. 'Who do you think you are, Fireman Sam?' Ranjit had joked. Mel said they might thank her for it one day, and they'd all fallen about laughing, Mel included.

It sliced easily through the seatbelt. Ranjit – unaware of eyes watching from within the trees – eased Karen out of the car.

She slipped the cutter into her back pocket, put Karen into the recovery position, and searched for her phone.

It seemed to be intact. The screen lit up and Ranjit pressed the "Emergency Call."

Nothing.

She waved it around, watching to see if any of the little bars would light up.

They didn't.

She moved back to Jo, slipping in the mud as she went. Her skin was still cold to touch. Ranjit checked for breathing but there was none.

She managed to get Jo free without issue, laying her on the ground.

There was still no breathing. She looked lifeless.

The screen of Jo's phone was cracked. It wouldn't turn on. Ranjit's dispassionate façade began to crumble. What should she do?

She thought back to her CPR training. Was she supposed to do mouth to mouth? How many chest compressions should she do, and for how long? She couldn't remember.

She placed her lips over Jo's mouth, closed her nose between her fingers, and exhaled. Jo's chest rose. She moved away and watched the chest fall. As the air came back it sounded wrong. She gave one more breath before placing her hands over the centre of Jo's chest to start compressions. It felt easier to administer to her friend than on the creepy practice dummy.

She settled into a calm rhythm, stopping occasionally to see if there were any signs of life. There never was. Her arms began to ache as the depth of each compression diminished.

It was no good, there was nothing more she could do. Karen was in the recovery position and still breathing. If she didn't respond this time, then Ranjit would go to find help.

Ranjit went over and gently stroked her friend's forehead.

Karen opened her eyes. They were distant and full of confusion.

'We've been in an accident.'

Karen began mumbling indistinct noises. Eyes fixed somewhere over Ranjit's shoulder. She started struggling, trying to get up. Ranjit tried to ease her down.

'Please, you might be hurt. We'll figure something out.'

Desperate hands grasped her own, digging their nails hard into her skin. Ranjit held on.

'Karen! Will you SIT DOWN!'

She did, recognition returning to her face.

'We crashed.' Karen looked around, her eyes settling on the upturned car. 'How do you feel? You've been unconscious.'

Karen rubbed her forehead. 'Okay… I think. Hey, is that Jo?

Is she unconscious too?'

'I don't think so. I tried to help her, but I think she's...'

Dead. Until now Ranjit had felt like she was the subject of a rushed drawing, quickly drawn lines creating clever illusions of what might be there. Now she was immersed in a horrific masterpiece of shade, depth, and texture. A scene of carnage painted upon a wash of impressive foliage, gnarled branches, and mottled shadows that beckoned from the distance.

'*I couldn't save her.*' Ranjit's eyes brimmed with tears. She struggled to form words between increasingly rapid breaths. 'Mel's dead too. Oh God–she's still in the car.'

Karen fought the urge to panic. She just wanted to lie down. Close her eyes and wait.

'Have you called for help?'

Ranjit sobbed quietly and shook her head. 'None of the phones work.'

'There must be a farm or something nearby. Maybe we should go and see.' Karen's eyes rested on the body of her friend, lying motionless in the mud. It didn't seem real.

Ranjit remembered reading once that if you were lost it was better to stay where you were rather than moving but that felt like madness. They were stuck at the bottom of a ravine and there was no way to get back to the road. The trees were densely packed, knotted between relentless foliage; it wasn't the kind of area where tourists would be rambling.

'Yeah, don't think I can just sit here waiting. Can you walk?' Ranjit asked.

'I'll be fine. What should we take?'

'There's some water in my bag and our jackets are in the boot.'

'I'll check the boot; you get the bag.'

The sun still hung high in the sky, but evening was fast approaching.

They decided on following the line of the cliff, hoping to

find some way of reaching the road.

Karen covered Jo with her coat, not so they didn't have to see her, but because it felt right; more respectful, less dehumanising.

They couldn't afford Mel any such dignity. She remained in the car, and though Ranjit and Karen did all they could to avoid looking at her broken body, it still felt wrong to leave her.

'Anything?' Karen was peering into the forest. The trees were tightly packed, but the ground looked level. Ranjit was pacing, checking for a phone signal one last time.

'Nothing. We'll try again later.' Ranjit wrapped her jacket around her waist and dropped the phone into her bag.

'Let's go.'

They followed the cliff face for about an hour. Twice they heard the sound of a car as it passed on the road above; twice they called out with no success.

'Watch it!' Karen reached out and grabbed Ranjit's arm, preventing her from falling into a tangle of tightly wound barbed vegetation. 'Nearly.'

Clusters of brambles and gorse were making their chosen route increasingly hard to follow.

'I'm not sure we can get much further this way.' Ranjit stepped, leant against the cliff, took a long drink of water, and passed the bottle to Karen.

'Should we try through there?' Karen nodded towards the forest. 'We're bound to find something: a stream, a trail, or even better, a Maccy D's.' Karen regretted the joke the moment it left her lips. It hung awkwardly in the air between them until Ranjit smiled. They both relaxed. Humour rarely solved anything, but it often provided a light in the darkest of places.

'I'd prefer a Greasy Spoon.' Ranjit replied.

They worked their way around tight knots of ancient trees, over carpets of decomposing leaves and wild garlic.

'I'm not sure this was such a good idea.' Ranjit was holding back a low hanging branch so Karen could pass.

'It was your suggestion.' Karen replied. Her wry smirk was cracked by the anguish beneath.

Eventually the trees retreated, revealing a small patch of land bathed in golden sunlight.

'What's the time?' Karen asked.

'Ten to five. No signal though.'

They squinted through the trees, looking for signs of civilisation.

Ranjit picked a small piece of moss from a tree and rolled it between her fingers. 'We should carry on the way we've been going. It'd be shit if there was a house just through there, and we turned away at the last minute.'

'And what if there's a house that way?' Karen pointed to her left.

'Fair point. I still think we should carry on; it just *feels* right.'

'It's as good a plan as…what was that?' Karen pointed left again.

'What?'

'There, I saw someone.'

'You're hallucinating now mate.'

'I swear … look, it's a woman.' Karen didn't wait for acknowledgement. '*Hello!*'

The woman continued walking. Ranjit caught sight just as she disappeared behind a tree.

'*Hello!*' Ranjit cupped her hands around her mouth as she called. 'We've been in an accident, we need help!'

They rushed to where the woman had been. Neither noticed the phone as it fell from Ranjit's bag.

'She can't be far.' Karen scanned the area. 'Why didn't she

answer?'

A low wailing cut through the stillness of the forest.

'What the fuck is that?' Ranjit said, 'It's coming from over there. Let's go.'

'Maybe we should just go back.'

'She's probably just an old hippie, doing some earth–mother ritual or something.' Ranjit tried to sound confident.

'I don't think we can afford to be too fussy. We need help.' Karen said.

The wailing continued, quivering through the trees.

They walked towards it, glancing nervously at each other.

'There she is.' Ranjit found herself whispering. The woman was standing between a small cluster of trees, facing away from them. Her long dark hair looked unkempt and matted; her white dress ragged and torn. One arm was pointing forward.

Streaks of sunlight pierced the canopy. A mottled pattern of light danced around the floor, moving in time with the leaves above.

'Let's just go.' Ranjit grabbed Karen by the hand and stepped backwards.

The woman turned towards them. Her lips were parted, her eyes wide.

The moaning stopped as she slowly opened her mouth. Held open wider than should have been possible and maintaining eye contact for several agonising moments.

The woman's face remained motionless as the mournful wail returned, swelling to a guttural howl. She raised her arm again, pointing directly towards them.

They both turned and ran. Fear had chosen its course. Neither noticed the pallid shimmer now encircling the strange figure, flowing from her, embracing the air behind them. The unearthly sound grew quiet, eventually slipping into the distance.

'I can't do this anymore.' Karen slumped against the remains of an old wall. A dead rabbit was splayed out on the floor, beside the lichen–encrusted bricks. 'Someone must have noticed that we're missing.'

'Maybe,' Ranjit said, although she thought it unlikely. 'They could even be looking for us now, but we need to keep moving. They won't find us here.'

Karen held her head in her hands. Ranjit wasn't sure she was listening.

A butterfly danced playfully around them. Quick flashes of electric blue. It landed on the rabbit to probe the sunken hole in its abdomen, as if the decomposing tissue were the nectar–rich stamen of a flower.

Normally she'd make sure Karen got a good look, receiving a slap on the arm for her troubles. She decided to check the time instead.

Ranjit bit her lip as she searched her bag. Then she began scanning the forest floor, her eyes darting to and fro.

'What's wrong?'

'The phone. It must have –'

Ranjit froze, looking between two tree trunks.

At first, she thought it was a large black dog standing amongst the trees, watching them. But as she got a better look at its large stocky head, hung low to reveal broad muscular shoulders, it was clear this was not a normal dog. The desolate black coat consumed any light unfortunate enough to fall upon it. Ranjit looked into the beast's eyes. Deep crimson shimmered within their blackness; she was transfixed.

Karen lifted her head and gasped. The beast snapped its head toward her and launched.

Ranjit was rooted; an unfortunate prey animal whose fight or flight refused to engage. It launched itself towards Karen, barely making a sound despite its vast size. She lifted her arm to protect her face.

Yellowed teeth tore into the flesh. Her legs thrashed helplessly, seeking purchase. The free hand, as if acting on its own initiative, explored the ground, looking for something heavy, or something sharp. It found nothing but damp clumps of leaves and dirt.

There was a small rock just beyond Karen's reach. Ranjit lunged forward, scooping it from the ground as she passed.

The beast twisted away causing Ranjit to gouge the side of its head rather than land a clean blow. A spatter of blood hit Ranjit's face. The beast released Karen's arm, which fell limply to her chest.

Ranjit staggered, narrowly avoiding the brutal jaws as the creature swung toward her. It drew back, readying its next assault.

Karen saw her moment.

She thrust her feet forward, catching the beast off guard. It fell sideways, thrashing wildly as it tried to get back to its feet.

Ranjit pulled Karen up and they both ran. The ground ahead of them dropped away. It was a sharp descent, but not too steep to risk.

They tumbled forcefully over coarse earth and rocky outcrops. Ranjit felt something tear through her jeans and into her calf, but they made it in one piece. She looked back up the hill as she hit the bottom. No sign of the beast.

It was only as she eased Karen up from the floor that Ranjit noticed the extent of her injuries. Her own leg was bleeding, but it was nothing in comparison to Karen.

Blood curled around the ragged flesh of what was once her forearm, spilling out in rhythmic gushes. Down the arm, onto the ground. Is *that bone?*

Karen's face was white, her expression blank and distant. Ranjit unhooked her jacket and pressed it onto the wound. 'That dog took quite the chunk out of your arm.'

Karen smiled vacantly.

Within seconds blood had started leaking through the makeshift bandage. Ranjit pulled off her belt, fastening it tightly around Karen's arm. It seemed to work.

The sun was sinking into the horizon. Pale light weaved through the wilderness as clusters of foxgloves swayed gently in the humid breeze. They needed to move.

Karen couldn't walk on her own, and despite Ranjit supporting her, she still fell several times.

'It's no good,' Ranjit finally said. 'I'll go and see if I can find anything. If not, I'll come right back. We can wait here until the morning.'

'What about…' Karen looked back towards the incline. Her voice was cracked and quiet.

'I don't think it'll be back.' Ranjit tried to hide her doubt before resting Karen against a tree and setting out on her own.

Had it not been for an unearthly shriek, echoing from the depths of the withering light, she would have walked straight past the road which cut a well camouflaged course through tightly enclosed trees.

Its surface was cracked and uneven. Potholes were filled with murky water, allowing little clue to their depth. It hadn't been repaired for years yet remained clear of the encroaching thicket. Someone had been cutting it back.

There was no telling how frequently it was used though. But it had to lead somewhere. She silently thanked the fox – or whatever had made the noise – for spooking her into changing direction and started to walk.

As the sunlight faded Ranjit was thankful for the illumination of the moon, though the longer time went by the more leaving Karen felt like a bad idea. She should go back. Try again in the morning.

Just one more corner.

An orange glow, shining through the trees, provided a

welcome answer to unspoken prayers. Doubt scurried away like a cockroach escaping the flickering brilliance of a fluorescent bulb.

She quickened her pace, the wound in her calf stretching with each stride. She barely noticed the warmth of fresh blood and she tried to ignore the intermittent stabs of pain.

The road came to a tall, expensive looking gate. Beyond it a well–manicured gravel drive led to a large house from which several expansive windows spilled light into the night.

There was a car on the driveway and movement inside the house. The gate was locked so Ranjit called out. No one came out, so she decided to climb.

As she approached, a man, probably in his late forties with slightly receding hair and a well–trimmed beard, stepped out of the front door. He walked to the car and opened the boot. Ranjit called again and he looked up, startled.

'This is a private drive,' he shouted, 'you shouldn't be here.'

'Wait!' Ranjit called, limping forward.

A woman with long auburn hair and a glass of wine in hand appeared at the door. 'What's going on?'

'Nothing, just stay inside.'

She did as she was told, and the man made a dash for the door, dropping a suitcase as he stumbled up the stone steps.

'Stop! Please, I need help!' Ranjit cried again, but it was no use. He took one frightened look at Ranjit as she pleaded for him to wait and closed the door.

What are they doing?

Ranjit limped over the fallen suitcase and slammed angrily against the door. '*I need help! Please, my friend needs an ambulance!*' The light on the other side went out, so she moved to the window. The woman peered from behind a curtain, eyes bulging with terror. A rabbit trapped in the gaze of a rabid dog. She stepped back, pulling the curtains closed.

Ranjit smashed her hands on the window leaving dark rusty

smudges on the glass. '*Please!* My friend needs help!'

They weren't coming out, but they might have called the police. She went to sit on the porch, and rapped the door every few minutes, just to remind them she was there.

The only evidence of their existence was a tiny slither of light from a first-floor window, escaping from a small gap in the curtains.

Hours passed; it didn't seem like the police were coming. The moon had disappeared behind thick clouds. Ranjit didn't even know if she could make it back to Karen. At least the night was warm. Hopefully her bleeding had stopped.

A strange sound pierced the tranquil night.

What's that?

High pitched. Rhythmic. *A siren?* It sounded far off but getting closer. She stood, hoping to see the cadent swell of neon blue, but there was nothing. The sound grew louder. She'd heard it before, organic, like a cat, or bird, or …

A pale glow was coming from the side of the house. Ranjit wondered if the couple had a change of heart, knowing instinctively that they hadn't. She walked onto the driveway for a better view. A leaden ball of panic swinging freely in her stomach. One part of her knew exactly what she would see, the other was only just becoming aware. The sound, not a siren but a mournful wail, had reached a piercing volume.

The woman was standing at the corner of a tall brick wall that jutted out from the side of the house, securing the property's extensive perimeter. Her pale skin appeared to glow in the oily night, like she had consumed the moonlight only to release it again; a washed-out memory of what had been, her mouth a contorted "O". Torn clothes hung loosely from a skeletal frame, quivering gently in a breeze that could not be felt.

Ranjit turned and headed for the gate – the only obvious way out. She didn't know what she would do once back in the maelstrom of the forest; unable to see, lost – but that didn't feel like a priority.

A few more strides. Ranjit tensed, ready to haul herself over the iron frame. And then she saw it, crouched on the other side; also tensing, ready to jump. The black coat that had contrasted so starkly with the daylight, made it almost invisible in the dark.

She skidded, taking a few awkward strides as she came to a stop. The beast was motionless. Holding her with barely visible eyes. She was transfixed again.

From behind her came that terrible moan, more intense now, more urgent. A corrupted harmony of low mournful drones and high–pitched shrieks.

The beast's eyes flickered and Ranjit was momentarily free. She turned to run back to the house; she would smash through the window if she had to. The woman hadn't moved. For some reason Ranjit found herself careening, not towards the house, but towards her. The ethereal spectre was pointing to a small cluster of bushes.

Ranjit didn't look back, didn't question. She couldn't hear the beast but knew it had already scaled the gate. She knew it wasn't far behind, bearing down, as the gaunt face ahead grew nearer. Sunken eyes. Distorted mouth.

Ranjit remembered a show she'd binged. The main character had said something about having to choose between one evil and another and preferring not to choose at all. Well *lucky him*, with his huge swords, great hair, and preternatural abilities. She could afford no such luxury.

The pale woman was nearly within reach. *What am I supposed to do now?* Perhaps it would just be better to stop. Hit the ground. Curl into a ball and let fate take its course. The piercing drone had become deafening. Up close the woman seemed translucent, like she was fading away. She remained motionless, still pointing her slender finger towards … what was that?

There was a gap within dense clusters of holly, the type she'd point out to her kids, *what animal do you think made that?* Either too old, too cool, or just plain bored of the same question being asked for the past ten years, they rarely gave a reply. Ranjit always suggested "badger".

She dropped to the floor and scrambled through, using her hands to navigate the well-used trench. She caught the pungent fragrance of rosemary. For a moment she was home; John was cooking roast lamb on a lazy Sunday afternoon, the kids were playing in the garden. Wooden fingers hooked into her hair, ripping clumps out as she passed. Bringing her cruelly back to the present.

She made it underneath and then came upon the wall that circled the property. It was neglected. Tall. Coarse fragments of brick came away at the lightest touch. She didn't think it would hold her weight. Clearly whatever made this trail didn't go over. Ranjit searched the ground.

There it was. The opening wasn't particularly big, perhaps four or five bricks were missing, but a channel had been dug beneath.

Her head pushed through with ease, but the shoulders brought her to a stop. She hunched them up, anchored her feet in the dirt and pushed. Her body shifted and then stopped. There was a rustling from behind.

She pushed her head down, squeezed her shoulders and arms hard into her body and pushed again. Ragged masonry scraped her arms and gouged her back. The pain was intense, but she kept moving. Once the shoulders were through the rest was easy.

She expected jaws to clamp around her feet, but they didn't. It had gone again.

The trees became less dense as she walked, giving way to

increasingly open stretches of land leading to a small dry-stone wall which marked the end of the forest. Ranjit stood behind it, looking out over a landscape of rugged pasture. The cloud filtered moonlight quivered across the ground. There was a house on the other side. Its lights were on.

She lifted herself over and headed for the fragile glimmer of hope.

The ground was soft. Boggy in places. Ranjit nearly lost balance when her foot was swallowed by the spongy land.

The house was nestled amongst a small complex of other, darker, buildings. There was a stench of wet hay and urine.

A blow to her side launched Ranjit into the air. Pain erupted in her hips, radiating out across her spine, into her abdomen. She hit the ground. Cold wet mud covered her face. She couldn't breathe. She couldn't see.

Spitting clumps of acrid sludge, she tried to get to her feet but was knocked down again. This time something had hold of her side, pinning her to the ground.

There was a low growl, becoming louder as the mouth clamped tighter around her pelvis, pushing enamel daggers into flesh. Ranjit roared as pain turned to agony.

Eyes still smothered in thick mud; Ranjit thrashed her arms wildly. She bashed her fists against the beast's head, but it was no good. It felt solid.

Her hands searched the ground for something she could use, but there was nothing. They just slipped around uselessly in the filth.

The jaws clamped tighter as the beast began to drag her away. She cried out again, reaching to grab the small of her back, hand brushing against the rear pocket of her jeans – against the seatbelt cutter she'd put there earlier.

She pulled it out and swung, connecting sharply with the side of the beast's face. It continued dragging, biting down harder. She tried again, smashing the spiked hammer down repeatedly. Breaking rocks with a wooden spoon.

Her body was becoming numb, she could feel herself slipping away. There was nothing else to do but hope that she passed out sooner rather than later. She should at least be granted that small mercy.

Her hand slipped down, still gripping the small safety device. It stopped as it became hooked around a belt loop.

Ranjit tugged, ripping the denim strip with ease. She swung it again, this time lashing at the creature's mouth. To anyone watching it would have looked desperate and random, and while it was certainly desperate, it was anything but random. All she need was to just catch its–

There. The bladed hook slid around the taught skin at the side of the beast's mouth. Ranjit felt steel slice into flesh. The beast gave a sharp growl, but the blade stopped, just a few millimetres in. She tugged again but it didn't move. This *had* to work.

Drawing on her final reserves, she suspended her whole weight on the handle. She felt bloodied breath on her face. Her arm tensed, holding her upper body off the ground. She swung back and forth as the beast continued pulling her across the field.

Deep breath. Hold it. Wait.

On the downwards swing she threw herself towards the ground, arm locked tight. The cutter followed, slicing neatly to the back of the beast's jaws. This time it howled and let go.

Ranjit felt herself drift, but the jaws didn't come again. She heard a shout. A deafening crack. She couldn't hold on any longer. The filtered moon was shining overhead. It was the last thing she saw before the allure of unconsciousness became too much to resist.

***

Llewella was in her bedroom when she heard the shouts. She looked out of the window. The field disappeared into the shrouding blackness. Nothing to see. She went downstairs, grabbed her shotgun, slipping a cartridge into each of its barrels, and went to the back door. She lifted a large torch off the wall and headed out in the direction the sound had come from.

She heard Ranjit before she saw her: arduous grunts, something being dragged through mud, snarling.

When the beam of the torch found her, Ranjit was face down in the mud.

Llewella almost didn't see the beast that was there too. She'd seen it before. From time to time the odd tourist would disappear. Not knowing how to keep themselves safe, they would fall prey to the fearsome creature that stood before her. Their disappearance was usually put down to a combination of inexperience, mountainous terrain, and weather that could switch to dangerous extremes in a matter of seconds, but she knew this wasn't always the case.

The woman looked like she could still be alive. That would be a first. Stories had been passed down for generations, telling tales of unearthly creatures that haunted these ancient woods and unforgiving mountains. It was more than a means to pass the time during cold dark nights, they could mean the difference between life and death. Those who knew listened and listened hard.

But it was one thing to protect yourself, and those you knew and loved—that was easy. It was quite another to risk one's own life to protect that of a stranger—that took real compassion. That took courage.

I'll be damned if this poor soul is going to die on my land.

'Get out of here.' Llewella snapped at it. It didn't move.

Llewella held the gun to the sky and fired. Darkness was momentarily expelled, sound reverberated for miles.

The beast fled back towards the forest.

Ranjit was bleeding and unconscious. But she was alive. Llewella scooped her into her arms and carried her back to the farmhouse. She tended to Ranjit's wounds whilst waiting for the ambulance, hoping they weren't as bad as they looked.

***

It was morning when Ranjit woke up. The police were hanging around outside the hospital room, eager to quiz her about what had happened. What had led to three of her friends being found dead in the forest? There had been a crash, obviously. But what else?

The nurse had told them they could wait until her family had arrived. Until she was strong enough to talk.

Ranjit ached all over. She wanted to know how Karen was but couldn't find the words to ask. The nurse said that someone would explain everything later and until then she should rest.

John and the kids were on their way. The thought made her smile, but her mind was full of horrors. Disjointed images flooded her morphine–soaked brain. She couldn't focus, couldn't make sense of it. She tried to keep her eyes open but despite her resistance fell into a deep and comfortable sleep. There was more horror to come, but for now it would have to wait.

Brett Always Dies

Brett O'Reilly

The three young men with *Seattle Estate Auctioneers* embroidered on their overalls sifted through the contents of the dead man's kitchen, cataloguing wares no longer needed.

'I'm telling you, every time. *Every time.*' A flash of light bathed rows of silverware, sealing the image on the Canon EOS R50's SD card.

'Here we go again,' Jayden muttered from the kitchen's island, his Jamaican accent smooth and low. The keys on his laptop rattled as he entered inventory from a stack of hand-filled forms.

Brett pretended not to hear and adjusted the camera for another shot. Mark shuffled nervously at the far end of the table, unsure of what to say. After two more bursts from the Canon's Speedlite EL-1 flash, he finally asked the inevitable.

'...Every time?'

It was the invitation Brett was waiting for.

'Every time. Starting with *Alien.* Brett—played by Harry Dean Stanton—gets sent by Ripley and Parker to corral Jones, the damn cat, only to have the alien come down from the air ducts, drive its second set of jaws into Brett's skull, and pull him—still alive and kicking and screaming—into the air ducts.'

'So you don't actually see him die,' Jayden said, still leaning over his screen.

Brett shot him a look and turned back to Mark.

'*Pulp Fiction.* Jules and Vincent show up at Brett's apartment, pop his friend who's lying on the couch in the head, then open up on Brett.'

Brett paused for a moment, looking down at the flatware.

'You can pack these up now, I got 'em. J', sending you the pics.'

Mark hesitantly moved forward and began packing away the knives, forks, spoons, and serving utensils into an antique cherrywood chest.

Brett fiddled with his camera before continuing.

'Then there's *Rampage*, the one with Dwayne Johnson and the giant gorilla? Based on the video game. Anyway, Jeffrey Dean Morgan's character lets Brett, who admittedly is a villain, go. Brett runs outside *just* in time for a chunk of building to fall on him. Again—*Brett dies.*'

Mark nodded in agreement, uncertain what else to do. Jayden lowered his forehead into the palm of his hand. Brett continued.

'*Archer*, season five, episode one. Brett dies in a hail of FBI bullets. *Teen Wolf,* season six, episode thirteen. Brett the werewolf gets poisoned with wolfbane, but is that enough? No! He gets hit by a car! Why? Because *Brett. Always. Dies.*'

'Ay, caramba, this again?' a voice spoke from the doorway. All three of the kitchen occupants turned to Luis, who leaned against the doorjamb, arms folded over the word Supervisor, which was embroidered onto his overalls above his name.

Jayden, who also wore the title *Supervisor* on his overalls, waved a hand in Mark's general direction. 'Fresh meat.'

Luis snorted as Mark turned flushed a deep red. 'Hey man, don't buy everything he says. Brett lives in *Suicide Kings*. Gets shot in the leg, but he lives.'

'Yeah,' Jayden chipped in, 'Wasn't Brett the kid who owned *Cujo*? Pretty sure he survived.'

'Oh! And Brett from *Jinxed*! He lives!' Mark added.

The sour expression on Brett's face curdled the smile on Mark's. Jayden and Luis burst into laughter, deepening Brett's scowl.

'Relax, Brett,' Jayden said. 'It doesn't matter what your name is—we're black, and unless we're in a Jordan Peele movie, brothers never survive past the second act.'

Luis smiled. 'That's why you never see us Latinx in horror movies. We're too smart to get caught up in that shit.'

'Right,' Jayden leaned back in his chair. 'Someone obviously missed *Breaking Bad*.'

Luis gasped in mock horror. 'Ese, you wound me! To paint my people with such stereotypes—'

Both Brett and Jayden fixed Luis with stony stares.

'Alright, alright, I know—I think I'm going to walk away now. Besides, it looks like the newbie is going to have an aneurysm.'

Brett and Jayden turned to Mark, who had begun to emanate crimson heat through his cheeks, entirely in contrast to his apparent desire to become invisible.

Brett gave Mark a comforting smile. 'It's all good, Mark. They're messing around. We're just not used to having—' Brett shrugged, '—*white* people in the room.'

'Yeah man,' Luis said, 'We're just playing. Maybe one day we'll even let you play.'

'Play what?' A voice spoke up from behind Luis, who jumped forward.

A girl, a year or two shy of her teens, stepped into the kitchen. Knee-high overalls and a dark blonde ponytail gave her a tomboyish look, which contrasted with her pale complexion and dark intelligent eyes. A big paper bag filled her hands.

'Hey Emily,' Brett said. 'We were just joking around with each other. How are you?'

Emily nodded and surveyed the room's occupants solemnly.

'I'm good. How are you?'

'I'm—good. So—where's your dad?'

Emily's neutral expression turned slightly sad. 'He's at the gate. Talking to the neighbourhood watch.'

Brett frowned, as did Luis and Jayden. Mark blinked in confusion.

'I feel like I'm missing something here—'

Emily spoke. 'The neighbours think Brett and Jayden are robbing the house. And that Luis let them in to do it.'

Luis crossed his arms and shook his head angrily. 'Let me guess. I'm the gardener. Right?'

Emily nodded. 'Sorry.'

'What about me?' Mark said.

'I don't think they even know you're here,' said Emily.

'Don't sweat it, Mark. David'll handle it. This is his daughter, Emily. Emily, this is Mark, the new guy.' 'Hi,' said Mark.

'Hi,' Emily said back.

'So—uhmm—your dad—'

'—has an antiques shop, yes,' Emily finished. 'We're here to window shop ahead of the auction. And—' she held up the brown paper bag,'—we brought you lunch.'

All four men broke into smiles. Emily handed the bag to Luis, who took it to the island and began unpacking.

'Muchas gracias, l'l sis!' Brett fist-bumped Emily.

'Ain't no thang, bro,' Emily deadpanned.

'Alright! A Reuben!' Luis said.

'Hi Daddy,' Emily said to the man standing there. David appeared to be in his late forties, streaks of grey lining his dark hair. A cardboard tray of fountain drinks rested in his hands, which he handed off to Brett before introducing himself to Mark with a handshake.

'With extra pickles,' a new voice said from the doorway.

'David, you are the best,' Jayden said, liberating a coke from the tray. His face turned serious. Everything okay out there?'

David's expression became grave. 'About that—'

Brett sipped on a coke and grimaced. 'Emily gave us a heads-up. How bad?'

'Well, it seems the neighbourhood pay for its own security,' David said. 'And that security appears to be scarily representative of the neighbourhood.'

'White and wanting to keep it that way,' Luis said around a mouthful of corned beef and sauerkraut.

'Pretty much,' David agreed. 'Judging by the two I talked to, they're either ex-cops who outlived their welcome on their force, or they didn't pass muster to begin with, and went into security.

'Listen guys, I really hate to say this, but stay inside as much as you can. If you have to go out for anything, send him,' David said, gesturing at Mark. 'And when you leave, let him drive. If they stop you, let him do the talking.

'It makes me sick having to say that. But I'm certain those two are looking for an excuse. Please don't give them one.'

'It's all good, David. You're pretty fly. And that's what counts,' Jayden said.

David gave a wry smile. 'Pretty fly? Isn't that so nineties?'

Everyone laughed, even Mark. Everyone but Emily, who simply watched, her dark eyes inscrutable.

'So David,' Luis said, wiping sandwich dressing from the corner of his mouth with a paper napkin, 'We don't want to hold you two up—how about I give you the tour while these pendejos finish their lunch?'

'Hey, güero, there's a kid present!' Jayden retorted.

'Ah, she don't speak Spanish. You don't speak Spanish, do you Emily?'

'Pendejo means pubic hair,' she said flatly.

Luis turned a deeper red than Mark had all morning.

'Luis. Perhaps you and I should talk about your language around my daughter.'

'Ah man—David, I had no idea—'

'Mm-hm.'

'I think we should get that tour going...' Luis sidled out of the kitchen.

David turned to the others. 'Thanks for setting such a great example for my daughter.'

The ghost of a smile played around the edge of his lips.

All three flushed red.

Emily turned to Jayden, 'Bye Jayden.'

Jayden smiled. 'Bye Emily.'

She turned to Mark. 'It was nice to meet you, Mark. I'm sorry about your leg.'

Mark blinked uncertainly. 'Uhm—thank you? It was nice to meet you...'

Emily walked over to Brett and to everyone's surprise, hugged him,

'Goodbye Brett.'

'Uhmm—bye Emily,' he said, navigating a mouthful of turkey club.

Emily slipped out the kitchen door. David glanced at the three young men and shrugged before following her.

'What did she mean "sorry about my leg"?' Mark said.

'Emily—is just Emily. She's a little—different.' Brett said.

'What Brett means to say is she's downright spooky,' Jayden said.

Brett looked at Jaedyn, then sighed. 'Emily—knows things. Or at least she seems to. She knew when Luis's wife was pregnant before either of them did. Told him congrats two weeks before Carla confirmed with a pregnancy test.'

'Don't forget my grandmother,' Jayden said. 'One day, David and Emily come by the office for some paperwork. Child walks up to me and says in a perfect Jamaican accent, "Muma Gabrielle wants you to know she is movin on, but you have always been her boonoonoonoos, and she loves you more than heaven and earth".'

'Before I can say a word, my phone rings. My Auntie Rachelle in Jamaica. Calling to let me know Muma Gabrielle had passed in her sleep.

'The child knew before I did. From Jamaica.'

Wide-eyed, Mark turned to Brett.

'What does *boonoonoonoos* mean?'

'I don't know. Do I look Jamaican?' Brett answered.

Jayden frowned at the both of them. 'It means *special person.* The point is, Emily is touched by *Obeah.* Magic. No child can know the things she knows.'

Brett shrugged. 'I don't know about magic. More like some kind of psychic ability. But the fact is, she's a kid. Her life's going to be hard enough without us calling her creepy.'

Jayden raised his hands in surrender. 'Point taken.' He turned to Mark, 'Brett's got a soft spot for kids. He'll make a great father someday—unless he *dies.*'

Brett frowned. '*Supernatural,* season fourteen, episode nine, Brett the vampire—'

***

Emily stood in the centre of the library and hugged herself as Luis showed her father around the room, stopping here and there to investigate various small, monstrous sculptures scattered all about, apparently the creations of the mansion's late owner.

'The boss says there's some horror film producer up in Vancouver interested in these—' Luis was telling David, as they peered into a glass case containing three statuettes.

What troubled Emily wasn't the grotesque figurines, but the giant fireplace that occupied the back wall of the library. Void of dust as well as wood and fireplace utensils, the firebox didn't fill her with dread so much as what she felt beyond it.

What exactly that was, she didn't know. Only that dark secrets held sway on the other side of the fireplace, and before day's end, someone was to die.

Not knowing how to explain to her father or Luis any of what she sensed, she held her silence.

David and Luis exited the library with Emily trailing after, hoping that maybe, just maybe this time she was wrong.

***

Brett let out a low whistle as he stood in the doorway of the library. 'Wow.'

The room was immense.

Glass-fronted bookcases lined the walls, filled with hundreds, if not thousands of tomes. On the wall to the left, sandwiched by bookcases, heavy velvet drapes standing sentry, mid-afternoon sunlight filtered through a colossal bay window; Brett could almost smell the salt air on the other side of the glass.

Opposite the double doors in which he, Luis, and Mark stood, a massive fireplace squatted, its chamber empty of wood or ash. Two luxuriously upholstered wingback armchairs crouched a few feet from the hearth, a pair of mahogany end tables accompanying them. Scattered through the centre of the room at seemingly random points, six freestanding curio cabinets imprisoned several small statuettes, each approximately eight inches tall.

The three men surveyed the room. Mark broke the silence.

'It feels a little—'

'—staged.' Brett finished for him.

'Yeah, that's exactly what David and I thought,' said Luis. 'Everything's almost too perfect. The chairs look like they've never been sat in. At least half the books have never been cracked open. His sculpting workshop's the same. Everything's pristine, like it's never been used.'

'Like it's all for show,' Brett said.

'Yup,' Luis continued, 'But wait until you get eyes on the main attraction. Not sure how he did 'em given the pristine state of his workshop, but you have to see 'em in order to truly appreciate Prevost's mad genius.' He led Brett and Mark to one of the cabinets and pointed at its contents.

The occupant of the top shelf immediately sent a shudder through Brett. Carved from stone the colour of curdled cream, the figure was a man in a trench coat with an oversized fedora crowning his head. Webbed feet poked out of rumpled trousers; the hands, clutching a book to the figure's chest, also displayed thin membranes between long, scaly fingers. Bulging eyes rested in a face of too much flesh; the loose-hanging jowls reminded Brett of a grouper fish he'd seen at the Seattle Aquarium as a kid.

What made the figure horrific was the attention to detail. The meticulous sculpting of each feature gave the fish-man a sense of vitality—so much so that Brett half-expected it to lunge at the glass, a caged predator intent on savaging its captors.

'*Arlo Myron. Lords of Cantabria.*' Mark read aloud the small brass plaque mounted on the statuette's base.

'Mirón,' Luis corrected him. 'It's Spanish for "lurker". Arlo Mirón is one of the characters from *The Lords of Cantabria.*

Jayden and I saw it last week at the Metro. Prevost did all the creature design for it.'

Brett's face wrinkled in loathing as he gazed at the figure on the second tier. 'What the hell...'

Luis practically beamed. 'Madre Miróna. She's the Queen of the Lords—the fish-men. They bring her unsuspecting human men to mate with, then she eats them.'

'That is seriously messed up,' said Mark. 'I'd hate to run into her in a dark alley.'

The three studied the figure with wonder and revulsion. Sculpted from the same cream-colored stone, Madre Miróna was Arlo taken to an extreme. Bulbous, lidless eyes seemed to study them back. Her face was heavier than Arlo's, her thick lips lined with tiny, pointed teeth. The webbing between fingers and toes was more pronounced, and sharp claws adorned both hands and feet. A tattered wedding dress hung over her bloated frame, doing little to conceal her swollen, mottled belly.

Brett felt slightly nauseous. Again, the attention to detail was so fine, so specific, he half-expected the Madre to step down off her pedestal, lurch forward toward the glass, and offer him a kiss—

'What's up?' spoke a voice directly behind him.

The trio jumped in unison, almost upending the curio cabinet and its contents.

'Dammit amigo! Don't sneak up like that!' Luis glared at a puzzled Jayden.

'You boys need to chill. You'll be in your graves before you're thirty.' Jayden shouldered his way in amongst them. 'I see you found Prevost's collection. Lovely bunch, aren't they? The bottom one looks like Luis.'

Luis snorted as Brett and Mark bent down to study the statuette on the bottom shelf. The now familiar features were all there, taken to their unnatural conclusion. The legs and arms were shorter, wider, and flattened, approaching, but not quite achieving the likeness of fins. The thing's trunk was rounded, with little in the way of a neck to separate torso and head—and no remnant of humanity existed in the latter. Bulging eyes mounted either side of a gaping maw full of those same small, pointed teeth that lined Madre Miróna's own mouth.

The inscription below the final statue read *El Cazador*.

'The Hunter,' Luis translated.

'This Prevost guy seems kind of messed up,' Mark said.

Jayden responded, 'Keep in mind, this was his job. Creature design for horror movies. And he was one of the best. Like H.R. Giger, who designed Brett's beloved Alien. It's still art, it's just—'

'Macabre art,' Luis interjected. 'If you check out that case—' he gestured toward another glass cabinet, '—it's full of his take on the classics—Dracula, the Wolfman, Frankenstein's Monster, the Mummy—even the Creature from the Black Lagoon. The cabinet near the fireplace has his Latin trio in it— El Cucuy, La Duende, and El Chupacabra. The man was a genius within his field. His field just happened to be the creepy monsters that want to eat you.'

'And our field is estate auctions,' Jayden said. 'There'll be plenty of time to admire the artwork later. Right now, we have a lot of work to do. Luis, can you show Mark how to catalogue the books?'

Luis nodded and waved his MacBook. 'Let's go rookie— you'll read while I enter. And hey, pull up one of those armchairs for me. Might as well be comfortable while I work.' He grinned at Mark.

Jayden turned to Brett, who spoke first. 'Statuettes first, got it. Multiple angles.' He glanced at the case with the fish-men. 'Who would buy these things, anyway?'

'Movie buffs, mostly. Collector pieces like this can for a lot. In fact, the boss already has a collector who's interested. Some guy by the name of Desmond Kelly, up north.'

'To each their own, I guess,' Brett said.

'Wait,' he continued, 'you and Luis, you two would totally buy these if you could afford them, wouldn't you?'

Jayden glared at Brett. 'Get to work.'

***

An hour passed as the four laboured away. Mark called out titles, authors, editions, and publication dates to Luis, who entered them into his MacBook. Jayden uploaded the contents of Brett's kitchen SD card to his own MacBook and wrote draft item descriptions to match each photo. Brett worked the room with his Canon, photographing all the statuettes from multiple angles before turning his lens to the stacks of books Mark and Luis had been setting aside.

After donning a pair of white linen gloves, Brett photographed each book individually, front cover, back cover, title page, and edition notice. Before long, he'd caught up to Mark and Luis; to pass time and give them a chance to pull ahead, Brett went to inspect the fireplace at the far end of the room.

The hearth and mantle were carved out of dark marble, with the firebox and flue fashioned from unmarred firebrick.

How weird, thought Brett, as he stepped onto the hearth. It's so clean, it's like it's never been used.

Ducking his head, he peered into the flue, again surprised at how clean everything seemed. And spacious. Curious, he stepped fully inside the firebox and stood straight up in the darkness of the flue. A flick of his thumb turned his camera flash on to the continuous light setting. The flue continued far above his head, the only marring in the brickwork being a crank wheel in the back wall, two inches above eye level.

'What the—?' Brett reached up and touched the unexpected protuberance. The size of a small dinner plate, it was black as midnight and cold to the touch, solid iron with no soot or residue attached to it.

Intrigue overrode common sense. Letting the Canon hang loose around his neck, Brett reached up with his other hand and took hold of the wheel.

Rightie tightie, leftie loosie—

Expecting some resistance, Brett turned the wheel to the left with enough force to launch himself into the wall. The wheel spun whisper smooth as a rectangular section of the back wall split and swung inward on silent iron hinges. The brick panel stopped with a soft clank, leaving a space large enough for two shorter than average people to walk through.

Darkness reigned beyond.

Brett took a step toward the aperture, rubbing his shoulder. 'What the f—'

'What the f —' Luis' head appeared in the chimney. 'What the hell did you do, man?'

'I—I turned the wheel —' Brett shone the Speedlite at the iron circle protruding from the wall.

Two more heads poked their way into the firebox.

'What happened?' said Jayden.

'A secret passage! Cool!' Mark said.

Both Luis and Jayden turned and looked at him.

'You realize this is why white people die in horror movies, right?' Luis said. 'You hear a noise in the basement, "Ooh, let's check it out!" You hear a noise in the attic, "Ooh, let's check it out!" You hear a noise in the secret passage in the fireplace, "Ooh—'

'I'm gonna check it out,' Brett stepped across the threshold, flash before him.

Luis stared in disbelief. 'You know, this! This is why Brett always dies!'

'Wait for me!' Mark scrambled after Brett. Luis looked at Jayden in shock. Jayden shrugged.

'One of us has to go after them.'

'You're kidding me, right?' Luis shook his head.

'We are their supervisors. One of us has to keep them out of trouble. Imagine how deep in it we'd be if something happened to the new kid.'

Luis grimaced.

'How about Rock-Paper-Scissors?' Jayden offered.

'Ese, I said it before. Lantinx don't die in horror movies for a reason. He tapped his temple. 'We're too smart.'

Jayden couldn't hold back his grin. 'Alright, fine. I'll be back soon.'

Luis slapped him on the back. 'Be careful, man. Call if you need me.'

It was Jayden's turn to grimace. 'Yeah, right.' He pulled a small flashlight from his back pocket and plunged into the darkness beyond.

***

From the landing on the opposite side of the fireplace, Brett and Mark descended a flight of worn stone stares that matched the walls and ceiling. The passage was broad enough for the two to stand side-by-side, though Mark remained behind Brett, whose light guided them down.

Less than a minute passed before they found themselves on a flat plane, a wooden door mounted into the rock. The door appeared old but solid, bands of slightly rusted iron holding it together. A small window was set into the wood approximately five feet up; a shutter for the aperture hung loosely on the same side as the two young men.

In sharp contrast to the rest of the door, a stainless-steel Mastercraft deadbolt gleamed in the flash's illumination, with a stainless-steel handle screwed into the wood above it.

'What the—' Mark stared at the door.

Brett snapped his fingers. 'Smugglers. I bet you this is a smuggler's tunnel. From prohibition days. There're probably more tunnels that lead right down to the water—they'd bring rum and whiskey in by boat and carry it up the tunnels to the house. I'd betcha anything!'

'Is that really a bet you want to take?' a voice whispered from behind Mark.

Brett and Mark both yelped and jumped, any hope for escape thwarted by the locked door. Their hearts began to assume a normal rhythm as the flash found a chuckling Jayden standing behind them.

'Bro! Not cool!' Brett said.

'Ditto!' Mark added.

'Ditto?' Jayden laughed, 'Well, you do look like you've seen a ghost! Any whiter, and you'd be one yourself!'

'Yeah, you're funny,' Brett said. 'We found a door—'

Leg of 'Why don't you and Casper move over and let me have a look.'

Brett and Mark gave Jayden sour looks as they moved aside to give Jayden access.

'Now let's see what we have here—,' he shone his light through the window in the door and let out a low whistle.

'What? What is it?' Brett said, as he and Mark strived for a look.

'Back off, man, you're crowding me,' Jayden said, 'Let me see if I've got the key for this lock.'

Jayden pulled a ring of keys out of his pocket and began trying a handful of unmarked ones while the other two shifted impatiently.

The third key slid into the lock but wouldn't turn it; likewise, the fourth didn't bear out on its promise. The fifth however turned the deadbolt smoothly.

Jayden stepped back and pulled the door open. A rush of air carried the faintest scent of something rotten, laid underneath a chalkier odour.

'Ugh, what is that?' said Mark. 'Smells like something died in here.'

'Maybe something did,' said Jayden, as he crossed the threshold. Brett followed immediately; after a moment's hesitation, Mark followed suit.

The beams from camera flash and flashlight swept through the darkness haphazardly, highlighting familiar, yet indefinable shapes.

The three men moved further into the room trying to make sense of the murky tableau, when Brett spotted a battery-powered generator in the corner nearest them. With a flick of the "On" switch, bright white luminescence flooded the room, its source three pairs of work lights, each mounted on a heavy-duty yellow tripod, stationed in the other three corners.

All three men blinked and shielded their eyes at the sudden burst of light; their blindness lasted only a moment, as the lamps faded to a dull glow, the generator's battery being heavily depleted. The subsequent impression was of a haunted space, where strange shadows lurked in the corners and dust motes floated in the light like an eerie mist.

It was immediately apparent they had found Prevost's real workshop. Along the walls, old barrels supported planks covered in sculptor paraphernalia; respirators, unopened bags of replacement filters, and brushes of all different sizes and appearance made up the bulk of the objects scattered about. On one such makeshift workbench, a ragged fedora rested amongst the paraphernalia.

Three large blocks of stone, all the same cream colour, sat on the floor against one wall next to a small hand truck with a motorized lift on it. A fourth such brick sat on a barrel near the centre of the room, a director's chair between it and the door through which the trio had entered. On the opposite side, a smaller keg was positioned, as if waiting for a model to take their place on it.

On the far side of the room an open doorway was carved into the rock wall. Forbidding blackness crouched in its depths.

Brett turned off the camera flash and circled around the chair for a better look at the stone block. Studying it, he let out a low whistle.

'You don't happen to know anything about a *Lords of Cantabria* sequel, do you Jayden?'

Jayden and Mark followed Brett's trail to view the unfinished sculpture.

Most of the block still retained its square shape, however, from the centre on the far side, webbed hands, open with palms up reached out in what struck Brett as a gesture of supplication. The rest of the creature's form remained eternally imprisoned in alabaster, it's creator no longer alive to wield chisel and brush.

'There were rumours of a sequel, but nothing definitive,' Jayden said. 'Then Prevost died, and the rumours went on hold.'

'Hey,' said Mark, 'How did he carve anything? There's no chisels.'

The three glanced around. 'You're right,' Jayden said.

'Unless…' Brett moved toward the wall right of where they'd come in, having noticed an aberration in the wall—a patch that seemed darker than the surrounding wall.

'Jayden, shine your light over here.'

Jayden did so, revealing a small recess in the wall—an alcove. In the alcove stood a door just like the two others—with the exception of excessive gouge marks spread across its surface, and scratches on the deadbolt. Littered at the bottom of the doors was a small pile of broken chisels.

'Wow,' said Mark, 'Someone really wanted in there.'

'Whoa!' Brett scrunched his face as he neared the door, 'I think I know where that smell is coming from.'

'Maybe Prevost had someone locked up in there! And they starved to death because he never came to feed them! 'Cause he died!' Mark said.

'That actually doesn't sound that far-fetched right about now,' Jayden said, stepping up beside Brett and shining his light through the door's small, paneless window. 'Ugh,' he said, recoiling from the stench seeping through from the other side of the door.

'Nasty, eh? Shine it in there, so we can see,' said Brett.

'What is that? Is that a—it looks like a pile of dead fish.' Jayden said.

'Let me see.' Brett shouldered Jayden to one side and peered into the room beyond. The beam from Jayden's flashlight rested on a pile of fish skeletons, some still sticky with scales and gobbets of flesh. 'What the hell—'

Mark stood to one side, eyeing the open doorway. Shiny steel hinges clung to one edge, their lines warped, as if some force had exerted itself on them.

'Guys,' Mark said, 'Isn't it a little strange that that door seems to be—missing?'

'Wait—shine the light over there—,' said Brett.

Brett and Jayden froze in unison.

Inside the locked room, Jayden's flashlight had found the still form of a little girl.

Brett spoke first. 'Keys.'

'On it.' Jayden scrambled with the keys, seeking the right one for the lock.

'Guys—what's wrong...' Mark looked at them worriedly. As if in response, the work lamps dimmed further, their power supply diminishing.

'Got it.' Jayden slid a key home and turned the lock. Brett pushed the door open and rushed in. Jayden pulled the key from the lock and handed the ring to Mark, along with his flashlight. 'Hold onto these. I gotta make a call.' He pulled his cell phone from his back pocket and started dialling.

The girl lay on the floor against the wall, curled up in a foetal position. Long black hair framed a gaunt face; a too-slender figure was draped in a stained and ragged sundress. Her eyes were closed tight. Brett guessed her age at four, maybe five.

Don't be dead. Don't be dead. Don't be dead. Brett knelt beside the girl, adjusting his camera so it hung behind him as he took the girl's wrist and felt for a pulse. Her skin was clammy and cold—too cold.

The girl's arm hung limply in his hand. Brett felt his heart and throat tighten, when a surge, slight, almost undetectable, passed under his fingertips.

'Is she dead?' Mark knelt down, eyes wide. Behind them they could hear Jayden swearing about a lack of reception.

Brett held up his free hand in a halting gesture. He waited.

Again. Faint, but there.

'I saw her chest move! She's breathing!' Mark said, flashlight trained on the girl.

'Goddamn piece of junk!' Jayden said from the doorway, looking at his cell phone. 'How is that possible, anyway? Prevost has been dead for over two months. The house has been empty. She should've starved to death by now.'

'Well, *someone's* been feeding her…' Mark's voice trailed off as he shone the light on the charnel heap of fish remains.

'Let's worry about it later,' Brett said, as he slid his arm underneath the girl and gently lifted her up. *Good god, you're almost nothing but a skeleton.* 'We need to get her out of here and call 911 on a working phone.'

Jayden backed out of the doorway as Brett carried the girl through, Mark immediately behind, only coming to a stop as his flashlight beam landed on the face of the creature behind Jayden.

'Ah, shit—' said Mark.

Brett looked up from the girl and jolted, stumbled backwards into Mark.

'Holy shit!' he said.

Jayden froze. 'That's a lot shit from the two of you...' Hands shaking, he turned around.

Arlo Mirón, Lord of Cantabria, shielded his bulbous eyes from the light with one webbed claw. Brett knew it was Arlo by the ragged shreds of trench coat and the old dusty fedora, which Brett suspected was missing from its perch on the workbench. The fish-man's other talon gripped an old crowbar, rust flakes peeling from it like scabs.

'Run!' Jayden leaped forward and grabbed the crowbar, which remained resolute in Arlo's webbed grasp.

Brett turned to dart towards the door to the fireplace and found another face looming out of the dark. The utter lack of human features told him he was face-to-face with Elcazador, "The Hunter".

'Get back!' Brett yelled as he scrambled in reverse towards the room where they'd found the girl. The door swung closed with a solid "clunk". Mark inserted the key and twisted; his face white enough to almost be luminescent in the flashlight's glow.

'Jayden! Jayden's out there—'

Mark bit his lip, his voice suddenly small. 'I don't think he is anymore.'

They both stopped and listened. Only silence held court beyond their ragged breathing.

'What are we going to do?' Mark whispered in a shaky voice.

'I don't know,' Brett whispered back. His mind reeled with too much information—or lack of it. The fish-men. The girl. Jayden—*dead? alive?* Too much at once, and none of making it sense.

'Shine the light around. Let's see where we are.' *Focus on the situation. Sort out the rest later.*

- 103 -

The room itself was quite large, and mostly contained scattered wooden and metal debris. A few old barrels still held their shape; a small cluster of these took up the far corner of the room, away from the door.

Mark tracked the flashlight beam back across the room and to the small window in the door, where Arlo Mirón was intently watching them.

Brett and Mark both jolted in surprise and horror.

The fish-man recoiled again from the light, and a string of burbled gibberish streamed into the room. This was answered in turn by more nonsensical syllables, only in a deeper voice.

An exchange took place in the darkness on the other side of the door, than another pause occurred, followed by the scrape of metal on stone.

'What are they doing?' Brett said.

Mark spoke. 'I think they're using the crowbar.'

A solid "chunk" shook the door as metal bit into wood.

'Shit! We need to get out!'

'Maybe we can hide?' Mark said, as he moved to the barrels in the back corner and started pulling them out in jerky, desperate motions.

Brett joined him. 'I don't think hiding in barrels is going to work.' He eyed the door, a rectangle of darkness framed by the deeper black of the walls.

'No—,' Mark said,'—but that might.' He shone the flashlight down on the iron ring of an old oak trapdoor.

At the door, wood creaked and splintered.

Brett put the girl down and helped Mark shift barrels to one side. The two leaned down and hoisted the trapdoor up, a task much easier than either expected.

'Rumrunners again. This must be an escape tunnel in case they ever got caught between the fireplace door and the main entrance,' said Brett.

Mark shone his flashlight into the void. 'There's a ladder.'

Behind them came a horrible wrenching noise. The door to the room shifted slightly inward.

'Go!' said Brett, 'I'll lower her down to you!'

The sounds of breaking and entering at the door intensified as Mark clambered down a set of rusty iron rungs driven into stone. Hurriedly but gingerly, Brett passed the unconscious girl down to his companion as the door burst open.

Dropping his own legs into the hole, Brett sat on the lip and turned to face the sensation of movement coming for him. Raising the Canon, he fired off a succession of photos, the Speedlite EL-1 hammering out a barrage of flashes which burned themselves on the lids of his closed eyes.

Satisfied with the warbling cries of distress and the tripping crashes of bodies amidst unseen debris, he reslung his camera and scurried down the ladder, pulling the trapdoor closed behind him.

Mark stood at the bottom, holding the girl and Jayden's flashlight.

'Here, give her to me. You lead.' Brett took the girl from Mark's arms, leaving the latter free to look about; they appeared to be standing in a tunnel with no ends in reach of the flash-light's beam.

After a split-second, Mark announced, 'You can't go wrong if you always go right.'

'Hurry!' Brett said. Already the sounds above were normalizing into deliberate movements.

They ran.

Seconds later, the tunnel ended in a T-junction; Mark turned right again. This led to a set of stairs leading down, which the two descended at speed. Another undiscernible distance passed before they found themselves at a four-way intersection. In the darkness behind, silence.

'I need to catch my breath, dude,' Mark said.

'Alright,' said Brett, his own breath playing cat-and-mouse with him. His arms were starting to ache from carrying the still unconscious girl, but he couldn't bring himself to put her down.

'What the hell is going on, man?' Mark looked plaintively at Brett.

'I don't know. I don't. Maybe Prevost somehow brought his sculptures to life. The ones we saw were just miniature copies or something.'

'Like Pygmalion and Galatea.'

'Who?' Brett said.

'It's a Greek myth. About a sculptor who—wait. Did you hear that?'

Brett listened. Hard.

Somewhere down the corridor they'd come down, a soft, squelching sound could be heard, as if someone in diving fins was trying to sneak up on the two young men and the girl.

Brett and Mark turned to each other; eyes wide with horror. The flashlight beam travelled down the hall to land on the bloated form of Elcazador, a mere twenty yards away.

'Go!' Brett cried.

The two of them ran. Again. The old smugglers' tunnels were a maze—one corridor after another, intersection after intersection, Brett and Mark ran, any sense of direction long abandoned, their only intent to lose their pursuer. Stairs and slopes seemed to abound throughout the tunnels, both up and down, leaving the two feeling like they were trapped in an Escher painting.

After what felt like an hour of running, both took a desperately needed break. This time, Brett had to lay the girl down to give his arms a rest.

'She's still out of it. Do you think she's even still alive?'

Brett laid his head on her chest and listened.

'She's got a heartbeat. It's—slow, but it's definitely there. It's—it's like she's been placed in a trance or something.'

'Weird. Maybe there's a spell on her. Like Sleeping Beauty.'
Brett gave Mark a look but said nothing.
The two sat in silence for a minute.
'You know, I've been thinking—,' Mark started.
'About what?'
'There's a lot of these tunnels. A lot. Like, more than smugglers would use.'
'So?'
'So maybe the "Lords of Cantabria" weren't brought to life by Prevost. What if they were here all along? And he just happened to discover them?'
'So, a race of fish-men has been living off the Washington coast and using these tunnels, but they were only discovered by Prevost, who kept them a secret so he could sculpt them for his horror movie creature designs.'
'Dude. Does that really sound that much crazier than the idea he sculpted them and brought them to life?'
Brett opened his mouth to speak, stopped, then sighed. 'You're right. It's all crazy. From any angle.'
Somewhere in the distant darkness, a strange voice warbled. A second, deeper voice answered back.
'I'm starting to understand why they call him "The Hunter"!' Brett said.
Mark took a deep breath. 'I have an idea. Do you have a light?'
'I've got my camera flash, but I'm not sure how much battery is left. I'm afraid I left my phone charging in the kitchen.'
'Your flash will have to do, I guess. Take the girl down that tunnel as far as you can without a light.' Mark pointed an opening in the wall. 'I'll use the flashlight to lead them this way.' He pointed to the right. 'Mark—'

'Don't worry about me. Worry about her. Get her to safety. Besides—,' he grinned, 'I'm the white guy. I have to live right?'

Brett couldn't help but grin back.

'Now go,' said Mark, 'Fast as you can without a light!'

Brett picked the girl up and draped her over his shoulders in a fireman's carry, then entered the other passage, one hand tracing the wall. Tripping despite the smooth stone floor, he wondered how long until it would be safe to turn on a light, and prayed he didn't stumble into a set of stairs before then.

***

Mark counted to five, which was time enough for the sounds of flipper-like feet slapping on stone to near the intersection where he lurked. With a quick prayer of his own, he darted down the corridor waving his flashlight haphazardly, and called out, 'Quick, Brett, this way!'

The ascending slope barely registered in his brain. He knew his gamble had paid off by the warbling cries that pursued him down the tunnel.

Maintaining a fast jog to keep distance between himself and his pursuers without actually losing them, he turned down different corridors to draw them away from Brett and the girl, always choosing the right path, not realizing that each choice he made was leading him further upwards.

Mark burst out into a larger tunnel, one well-worn with bits of old wooden debris strewn about. Old, rusted sconces, empty now of any torches, lined the walls, each a dozen feet apart.

He stopped and considered for a moment before declaring aloud, 'You can't go wrong if you always go right.'

This new passage led on another twenty yards before ending at a set of broad shallow stairs leading upwards. A wooden door rested against the wall at the base of the stairs, a steel deadbolt catching the flashlight's dimming beam.

'I'll be damned,' he said, grinning. He charged up the stairs to the Prevost's hidden workshop—only to stop short as his dying flashlight beam fell upon the face of Madre Miróna, standing in the doorway above him.

'Oh shit,' Mark said.

The flashlight died.

***

Brett slowed down to a walk when he realized he'd begun running, carried on by the downslope of the tunnel. Stopping, he took a moment to listen for the sounds of pursuit, but only heard the sound of his own laboured breathing.

After a moment's consideration, he turned the Canon's flash on and shone it the way he'd come, fully expecting to see Arlo lurching out of the dark towards him.

The tunnel was empty.

Brett considered turning back, attempting to backtrack his way to Prevost's workshop.

He decided against it—the chance of running into one of the Lords of Cantabria was too great. Besides—the smell of seawater had begun to seep into the tunnel. There had to be an exit somewhere close.

With the unconscious girl still slung over his shoulders, he continued on down the tunnel, the scent of escape lingering at the edge of his senses.

Brett soon found himself lost in the labyrinth. The tunnel he had ran down had dead-ended quickly, forcing him to go back to a T-junction, where the other tunnel joined on the left side. This led to another tunnel with three different branches along its length before it too ended abruptly.

Like that Greek myth about the minotaur. What was the hero's name? Perseus? Orpheus? Mark'd know. Sure as hell wasn't Brett.

The charge on the Speedlite flash was depleting. He began to orient by slope and scent; always choosing paths where the floor leaned downward, or where the scent of the sea seemed a little stronger. He took to turning the flash off to save the battery, only turning it on when unsure of the next twenty to thirty feet of footing.

Once he stopped in his tracks, finger on the "On" button, as he heard the warbling of several creatures pass through the intersection, he was a few yards away from entering. With eyes closed, he waited for them to pass, hoping against hope that whatever sense allowed them to navigate the tunnels in the dark would not reveal him to them.

They passed on, seemingly oblivious to his presence.

Brett continued on, using the flash more sparingly, not only to conserve the battery, but to reduce the possibility of discovery.

All sense of time had fled by the time he stumbled into the grotto.

The saltwater in the air seemed to burn his lungs, just as his arms and shoulders burned from carrying the girl. His flash reflected off the underground lake, revealing stone walls and nothing else.

He gently lowered the girl to the ground and sat beside her. He knew if it wasn't for her, he might just lie down there, wait for the fish-men to find him, and let the nightmare end.

He couldn't give up. Not with the girl's life at stake.

I just need to rest a minute.

He glanced at the prone child—and stared. The little girl was stirring—finally. One webbed hand flexed in her sleep.

Brett looked on in horror as the girl rolled over and squinted at the light, her eyes large and aqueous beneath heavy lids.

Comprehension came quickly.

'Prevost, you fucking bastard,' he said.

You took a page right out of Lovecraft, didn't you, you bastard. Only a photograph wasn't good enough. You had to have a hostage to force them to pose for you.

The girl lay still, studying him, her face clearly etched with fear.

'Grob?' she said, in the warbling language he'd heard in the dark.

Brett climbed to his feet, then reached for the girl, who cringed and shied away from his hand.

'It's alright,' Brett said. 'It's alright. Let's get you back to your people.'

Again, the fish-girl whimpered when he held out his hand.

'It's okay. I get it.'

Brett turned to the mouth of the grotto. 'We're here!' he yelled into the yawning darkness. 'We're here. I'm—I'm so sorry—I—I didn't know...'

He fell to his knees, his heart as heavy as a stone. 'I'm so sorry. I didn't know.' He looked at the girl with tears welling up in his eyes; she in turn studied him curiously.

'It's okay. Your people will be here soon. They'll take care of you. You'll be free again. You *are* free.'

A figure appeared at the mouth of the grotto, at the edge of the Canon's flash. A warbled cry issued from thick, rubbery lips as Madre Miróna rushed across the threshold, arms open.

'Grob!' The girl shot to her feet and threw herself into Madre's arms, mother and child reunited.

The two embraced for a long moment as looked on, his own heart a maelstrom of compassion, regret—and fear.

Madre Miróna broke her child's clutch and lifted the girl up into her arms. Carefully, she stepped up to Brett and hesitated before laying one cold, scaled hand on his cheek—then turned and waded into the saltwater lake. The girl watched the young man over her mother's shoulders as the two sank deeper into the water, leaving Brett all alone on the shore.

The Speedlite began to dim, it's endurance formidable, yet still finite. Brett turned to the grotto's opening, intending to at least exit the cave before he lost the light.

Arlo Mirón stood waiting for him.

The fish-man extended one webbed claw. In the flash's dying light, Brett saw the other was empty, the rusty crowbar discarded.

He looked at Arlo's hand and thought of a quote by Martin Luther King, Jr., one that his own father he'd always been fond of.

Faith is taking the first step even when you don't see the whole staircase.

As the Speedlite EL-1 gave way to the darkness, Brett reached out and grasped the hand of the Lord of Cantabria.

***

The path to the light was even more labyrinthian than the one that had led Brett to the grotto. And rougher—it seemed Arlo's assistance was not born entirely of good will, as he half-dragged Brett through pitch-black corridors of stone, seeming to care little for the latter's falls and scrapes.

Brett's sense of smell once again alerted him of escape before his eyes did; the air in the grotto had been denser, the taste of salt heavier, whereas the breeze that imperceptibly caressed him now brought the scent of sand and fresh air with it. Gradually, the light seeped into the tunnel around him, and the sound of seagulls rode across that of distant breaking waves.

A final corner brought them into another grotto, though this one was filled with sand and small tidepools and a distant light that crept in from an opening in the rock.

A pair waited in the grotto—Elcazador, whose image Prevost had perfectly captured, stood over Mark, who sat on the sand, one leg stretched out before him.

'Mark!' Brett started to run to his friend but was pulled up short by the claw wrapped around his hand.

'Hey Brett! Guess what! I don't think they're going to eat us. Or make us mate with Madre Miróna. And then eat us.'

'What happened to you?'

'I…found the stairs back up to the workshop—where I found the Madre waiting for me. Just in time for my flashlight to go out. I ended up falling down the stairs and passed out. When I woke up, my ankle hurt like hell, and the big guy here was carrying me.' He gestured at Elcazador, who continued to hover over his captive.

'Then he brought me here. Been standing guard over me ever since.'

Mark looked Brett up and down. 'Where's the girl?'

Brett grimaced. 'Where she belongs. With her mother.'

'With her—,' Mark looked at Brett quizzically before understanding dawned across his face.

'You mean—'

'I'll explain later. For now—do you think they're going to—'

Arlo released Brett's hand as Elcazador moved away from Mark and headed towards the opening Arlo had brought Brett through. The two Lords of Cantabria slipped out into the darkness—though not before Elcazador took one long, last look at the two bewildered humans.

'I guess that answers my question.'

Brett turned to Mark. 'Can you walk?'

'Not without help. Of that I'm fairly sure.'

Brett helped Mark to his feet and got Mark's arm over his shoulder. The two of them begin to make their way toward the light at the end of the grotto, in slow, lurching movements.

'When you found the workshop, did you see Jayden? Do you know if he's okay?'

'I don't know. I literally ran into Fish-Mom, and my flashlight died. I had a "whooshing" sensation as I fell backwards on the stairs, then it was lights out. Pardon the pun.'

Five minutes later, the pair struggled through the sandy mouth of the grotto and emerged onto a beach, the setting sun before them, rocky cliffside behind, and the mansion of famous sculptor and special effects maestro Howard Prevost far above.

Both Brett and Mark shielded their eyes against the sun's glare, unaware they were no longer alone.

***

Jerry cracked another beer and swore as foam flooded out of the can and spilled over his OverKnight Security uniform. His partner, Rob, cackled at the sight before taking a swig from his own half-finished lager.

'Yeah, real funny,' Jerry said, swiping liquid off his pants and onto the floor of the OverKnight Security jeep.

Rob took a final drag off his cigarette and flicked it out onto the pristine stillness of the beach. 'Still can't fuckin' believe that antiques dealer stickin' up for those thugs. What a fuckin' cuck.'

'Yeah, you see the camera that one kid had? Canon EOS R50. I got one just like it. No way a little shit like that could afford a camera like that,' Jerry said.

'Yeah, you're right,' Rob agreed, 'Punk probably stole it from another auction. Bet ya the three of them got quite the side hustle going, stealing from these estate sales and selling on the street. They're like grave robbers, if you think about it.'

'Yeah, totally,' agreed Jerry, squinting out the jeep's windshield. 'They—what the hell?'

Rob followed his gaze. 'What the hell?'

***

'I got a bad feeling about this,' said Mark.

Down the beach, Brett could make out a parked jeep and two figures running towards them, guns in their hands. Having never held a gun in his life, Brett had no idea what kind they were —the fact they were guns, and that they were pointed at him was more than enough.

'Freeze, motherfucker!' one shouted, a brass nameplate on his shirt reading "Jerry". He stopped and took up a shooter's stance a half-dozen yards away from Brett and Mark.

'Let him go! Hands in the air, motherfucker!' the other guard, whose own nameplate read "Rob", yelled as he dropped to one knee, weapon trained on his target.

Brett knew very well who they were talking to.

'It's okay!' Brett held one hand up while using the other to lower Mark to the sand. 'I'm unarmed!'

He raised both hands up in the air. A cool breeze trickled from the ocean through his fingers. The sun shone red and gold, though its brightness still made it difficult to see.

'I'm unarmed!'

The Canon EOS R50 bumped against Brett's hip.

'Gun!' Jerry screamed.

'Motherfucker!' screamed Rob, in response.

The first two shots destroyed the camera and flash; the second also grazed Brett's side with fire and agony.

Brett staggered. *At least they didn't call me a n—*

The next two rounds hit centre mass, stealing away the thought and leaving only pain.

A fifth shot rang out, leaving nothing at all.

We Two Must Part, With Sad Reluctance

Karen Heuler

C elia caught her reflection in a store window and there she was, slightly bent, a little stooped. She came to a surprised halt and forced herself to stand tall and straight, not a difficult task normally, as she was just 48. Still, she had to use all her concentration. There! She was straight. But as she turned to continue on her way, out of the corner of her eye she could see her body settle back into its new curve.

That night she asked her husband Charles if he had noticed anything. He looked up quizzically from his paper. His eyes measured her. 'Ah, now I see it. Just a little stoop. I wouldn't have noticed it if you hadn't asked.' He turned back to his paper. Dispiriting to consider that she was, of course, aging. This was the first sign of the onset of middle age, of sags and strains and windedness. It had snuck up on her; she had assumed all that was far ahead, and here it was, arrived. Like a dark presence following her. Gloomy thought.

Celia was normally a reliable sleeper. But she woke that night with Charles hugging her right side as she lay on her left. How had he fallen asleep like that, his weight resting on her like she was a pillow?

'Move, Charles,' she hissed, but he stayed put. 'Move!' she said, loud this time, and she jabbed an elbow at him.

But the elbow hit nothing. She sat up and switched on the light.

Charles lay facing away from her, not even close, and sound asleep. Her right side still felt his impression, still felt like something was draped over her, or clinging to her.

Well, maybe there was something. She got up and went to the bathroom, washing her face to think a little more clearly, and then looking at herself in the full-length mirror. Maybe something was stuck to her?

She stretched to see her side and as much as she could of her back. Nothing. She shifted her nightgown off and checked again. Nothing. She switched to another gown.

She was leaning forward even more, she could see it in the mirror, and tilted slightly to the side. But she was tired. It was the middle of the night.

It took forever to get back to sleep; she couldn't find a good position. She kept feeling that there was something constricting her or her nightgown. It was hard to put a finger on it, but something wasn't right.

When she dressed for work the next day, she chose the loosest clothes she could find. She still had that annoying sense that something was stuck to her back and side.

At her job as an associate production manager, she sat stiffly upright at her desk and at meetings. Her secretary, Lisa, stood behind her once, looking over her shoulder as she checked a report and she snapped, 'Don't lean on me, Lisa!'

'I'm not touching you,' Lisa said, offended.

Celia sighed and apologized. 'I just feel off,' she said. 'Like there's something hanging on me all the time. Across my side and across my back.' She gestured.

'There's nothing there, Celia.'

'I know,' Celia said.

She sat forward in her chair at dinner. She leaned forward on the couch when they watched TV. She had trouble paying attention. She got up restlessly and changed her shirt and checked the mirror and even weighed herself, the sense that something was riding on her was so strong. She was terrified that the scale would add the weight of some invisible creature, but she was also disappointed that it didn't. Which was worse? To really have something there or merely to feel there was something there?

That night she slept with pillows piled along her back, because she could feel them, and it was better than feeling the other thing. That worked for one night, but then the next night she couldn't feel the pillows at all.

The next day Celia woke up with a tightness in her neck. Not her throat, her neck. The pillows must have made her sleep in a bad position. It felt like she'd pulled a muscle. She pushed the pillows away and got up, aching a little.

Her neck, her aching back—ah! She was coming down with something, then. She took some aspirin and Vitamin C and got Charles up and made coffee and fed the cat. Not too bad, really. Probably just a cold. Charles sat down at the table, yawning.

'Can't wait for spring,' he said. 'Winter's getting on my nerves.'

'I think I'm coming down with something. Feel all achy.'

He laid his hand on her forehead. 'You don't feel hot,' he

said. 'But maybe you should stay home and stay in bed.'

And feel again that something that was nothing? She'd had enough of it for one night. Maybe if she moved around, it would wear off all by itself. She shook her head. 'I don't want to give in to it,' she said.

She tied a scarf around her neck, to try to get rid of that strange feeling, like there was something there already, a piece of tape, a rubber band, constricting her skin. It felt better with the scarf on. At least she could ascribe the sensation to an object now, the scarf.

Her job was a desk job except for all the meetings, which were just as endless as they were pointless. A long time ago, she had found meetings interesting, and had watched to see the guy's jockey for one-upmanship at each one. The fast talkers, the interrupters, the jargoneers; all of them struggling to "win" the meeting. What was she? She was a sly commenter. She would ask, at the pivotal moment, 'Would that proposal work if the price of oil goes up? It's supposed to.' Or 'Which of our employees do you think would be able to do that?'

Most of her coworkers had moved on to other, better companies. Maybe she wasn't ambitious enough, but it was hard to see what ambition would look like in this profession. She preferred the people to the job, and when people she liked left, they were often replaced by other people she learned to like. She stayed because it was all she knew, and there was nothing wrong with it. Her life was good enough, and even, in some ways, good.

She could get through her job blindfolded, which was lucky because really, she was dragging.

Lisa came in with a second cup of coffee. 'Thank you,' Celia said. 'I'm no good today.' She sipped and sighed.

Lisa tilted her head. 'You do look a little off. Did you sleep all right?'

She shook her head. 'I seem to have lost the knack.'

'Does your back hurt? You look all hunched.'

'I feel all hunched,' she agreed. 'I wonder if this is arthritis or a disk or something.'

By the end of the workday, she was cricking her neck constantly. She leaned forward when she walked. She could straighten up only with determination.

'My,' Lisa said. 'You know, maybe you've pulled a muscle. Get a massage or a heat wrap or something.'

'I will,' Celia said. She looked up some massage places, chose a Japanese one, and stopped on the way home. They specialized in placing hot stones at pressure points.

It helped a little, not a lot, but she would come back again if it didn't all go away as mysteriously as it came.

She was late getting home and there was Charles, warming up soup and slicing bread. The soup relaxed her tension and spread a nice warmth inside her, and for a moment, it all shifted back into her ordinary life.

And then the moment passed.

She had a glass of wine and watched TV. It was hard to get a comfortable position; she kept having to shift her legs because her back felt odd, and she eventually got a pillow for her neck as well. She could describe the neck thing better, now. It was as if there were fingers around her throat, near her collarbone, pressing in.

'Like this?' her husband asked, gently putting his fingers exactly where she had felt fingers. It made her heart lurch. She cried out, and he jumped back. 'Did I do something?' he asked, immediately apologetic. 'I'm beginning to think you don't have a cold. What's wrong?'

'I told you,' she said, exasperated. 'It feels like I'm being choked. And I feel bent, too. I don't know what it is. I feel terrible.'

'Finish your wine,' he said. 'Have a second glass. If we

can't get you to a doctor tomorrow, we'll go to the E.R.'

She was absurdly grateful to him. She let out a long-relieved breath. Was her throat relaxing? Was her back better? She took another sip of wine. Maybe it was stress.

But in the middle of the night she woke with two hands on her throat. The fingers had advanced! She was frozen, paralyzed with fear. The odd thing was that she was on her back and the hands came from behind her, an impossible thing.

They seemed to tighten and loosen with her heartbeat, which was frantic now. She could only breathe in little pants, but gradually she tried to breathe against her heartbeats—she would wait for three thuds and take a breath and wait for three thuds again. She tried hard to accept the hands for a moment so she could keep from panicking, because all she really wanted to do was panic. She lay there trying to concentrate on naming everything that was happening to her, so she could describe it to the doctor in the morning. The hands are lined up almost finger to finger, across my neck but not quite yet on my windpipe. They come from behind.

Her back, or was it really her hips, also seemed weighed down as if she were carrying a heavy child slung to from the side.

Her heart crashed harder for a moment.

Or as if someone were behind her, wrapped around her, with its hands holding on around her neck.

All at once she broke free from her paralyzing fear and shouted out loud. She was awake. She sat bolt upright in the middle of the night, clawing at her neck, trying to remove the hands. Charles jumped up, grabbing hold of her frantic motions. 'What is it, what is it?' he kept asking until her breathing calmed down and she could answer.

'A dream,' she said. 'A nightmare. Whatever it is, it's still here.'

He turned on the light.

She was hunched over, the sheet flung aside, her hands at her neck. 'It's trying to choke me. I can still feel it.'

'There's nothing there. Take your hands away. There's nothing there.'

'It's there,' she said bitterly. 'I can't see it either, but I can feel it.'

He slowly lifted his hand to feel along her shoulder and throat. 'There's nothing there,' he said again. 'The doctor will know what it is. Maybe it's some kind of condition; I mean, maybe it's an illness. You know what I mean.' His voice had gotten conciliating; she knew what he meant: Maybe you're crazy. She understood.

She went to her regular doctor, who found nothing, but gave her a pill to relax. She went to a specialist, whose scans showed nothing wrong with her brain. Blood tests showed nothing out of whack, though a few things were at the lower end of normal. They found no evidence of disease. 'Do you doubt me too?' she asked Charles. 'Do you think this isn't real?'

'Oh, it's real,' he said unhappily. 'I can see what it's doing to you.' But his voice was a little restrained. She looked at him and saw his eyes swing away. He didn't believe.

She went to another doctor and then she went to palm readers, psychics, seers.

She bent forward further every day, soon panting with the effort of carrying this gnome around with her. She had to call it something, and it seemed bent and evil like some gnomes the garden centre had. And when she picked up one of these gnomes, they always seemed so heavy. That was, she was told, to keep people from stealing them.

Well, who would want to steal the gnome on her back, on her shoulder, at her throat? Not the doctors surely, who went over their reports and referred her to other doctors, including a psychiatrist who gave her pills that slowed her down even more than the weight on her back did.

She rarely went to work. Then she was put on sick leave. Then she didn't care.

She went to two spiritual advisers before she found a pair who worked together, a husband and wife who claimed their different aspects allowed them greater insight. They had her sit down in their living room, on a bench, in the middle of the room, while they circled her, occasionally diving in closer to sniff her or touch her shoulder or lift her hair.

'I see it,' the wife said.

'Yes,' her husband agreed.

They were solemn. 'I'm so sorry,' the wife whispered. 'Your soul is leaving you. Pulling itself out.' Her husband nodded, and they waited for her to respond.

She watched their faces, hoping to see some humour, some irony, some explanation. 'Nonsense,' she said. 'Souls leave when you die. And not before. I've heard all kinds of people say it.'

The wife sighed. The husband said, 'Normally, yes. That's better for you and for the soul. Less of an ordeal. You die, and the soul is free to do whatever it's supposed to do.' He opened his hands. 'But sometimes they leave on their own. Sometimes they decide. We've seen it before. Not often. Once in a while. It's a slow, sad process; they have to pull themselves out of the body.'

'It's nothing you've done,' the wife said gently 'and there's nothing you can do to stop it. At least we've never heard of anyone stopping it.'

Celia's eyes were dry as she stared at them. What they described was impossible, some New Age nonsense that nevertheless registered with her. If no doctor could find anything wrong, then maybe it wasn't the body's failure at all? She felt indeed as if there were something else at work inside her, pushing through. It sounded crazy and it sounded true.

'No,' she whispered. 'I won't let it.'

They looked at her sympathetically. 'Do whatever you can to soothe yourself,' the wife said. 'To keep calm.'

'Will that stop it?' Celia asked.

The husband and wife were silent.

'That won't stop it,' Celia whispered.

She left feeling weighed down by the soul she carried around her back and hips and spine (was it formed the way she was? Was she feeling it like a child on her back because of this?). She looked in a store window as she passed and saw she was bent far forward, like an old woman. Her face looked shocked too, perhaps because she wasn't getting enough air with each breath. She was gulping when she moved. She stopped, letting her breaths catch up with her.

Charles laughed at her harshly. 'How could you believe them? This is the worst nonsense. Taking advantage of the sick and frightened.' He went on, fuming.

Celia was startled to hear herself described as 'sick and frightened'. When had he switched to that description for her?

'We're going to another doctor tomorrow,' he said finally. 'We won't stop until we find out what's wrong. This is medical. What did they suggest, an exorcism?' His words were scornful, his arms crossed, his feet apart. Fighting stance, Celia thought.

'Exorcisms cast things out,' she said. 'We don't want that.'

He looked at her sternly, but his look relaxed into sadness. 'We'll find the right doctor,' he said. 'We will.'

She checked herself again in the mirror. Her eyes had a shaded look, a grey, empty look. '*Don't leave me*,' she whispered to the mirror, to whatever was moving behind her eyes. '*Don't leave me.*'

That night the hands pressed harder. She couldn't lie down

because it helped the hands, it gave them more strength. She bunched the pillows together and leaned back against them, trying to ease her breathing. She would stay awake all night if necessary. Charles had said he'd find a doctor, and he would. He had held her hand until he'd fallen asleep; she wished he'd stayed awake with her, but that was too much to ask.

He took her to the hospital the next day, reporting that Celia was having trouble breathing and trouble standing straight up, whether that was related or not. They ran tests, they took pictures. Her potassium was low, as was her thyroid level, much lower than her last set of tests. They gave her some pills, and she was kept overnight to make sure she responded.

In the morning a young doctor came in, making rounds. He picked up her chart and smiled at her, a practiced smile. 'Low thyroid can cause a kind of paralysis; low potassium can affect muscles, so it's very likely that the feelings will go away once you're on a stable dosage.'

'Is this common? This feeling I had?' she asked. She was in fact a little better. Certainly, she felt easier and safer. Why hadn't she acknowledged just how afraid she'd been?

The young doctor put her chart down. 'I wouldn't say common,' he answered. 'But everyone's different. And when your body starts acting funny, you automatically try to make it sound reasonable. People with heart attacks say it's like they're being crushed or someone's sitting on their chest. That's what it feels like; that isn't what it is. Same for you. Your body's suggesting something to you, that's all. It will go away.'

She was so relieved. She touched her neck, even stroked it. Inside her throat there did seem to be a bump, a lump, an interference, but she strongly swallowed a few times. That must be her thyroid, she thought, her thyroid not doing its stuff and just lying there, like a lump in the throat.

They gave her a mild muscle relaxant, to help her until she felt her thyroid kick in.

She took the pill the first night and slept halfway through. But then she woke again, her head splitting open in pain. A side effect? She grabbed Charles's arm and pulled at it; she didn't want to jerk herself enough to shake him.

He let out a long sigh before forcing himself up. 'What is it?' he asked.

'My head hurts. It's awful. Can you get me some water and some aspirin? And the pills. See if this is a side effect.' She was whispering. She put her hands over her forehead; it felt like her brain had swollen, pushing against her skull. The doctor would say, 'That's what it feels like, but that's just the body trying to come up with an explanation.' So, good, her brain wasn't swollen to an incredible size, squeezed up against the coffin of her skull. It just felt that way.

Charles brought her aspirin and water. He carried the pharmacist's printout about the medication's side effects, which he read standing next to her. 'It does say headaches,' he agreed, sounding a little surprised. 'But not under the "call your doctor immediately" listing. Just under possible side effects. How bad is it?'

'It's bad,' she whispered, resting back against the pillows. 'It's bad.'

'Well,' he said uncertainly. 'Well.' He frowned, his eyes studying her.

She shuddered once, twice, then lay limp. Her head rolled to the side, almost off the edge of the pillows. He hesitated, then lifted her head and removed a pillow. She nodded and said, 'That's better.'

He got a cool washcloth and put it on her forehead.

Her throat was clear. For a moment she felt a surge of hope. But if it had moved from her neck to her head...? Could this possibly be a good sign?

'Charles,' she whispered.

'I'm calling an ambulance,' he said abruptly. His voice was tight.

'It's almost done,' she said. 'It's letting go. This is the last of it. My hands are cold.'

He took her hands and began to chafe them. 'I'll get more blankets. I'll make the call and get more blankets.'

The strange part was that her legs felt so very light. They wouldn't move, and they felt made of paper. Her hands moved, though they felt made of ice. Paper and ice. Her head was made of some clanging metal. Charles's hands were hot, rubbing hers. She wondered idly if he felt himself burning up by fire. Would that be worse? The banging in her head (always remembering what the doctor said, there was no real banging) settled into heaviness. And then the weight of it all shifted. There was a distinct release, and she gasped.

Her husband came back in the room. 'I've called 911,' he said.

'Too late,' she whispered. Her body was limp. Her hands, her limbs, stayed in what must have been an awkward position since he straightened her out. 'Any minute now,' he said. 'Just hold on.'

Her jaw began to drop in a hideous grin. She felt the last grip letting go. There, it was free, was that a moment of joy she felt at last? Was it sharing its feelings or was this last final moment just gratitude that the pain had stopped, the fight had stopped? Her eyes were open, and she thought she saw it, stepping out bright and greenish-hued, thin, and supple, but again she heard the doctor say, 'The body makes up stories.'

Her fingers twitched as her body reached out to where the soul was, trying to grab onto it, her final reach.

And then it was gone. The doorbell rang and Charles called out to it. Celia's eyes stared, fixed, at the place where the soul had been, standing there in its own story, released.

Hell's Reach

Gregory J. Glanz

D usk settled around the foothills below the dark spire, a mantle of unwelcomed shadow rising toward the open window as the little grey man pored over old parchment and tattered tomes that held the lost secrets to his freedom. The ancient keep sat in the nethermost crook of upthrust crags, its broken windows and unhinged doors belying the fact that it was, if sparsely, inhabited.

Despite the rubble that sprawled everywhere in the broken courtyard below, a figure entered and sat, the beginnings of a small fire going in mere moments. The figure looked up at movement from atop the keeps stone steps, then allowed his gaze to rise a notch to the top crenelations where a lone light shone through a single window in the highest spire, and then higher yet toward the top of Hell's Reach. The peak rose to twice the height of any other in the range, a charred stalagmite thrusting itself through clouds as if it could pierce Heaven with sheer maliciousness.

From his un-shuttered window near the top of the main spire where that lone light shone, Flik set aside the journal he was translating and watched as the intruder, damned soon enough, stood to face those that emerged from the keep. There appeared to be no words spoken as six men surrounded the lone warrior, his dark skin twinkling with strange silver glints in the flickering flames of his small fire.

The small grey man, watching from five storeys above, leaned forward, chin thrust almost through the open window, and saw the bulk of Temzon Mass below, well behind what would be the skirmish line as the other six closed in for the kill. *A coward and a bastard.*

The lone warrior, a giant of a man Flik could now see, reached back, and pulled free a two-handed sword from the sheath on his back. Silently, he swung it in two large sweeping arcs to back up his foes, and then suddenly burst at full speed straight toward the centre of the line. With a powerful stroke, he cut clean through the shield arm of the first man he met and smashed a shoulder into another as he sped past.

Flik's grip tightened around his feather pen, his heart in his throat as the giant warrior sprinted toward Mass. The fat man fumbled with his sword but was too late as the barbarian's blade impaled deep into his prodigious belly. The warrior kicked the fat man off his blade, but it was too late for him as well, as the others closed from behind and began smashing at him with hammer and mace.

Flik saw one more of the six go down before the giant warrior's sword was ripped free and he fell to the ground, bleeding and unconscious. Leaning out the window, he found Temzon Mass sprawled in the rubble-strewn courtyard in a pool of his own blood. Dare he hope the fat man was dead? He would be free of the fat man's hostility, if not of the rest of Jesteel's crew.

Moments later, the four remaining guards dragged Mass and

the warrior up the stairs and into the keep, no doubt into the old audience chamber where Jesteel held her hellish court after happening upon this cursed place just three moons ago.

And certainly, the place was cursed; but not haunted. *Until it was.*

Flik's gaze lingered over the two bodies in the courtyard, left for dead, and knew they would rise at midnight of the new day not seven hours hence. A violent shiver rattled his bones, and he tore his gaze away, contemplating their fate.

They will be willing servants, without will. Death is no escape in the shadow of this God-forsaken mountain.

The Tomereader, as Jesteel had dubbed him, twitched with eagerness to descend to the lower level to see if Mass indeed survived. He knew the captured warrior would not. Even if he was brought alive before their leader, he would be tortured and left to die, punishment for all the ills that beset Jesteel's broken mind, as well as the crime of killing at least two of her mere eleven living guards.

Of all the creatures conjectured, whispered, and breathlessly rumoured to inhabit Hell's Reach, only thirteen were alive. A cursed number, to be sure. The rest, numbering maybe five times that, worked the mines, though not by choice. But choice is for the sane, and sometimes the living, but not those living in the shadow of this accursed mountain, nor among the scraps of its ruin. And death is no escape.

Not from the wielder of Death's Hand, though Flik never called it that in front of Jesteel or her men, merely referring to it as The Fist. It was too ominous a title, one he'd found while translating the ancient language of an unattributed journal.

Besides, Jesteel and The Fist already held her followers in thrall, though he suspected it filled her with a fear she loathed while holding her fast with the power she teased out of it, out of that rust red fragment of the Dearth Stone that lay embedded on one knuckle.

He finished the translation of the paragraph before feeling he had waited the requisite time so as not to appear too eager, and finally arose from the grey, ratty divan that sat in this once-magnificent library. He turned to take one last look out the window as the sun dipped behind a nearby peak, the last moments of daylight leaving the keep, though it still shone brightly on the kingdoms beyond.

His eyes lingered over the phrase just translated. *And pestilence will ride in its palm as death harbours its army.*

Sighing, he snuffed his lamp and skirted around piles of books, long since removed from their shelves so that he might pore over them. He grabbed a lit torch from the wall sconce before exiting into the stone, spiral stairwell that led to the lower levels. As he descended, Flik passed door after door. Some were locked, some broken, some ajar; most hid only aged debris from the previous inhabitants of this dark place over three decades past.

All of it useless but for the exception of the journal.

His right hand strayed to the pocket of his breeches where he fingered a rust red fragment of the Dearth Stone. *The missing fragment.* He held onto it ostensibly to counteract whatever Jesteel might do, though he knew his cowardice would not let him. Maybe it would protect him against the undead were it necessary. Maybe not.

But there was also the passage he recently translated: *One chance, have I, to end this scourge. If not, the second fragment must come into play and Hell's fury called forth.* Ominous sounding, and not a power he wanted to put into Jesteel's hands. So, he kept the fragment.

Six months ago, Flik thought he'd have a lifetime to study the place. Unfortunately, Jesteel and her crew showed up three months later. He'd watched, in hiding, from well above, near the top of the tallest spire, still a shadowed place for most of the day. He cherished midday when the sun rose high enough to shine its light into the library window for a few scant hours. In the end, he'd known he would either have to sneak away, or introduce himself. He could not hole up in the tower forever.

Would that I had left.

The doorway on the last level of the stairwell before reaching the courtyard was broken, piled with stone from the collapsed floor above. Flik hated going outside and making his way past the mines, but there was no other way. Once at the bottom, he placed the torch in a wall sconce and stepped outside. The sky shone blue, though dusk was already come to the base of the dark spire. The sun was well below the elevated horizon of nearby peaks, a crosshatch of monstrous shadows securing the place in a deep, bronze veil.

A creature shambled from the mines some hundred paces to his left, carrying a large rock. Then a line of them emerged. In the fading light of dusk, he could almost pretend they were alive. Almost. But the odd cant to their bodies, the tattered clothes, if they had any, and misshapen forms left no doubt that these were not creatures of natural life.

They worked to clear the mines of debris, day and night, like automata. Animated machinery that, under the bidding of Jesteel and that fragment of rust red gem embedded on Death's Hand, searched deeper and deeper for the Dearth Stone. Flik knew it had been purposely buried there, hidden from humanity after this kingdom's collapse at the hands of pestilence, famine, and inhuman hatred; caused by the Dearth Stone, Flik had learned, according to the journal he was translating, and the sparse letters he'd searched out in the keep.

As Flik made his way around the rubble of the courtyard, he heard a guttural grunt and clatter of collapsing bones, off key percussions to no recognizable tune. He looked over and saw one of the more skeletal looking undead lying next to the nearest pile of boulders, several of its limbs having snapped off as it lay helplessly twitching on the ground. There was no maintenance for this flesh and bone machinery, and Flik knew it would lie there until one of the living guards disposed of its various parts into a bonfire.

Flik turned away from the sorry creature and wound his way toward the keep's steps. The two bodies still lay on open ground, the giant warrior's small fire now but a glowing ember, dying.

He strode toward the massive iron doors that hung bent and useless from the scarred outer walls. A scream echoed down the main corridor, muffled by iron-banded wooden doors that stood, slightly ajar, some twenty paces ahead. Zole Sty and Mulbark Harag, lounging on either side of the doors, eyeballed Flik as the little man flinched at the scream, his heart missing a beat just as his feet missed a step and he stumbled.

'Careful, little man,' Harag chuckled.

'Nothin' to be 'fraid of in there, eh, Bark?'

'Nothin' at all. Unlessin' blood scares ya.'

Both men laughed and Flik straightened his shoulders and back, pulled at his drab tunic and strode between the two, his head barely reaching the bottoms of their long scraggly beards. They were two of the originals, along with Temzon Mass, that had arrived with Jesteel. Her trusted three. The others, mine-runners as she called them, rarely entered this chamber. *They should be thankful.*

A noxious, invisible plume swam between the two guards and their worn deer hides and greasy cuirasses, only a step above that of the undead mining in the caves. Flik's eyes wanted to water as he passed, but he did his best to ignore the duo. As he entered the room, another scream sounded.

Temzon's bulk lay mounded on a table off to the right where Jesteel stood, her head bowed just above broad shoulders. A rust-red glow, like an aura, enveloped her. The captured warrior, bloody back to cold stone wall to Jesteel's left, howled again, straining at chains and manacles around wrists, ankles, and neck.

Jesteel sighed and the glow faded as she turned to face Tomereader.

'He keeps yelling the same thing,' she said, 'though I think that will change once I turn my attentions his way.' Sweat dripped from her large, fleshy face, dark eyes narrowed with fatigue.

Flik glanced at the giant warrior, dressed in knee-high moccasin-like boots, some kind of hide skirt or loin cloth, and a leather vest that was torn and bloody, hanging like rent skin from his bruised torso. His entire person, from bronze plate to weathered knee, was covered in some kind of silver-coloured tattoos.

Temzon Mass sat up with the aid of Jesteel's left arm and Flik almost gasped. The fat man's skin was now sallow, his once dark hair shot through with grey. Skin now sagged loosely from his jowls, and he wheezed at the effort despite Jesteel's aid. A long bloody tear in his tunic revealed a vicious scar where the barbarian's sword had impaled him.

'Go get some rest, Mass.'

The big man heaved his bulk off the table and groaned under his own weight, both hands grabbing at the back of nearby wooden chair. He eyed Flik, his normal malice somewhat deflated, weakened as he was after the wound. His eyes, their filmy whites, squeezed shut as he gathered himself to leave.

'I'll be fine afore long,' he said, glancing at Flik as if daring him to disagree.

Jesteel strode to the ruin that was, at one time, a throne, and sat down heavily as she watched Mass shuffle out the door where Sty and Harag stammered momentarily, torn between helping their comrade and revulsion at touching whatever it was he had become.

'That's new.'

'What? Healing?' she replied, pulling the massive iron fist and attached bracer off her hand and forearm. Flik saw her shiver as she turned away to hang The Fist off the left arm of the wooden throne, the right having long since broken away. The slight glow of the embedded fragment of the Dearth Stone went dark, and Flik idly fingered the matching, rust red chip in his pocket.

He had found The Fist shortly after arriving at the keep below Hell's Reach, among the ruins of the throne room. It seemed a wholly surreal thing, and certainly too large a fit for such as he; and so, he had ignored it.

A few weeks later, as he scavenged through the keep, he'd found the journal. And with it, the second fragment of red stone. Only recently had his translations born readable fruit. *One fragment of the stone to shake Heaven and earth. Two fragments to summon Hell in all its fury,* he silently recited. Glad, at least, that he had not given up the second chip to Jesteel. He was still working on that part of the translation, but it seemed clear that the writer of the journal had goaded the wearer of Death's Hand into invoking the power of the first fragment, apparently killing him, and most everyone else, in an avalanche. It also buried the Dearth Stone deep in the mines. And those few who yet lived had left the accursed place behind forever.

'It seemed Temzon was destined for death had I not intervened with The Fist.'

The barbarian strained at his wall chains and yelled again. Flik cocked his head.

'Indeed, though he seems to have marched a bit closer to it regardless.'

Jesteel shrugged, the throne creaking under her wide, shifting hips.

'Well, it seems that thing gives me more power of life over

the dead, or even death, than I believed.'

'Certainly, there is now tangible evidence of that.'

The barbarian screamed again, and Flik definitely picked out coherent, recognizable syllables.

'I was going to let him hang there a bit, but I don't know if I can take the constant interruptions,' she said, turning to eyeball the giant warrior. 'Besides, he took down two of my men. He's going to pay with his balls and his eyes for that. And then some.'

'Freedom.'

'What?'

'Freedom. I believe that's what he keeps yelling. Or some sense of it.'

Jesteel grunted a laugh and held The Fist up momentarily before her face. Flik saw a visible shiver as she let it drop, hanging it from the iron chain that ran from its wrist up the inner forearm. 'No such thing. Not here. You understand him?'

Flik shrugged. 'It's some dialect of the north, I think.'

'Well, no one just walks away from this place.'

Flik thought of the power she held, because of Death's Hand, over the dead, now the undead, and even those of the living, unwilling, or maybe unable, to turn their backs on her. That kind of simple betrayal in itself took a defiant will, something none of the dead possessed, nor, apparently, her living company.

'Not even you?'

Jesteel's gaze turned to the outer corridor, her eyes upturned as if her perceptions soared over the mountains to the open plains beyond, a glimpse of her own freedom. But with a low growl she dismissed it and turned back to the small, grey man, the momentary crack in that door slamming shut.

'I might throw you up on the wall next, Tomereader, if you don't give me something new to work with soon.'

'Which is why I have come.'

'Hah! Not to check on your favourite tormentor? To see if he yet lived?'

Flik could see in the hard lines around her eyes that whatever momentary melancholy she'd experienced had fled, the power of Death's Hand driving her as much as she was driving everyone, and everything, else.

'I was unaware of Temzon's wound, Jesteel,' he lied. 'My apologies for not making my intentions immediately clear. I have found some documents that claim the Stone is buried in a place called Wayvern's Tunnel, at one time home to a rather rich vein of copper.'

Jesteel straightened in her chair, her impossibly broad shoulders straightening beneath the ermine cloak wrapped around them, her eyes boring into him. 'So, you know where it is?' she gasped.

'Unfortunately, I do not.'

Jesteel slammed a fleshy fist down on the left armrest of the rickety throne and it cracked, sagged beneath the weight of The Fist. With another low growl she snagged the symbol, and power, of her authority, and slung it over the back of the throne. But Flik saw again the shiver that ran through her.

'However,' he said, holding up one hand as if it could stop her fury, 'I am poring over personal documents for maps and other allusions to such things. I feel confident with this new information…'

'Just find it for me, Tomereader!' she bellowed, now standing before him, her large, flat belly, and pendulous breasts as much a threat to him as any weapon as he looked up through the laced leather vest at her grimy under-cleavage. The small man paled, could feel himself visibly shrink before her glower.

'Yes, Jesteel.' He replied, hoping he could hold his bladder until he was outside.

'Now leave me,' she ordered, pulling a thin stiletto free from a waist sheath attached to a wide, black leather belt. She turned her gaze on the chained warrior. 'I have other business to attend to.'

Flik made a quick bow and an even quicker retreat as she approached her captive, the point of the blade hovering inches from his left eyeball.

Neither Sty nor Harag made a comment as he passed, both of them trying studiously to stay out of sight while at the same time peering surreptitiously around the doors to see the gruesome proceedings inside.

He scuttled down the steps into a silent evening, the mere suggestion of the setting sun a bare orange glow around one peak to the west. As he turned the corner, a gruesome bellow exploded from the keep, reverberating around the ruined vale of human detritus. His stomach jumped to his throat, and with it blood and hot bile. He stumbled toward his tower, nausea overcoming him as everything in him rebelled. He skidded to all fours, vomiting everything up.

When he was done, snot and tears smearing his face and hands, urine soaking his breeches, and the contents of his stomach staining his tunic, he struggled to rise. The clicking of that lone, broken skeleton, as if in answer to the tortured call of a soon-to-be brother, started up again. There seemed a nervousness about it that Flik had not before noticed.

His legs, stomach, and chest aquiver, Flik stumbled back up to the library, his erstwhile home. He tried not to think about what Jesteel was doing, what pain and harm she would inflict upon the painted barbarian. But it was no good. The thoughts of it would not leave him, and the mere vision was dizzying, a brackish eddy sucking him down into despair as he sank onto his ratty divan and wept.

I wonder if madness will follow him unto death. Or me through these halls.

***

Flik arose the next morning, hungover as if he'd been drinking for a week. He shuffled over to a side room, set up with a cask of cold water for bathing, and stripped down before scrubbing himself clean. Donning fresh clothes, he went back to his divan, and stared idly out the window. The bodies of the two slain guards were gone, of course, no doubt having joined the small legion of undead miners in the caves below the mountain.

Feeling some urgency at Jesteel's last words to him the night before, he began to pore over fresh parchments, scrolls and books. Well, fresh to him. Certainly, nobody had laid eyes on the things for some thirty years, if the dates he'd found on some of the letters could be trusted.

He grabbed the ratty chronicle and flipped through brittle parchment, quickly locating the passages with which he was now familiar, though he had passed on little of the information contained therein.

'Pestilence in his palm...' he mumbled.

'Disease sprung forth from his gaze...'

'Power over the dead...'

Flik wanted to squeeze the little book, as if knowledge would flow from it like juice from an orange, but his trembling hand set it gently down. He exhaled in frustration, sorry to have ever told Jesteel about the damned Fist.

Greed had snagged him, he knew. Greed for all of the knowledge and lost history contained here. And so, he had gone to Jesteel, in those first few days after their arrival, some small knowledge in tow, hoping to strike a bargain. Not much of a bargain, just one that allowed him to stay... and alive at that. They seemed uninterested in anything but tormenting him for a time, especially Temzon Mass. Flik figured out quickly enough that when they tired of him, he would probably die.

That's when he told them of The Fist. *If only I'd have known what it was at the time!*

But he had not known, and even if he had known it was really called Death's Hand, he was not sure that he wouldn't have told them anyway.

Temzon Mass, believing his claimed knowledge was some ruse, had grabbed him by the throat and tossed him into a corner, stood over him with a raised boot.

'Let him finish,' Jesteel had interrupted, and Flik told her about The Fist, showed her where it was.

A month later, after beginning his translation of the journal, he'd imparted more knowledge.

'That rust red gem fragment,' he'd said as his fingers fiddled idly with his own fragment in one breech pocket, 'is part of a larger gem, buried in the caverns, the old mines. The Fist, and its fragment of the Dearth Stone, allow you to command the dead. The Stone itself, according to accounts I've found, has far greater powers.'

'Why is it in the caverns? Aren't they collapsed?'

'Indeed, and the Stone is why they were collapsed. Apparently, the previous holder of the Stone, and the throne,' Flik inclined his head toward Jesteel where she sat, 'was goaded into invoking the power of one of the stones and literally brought the mountain down upon them.'

Regardless of that cautionary tale, it did not take them long to find an unwilling test subject, brought back from town by Harag and Sty just to be butchered by Jesteel. Just after midnight, the creature rose up, sallow skin sagging around dimmed eyes and stood, his limbs somehow fundamentally askew, Flik thought.

Flush with the prospect of this power, Jesteel had idly mentioned that they needed to clear the mines and find the Dearth Stone. Haltingly, the creature began to shamble away.

Everyone jumped up, most drawing weapons, but Jesteel barked, 'Hold.'

They followed the creature out of the keep, down the crumbling stone steps, and around the corner through the littered courtyard to the mines where it began to pull stones out and place them some score paces away from the entrance.

Jesteel had laughed heartily at that and said, 'We need more dead.'

Since then, Harag and Sty began to take wagon loads of ore into Shanto to a processor and assayer across the sound. They returned with wagon loads of dead, and a few hand-picked guards to keep the undead on task. Jesteel found that anyone could command the dead if it did not countermand her orders. As long as she wore the fist, anyway.

Flik tried hard not to imagine the graveyard deals and undertakers on the take that supplied Sty and Harag with bodies. One full moon later, there were nearly a score of the undead creatures, and two living guards. Now there might be sixty of the damned and, other than Jesteel's crew, eight guards.

Well, six guards, Flik corrected himself, his eyes trolling across the littered courtyard below.

A week later, as Flik pored over another tome, he heard a wagon pull into the compound. He looked out to see Harag and Sty on the buckboard, a half-dozen bodies in the canvas covered back, no doubt, along with supplies, and two new, living recruits following on horses.

***

They told Norby Solomon it would take a few days to get used to the stench. They lied. Several weeks later, he still wrapped thick cloth around his face whenever he entered the tunnels. The freshly dead were the worst, the skin actively rotting off their bones as they hauled rocks away by hand, cart, or wheelbarrow. He doubted, even were the place empty of the dead, that the putrid odour would abate. The very rocks seemed to mock him with it, as if the caustic nature of the decrepitude leeched into them.

Norby was a small man, though wiry and muscular. His time in Shanto across the sound had come to an abrupt end. After a stint in the local jail for assault and robbery, he was told in no uncertain terms that he was no longer welcome in the coastal town. And upon his release, almost like fate intervening, there was Zole Sty, flashing coin and promising more, just to guard a few miners. Only when they arrived in the shadow of Hell's Reach and uncovered the seven dead bodies in the back of the buckboard did he start to question the true nature of his new position.

It was in his mind that he would run off at the first possibility. Of course, he would take the horse they had given him to ride. The least of payments they should expect after the lies he'd been told. But then he was introduced to Jesteel, and she ordered him to the mines where he was instructed as to his duties. And he tried to leave. Tried to walk away. But it burned. His brain burned and he was blinded by a dark crimson light whenever he tried to do other than he'd been told.

And his anger at it did not cease. Nor lessen.

Fate be damned. Everything else here is.

Norby once again entered the caverns to check on his rotting charges. He kept the lantern pointed straight ahead, trying not to focus too tightly on any one creature. He could almost pretend they were beggars trying to scratch out a living in the slums where open sewage oozed along the gutters.

One of the dead backed into him, its patchy hair and pealing skin exposing a chunk of its skull, one eyeball missing. He yelped and jumped back, instinctively swiping at the thing with his short sword. It caught the creature in the shoulder, nearly hacking the arm off, and the small boulder it carried fell from its weakened grip, crashed through one leg. The creature fell, pinned to the ground at the hip.

'Dammit,' he grunted, and put a boot to its skull, nearly severing that as well.

He moved on, deeper into the tunnels, making his usual rounds. *Unable* to do anything but make his rounds at the appointed times.

He skipped around another corpse that stood hacking at a large boulder with a pickaxe. Its skin hung like tattered clothing over exposed bone.

'A beggar,' he mumbled, and moved on.

He began yelling his orders at them, bullying them when whispered pleas would have the same effect. They took no offense.

Is it possible they don't understand what's happened to them? He shook his head.

He saw the bare femur of a bent over creature, mostly skeletal, as it tried repeatedly to lift a rock, unable to get it off the ground, but incapable of ceasing its feeble attempts. Pallid flesh, like lichen, clung to its ribs.

'Ah give it up,' he grunted, and kicked the thing below the hip, snapping its leg as he continued on. A momentary cloud of crimson filled his vision and his brain briefly burned, making his eyes tear up. Such were not uncommon moments as he went through the caverns, but Norby found they dissipated quickly enough if he kept moving.

After several skeletal piles were found following his rounds, some of them still twitching and clacking bone on bone, he was warned. This kind of labour was not easy to replace, Bark had told him, and unless he wanted to take their place, he would direct them only, not abuse them.

As if they haven't suffered the ultimate abuse already.

He was about to turn back when he heard the chink of a pickaxe farther on. Shining the light down the tunnel, he saw a massive creature bent over, hammering away. As Norby approached, it reached into a small niche and retrieved an object. There was a brief spark as he hurried forward and the same crimson glow that bloomed like a bloody disease in his eyes when he tried to disobey Jesteel flared in the tunnel.

Norby gasped. 'Whattya got there, dummy?'

The dead giant turned and stood, pickaxe resting on one collar bone with one hand wrapped around its shaft. In his other, sat a massive, rust red gem.

Norby watched as the scant flesh of the thing's hand burned away, melting like so much wax in a furnace, and the gem dropped to the ground, smoking.

He looked up at the creature, well-more than a head taller, and spat, 'God-cursed brute.' He bent over to fetch the gem, thinking of what kind of cruelty he might inflict upon this lout of an undead when a pickaxe cleaved his skull and kissed his brain with its point.

The giant creature reached down with the bone claw of his left hand and retrieved the gem, then straightened and began to walk out of the tunnels. Norby, his life abruptly ended, did not wait for midnight. He obediently stood and followed.

The giant undead warrior strode down the poorly lit, uneven tunnels, the rust red glow of the Dearth Stone held forth, wrapped in one bony claw. As he passed, each ghoul, flesh or no, stopped their mining and stood in the light of undead reason. With that clear logic in mind, the insanity of death flowed over them as it had to. Some raised pickaxes, others dropped small tools, rocks and boulders as wheelbarrows and carts were shucked aside.

As they moved, torches were extinguished and a wave of darkness followed them, the undead having no use for the lies of the light, their crazed perceptions cutting through the darkness like a mis-aimed crossbow bolt afire.

With a unity of purpose, they emerged from the tunnels as a cold wind swept down from the mountain top to meet them, snow, dust, and grit mingled in swirling eddies, blinding the mortally sighted and snapping tattered pennants to attention. The three guards on duty outside the entrance moved to intercept, ordering the emerging horde back into the tunnels.

'Get back to work, ya daft corpses!'

The guards were used to being obeyed unquestioningly. Overwhelmed by the sudden horde, they died before realizing that their will no longer held any sway with the dead. The horde grew by three.

With barely a twitch of his hand, the new lord of the undead ordered the horde to find the other guards and bid them, "Join us." They went forth, leaving a trail, a litter of bones and flesh; an arm rotted off, an eyeball jarred loose and crushed, genitalia dropped to the ground under the stress of the march. All ignored, inconsequential.

Only Norby stayed with his master, marching to the keep and up the steps. As they approached the massive stone doors, hanging askew from broken hinges, the keep's lights were snuffed, and a cold wind followed them in.

'Hey, whatsat?' a questioning voice echoed up the hallway.

As they approached the massive iron-bound wooden doors leading to Jesteel's throne room, another voice asked, 'Norby, is that you?'

'God's, they found it, Bark!'

Norby stood a step behind the undead giant, sword drawn, shadowed from the rust red glow, now the only light in the hallway.

'Here, give it up then. We'll take it to Jesteel.'

The giant warrior silently launched the pickaxe in his other hand toward Zole Sty's head, piercing deeply into his brain. His arms and legs went rigid as if pithed, his eyes watering instantly before he collapsed to the ground, waiting for death to completely take him.

'What the hell…' but Mulbark Harag never finished the thought as Norby's short sword slid up under his ribs and cut through the soft tissue of his heart. He too collapsed to the ground, a short wait from death.

'Rise,' the undead lord said, and they did, once again standing guard, though their purposes no longer bound to Jesteel's will.

The giant creature laid one palm on the doors and opened his lipless mouth, a ghoulish maw of rotting flesh and missing teeth, and a piercing scream erupted from impossibly deep inside it. The timber of the doors began to vibrate before suddenly exploding inward. Shards like tiny missiles flew away, and the impact echoed hollowly through the halls of the keep.

As the debris began to settle, a dusk enveloped the room, as if all light were being sucked into the darkness of the hallway. The cold wind whipped past the undead giant, driving dirt and grit in swirling eddies to all corners of the room.

Jesteel stood and her gaze became cold steel as she donned The Fist.

***

Flik sat upon his ratty divan taking notes, continuing to slog through the difficult translation of the journal. He felt a queasiness at what he'd found. All this time Jesteel had set her undead crew to clearing the tunnel in search of the Dearth Stone, something the anonymous author of this journal feared.

I need to finish this translation, so I know the root of that fear.

Flik's ears perked up as he heard the hollow thunk of the heavy door at the bottom of his stairwell echo upward. The little man sighed. It was probably Temzon Mass coming to harass him about his research, or rather the lack of insight he had provided to Jesteel these last weeks.

It wasn't that he didn't have anything to report.

However, in light of the information he recently gleaned from the journal, Flik feared such knowledge, and power, in Jesteel's hands.

It was, after all, the madness that gripped the previous owner that caused his court to betray him. Such power must warp a man. What would it be like to have your own dead walking around as vassals? Not vassals. Indentured undead?

Flik shivered as, in the back of his mind, he followed the slow, plodding echo of his visitor as they climbed the five long flights of steps. That climb, he always thought, was what stoked Temzon's rancour, as he had always been the one to act as Jesteel's liaison with Flik. Mass despised the climb, heaving his bulk up and down those stairs at his boss's discretion to check on her Tomereader. He always arrived sweating and winded, promptly plopping himself on the chair nearest the door, an old wooden thing that creaked threateningly under his weighty buttocks. Flik had been spared such visits over the last weeks as Mass recovered from what should have been a mortal wound inflicted by the sword of the giant warrior.

To be fair, however, it had only been a cruel dislike at the beginning. Then there was the defiant guard, recruited under less than candid circumstances, who demanded he be allowed to leave. He had stood before Jesteel, ranting about 'this accursed place' and how he wanted nothing to do with it.

Flik had the unlucky coincidence of being in the room at the time. He'd watched the man, squirming in obvious pain from this small defiance, as his eyes watered and thick, white spittle sprayed from his ranting mouth. As he squeezed his eyes shut, in clear agony, Jesteel donned The Fist.

'Enough,' she'd shouted, and smashed him in the face. The effect stunned everyone in the room as the guard's head all but exploded at the impact, a rust red glow flashing through the bloody debris.

Flik was of course horrified, as was Jesteel as she removed The Fist. Both hands shook violently as the blood drained from her face.

'Gods,' Temzon Mass groaned, and Flik's gaze turned to see the big man where he'd been standing before Jesteel's attack, only a few feet behind the beheaded body now lying crumpled in a ghastly heap at his feet.

It was in that next moment that Mass's cruel dislike blossomed with the flame of his rancour and loathing, as Flik, gazing up at the fat man picking bits of flesh and blood, bone and brains from his face and facial cavities, giggled.

Mass gave a broad wipe across his features with one hand and reached for Flik with the other. He tossed the gore aside and picked up the little grey man with one hand, murder in his eyes. Thankfully, he never found out what Mass had in mind as Jesteel barked at him to let go. But the damage was done, and that glint that promised death never left the big man's eyes whenever they passed over Flik.

'Leave us,' Jesteel ordered. 'Go back to your books.' And it seemed from then on that she had to suppress a shiver of dread anytime she reached for The Fist.

Not even the powers of Fist, Stone and Mountain could bring that poor soul back.

As the echo of footsteps neared his rooms, Flik felt an unseasonably cold wind sweep down off the cliff face above the keep and pour through the open window, lashing at cloak and candle. He shivered and quickly closed the shutter as Mass entered the room.

Flik noticed the big man was neither sweating nor gasping for air as was the norm after such a climb. He did, however, look much paler than usual, all of his hair now grey and much of the colour faded from once crystal, blue eyes.

'Well, it seems your time may finally be running out, Tomereader. Jesteel wants some answers. And if not...' he shrugged.

It was a cold appraisal, the voice without inflection, and Flik's bladder tightened. There was no malice in the statement, no threatening tone. Only deathly promise, he thought. No hate, only cold insight.

Mass grabbed a nearby book from a table inside the door and ruffled through the pages.

'I've, uh, I've got something very important,' he said, reaching for the journal and his notes.

The big man tossed the book back down upon the table, stared at Flik.

'Yes?'

'I've just got to, uh, got to finish the translation,' Flik stammered. Mass's cold stare sent shivers down his spine like his baleful glances never had.

'Whatever you've got, you'd best bring it down in short order, little man,' he warned, then turned and strode from the room. After a few thudding footfalls, the stairwell went momentarily silent.

'I don't want to have to come back up here for you later tonight,' a ghostly voice echoed up from the stairwell, then Mass continued on down.

An hour later, the blood drained from Flik's face as bile rose up in his queasy stomach. He stared at the finished translation of the latest passage from the unattributed journal. It was not something mentioned anywhere that he'd found, because it would never be allowed. At least not by any who knew the Dearth Stone's origins and power. And how long ago had anyone lived with true knowledge of Fist and Stone? But there it was.

The dead must not be allowed to possess Death's Hand, nor the Dearth Stone, lest the veil between Hell and Earth be torn asunder. And yet, death stalks us everywhere, the living in the shadow of the dark spire now far outnumbered by the dead.

And Jesteel had been using these creatures all along to find the damned thing!

Flik gathered himself and flew down the stairs, sweating despite the chill. At the bottom, he stuck his torch in a wall sconce and scooted out the doorway toward the courtyard in front of the keep.

After only a few steps he stopped, wrapping his arms around himself at the chill and the wind that swept down upon the courtyard. A preternatural darkness enveloped the place, bare starlight all that illuminated this nether domain of a keep. An eerie glow limned the stone lintel above the door atop the steps to the keep.

Flik went back for his torch and once again hurried toward the steps of the keep. He stopped at the bottom, staring up at the rust red glow that emanated from within. Fear poured instantly into his bones, weakened his limbs, his mind, his purpose. He took one sideways step toward the stable on the other side of the compound, readying to bolt. Unashamed of cowardly flight, though not unafraid.

'Best hurry on up.' The voice from behind made him jump to the first step and turn around. His stomach tightened around his bladder and his heart hammered his chest into damn near rubble as he faced Temzon Mass. The big man was paler even than an hour ago, his eyeballs now coated with a filmy, yellow cataract.

'Up you go,' he ordered, and took a step forward.

Flik backed up a few steps before turning and bolting up towards the keep. He scurried through the broken outer doors before slowing to a walk, and eventually a stop. The entire hallway glowed a very dim rust red, outlining the figures of

Harag and Sty outside the doors to the throne room.

His torch revealed sagging flesh on the paunchy frames of the guards, their heads cocked oddly to the side. As he stood there, contemplating whether or not to continue, he noticed that neither man any longer possessed eyeballs, the angry sockets surrounded in crusted blood.

'You won't need that,' Flik heard from behind, and turned to find Mass standing in the broken doorway as his lantern flickered out.

The creak of opening doors turned him back around as Harag and Sty motioned him forward. Mass laughed, a breathless, grating sound, metal rasping on bone. The big man trod slowly forward, Flik pushed along as if repelled by a polar opposite. His feet seemingly moved to another's volition.

As he passed between the hulking guards, their eyeless stare down the hallway, he saw how flaccid and pale they now were. Small wounds to either side of their sockets were crusted, but still bleeding, thin trickles like tears oozed down their cheeks and off their chins.

The throne now faced the back wall, its breadth and width bathed in darkness, though Flik made out a bare outline hanging from the chains. Broad shoulders and Jesteel's cloak jutted to either side of the back of the throne.

Again, he stopped, stammered before finally finding some small voice.

'I've found something, Jesteel!' he squeaked, his throat constricted with fear.

'Good.' It was only a whisper skipping across the gritty breeze impossibly swirling throughout the room.

The figure stood and stepped to the side of the throne, turning to face the little grey man. Flik cowered, cringing as if Death's Hand gripped his heart and squeezed, its rust red glow and iron form wrapped around the giant warrior's forearm.

'Do tell us.' The creature ordered, perfectly enunciated as if invisible flesh still housed the bony pallet that gleamed behind receding flesh, a grotesque maw of yellowed teeth in a cavernous mouth.

Flik stared at the sallow face, its puckered, lidless eyes, and empty sockets, devoid of sanity, and knew that he could not say what he had hurried here to tell Jesteel. *The dead cannot be allowed to possess Death's Hand, nor the Dearth Stone.*

As the giant warrior approached, Flik saw that each silvered tattoo on his tattered body moved as the undead, halting and oddly angled where torn skin and shredded sinew held little natural sway. A towering bear tattoo on the creature's chest folded over itself, its mouth opened in a silent, ghastly roar, its maw a tangle of jutting bone where ribs thrust through ragged skin.

A monstrous hand reached down and grabbed Flik by the scruff, effortlessly lifted him from his feet where he swayed as his eyes and his mind swam in some tortured current.

'Where's Jesteel?' he whispered, and the giant strode back toward the throne, the little grey man in tow.

'Behold.'

And Flik's eyes, adjusted to the dark now, saw her hanging from the same chains that had once held this giant warrior. She bled from myriad wounds, flesh and clothing intermingled so as to be indistinguishable. Her breasts hung in tatters, as if flensed of blubber, and her right arm was missing from the elbow down.

'Our Lady of the chains,' the undead warrior rasped, an apparition somehow released from his own chains, no longer holding him in Death. 'The dead reign here now.'

Well, death would come to Jesteel soon, Flik knew, and he would be the last one living among an army of the dead.

'Grief now has a body, and I am its Lord and Master,' the creature crooned at him. There was a susurrant moan and a sluggish shuffling of feet behind him and Flik turned to see the hallway filled with the undead, the faded light of unreason darkening their empty sockets.

But he felt no grief. Not for the poor bastards unwittingly conscripted after death by the crew that now stood, unwillingly, beside them. Not for Mass or Sty or Harag. Not for Jesteel. Not even for himself.

He reached into his pocket and fingered his hidden fragment of the Dearth Stone and recalled the passage he had long ago translated. *One chance, have I, to end this scourge. If not, the second fragment must come into play and Hell's fury called forth.*

It seemed insanity itself to give the fragment to this gruesome lord, lord of the mountain, Lord of the Lost, but as he'd known, choice was for the sane, and sometimes the living, but not those living in the shadow of Hell's Reach.

He pulled the fragment free and held it forth. 'The dead may reign in the keep, but Hell holds sway on the mountain. And this fragment, placed in the empty setting of Death's Hand next to its twin, will bring forth Hell's fury at your summons.'

'Place it in the setting,' the Lord of the Lost demanded, lowering Death's Hand until it wavered before Flik's face.

The little grey man did as he was bid, and Fist and Stone began to glow. The giant warrior arched his neck, moaning as the rust red glow suffused its body, shot through those bony cavities now void of flesh.

The earth trembled at his summons, the pressure slowly building as lava rose up to the call, filling a thousand little tunnels dug over the centuries as a long line of now-dead kings, queens and dukes had mined it for all its natural wealth.

The undead creatures all stood in thrall, unaware of anything but their master's will, the revenant of his ecstasy filling with newfound nightmares. To be sure, there was a shuffling of mangled and rotting feet as the ground beneath them shook with growing fury, and the mountain above quaked as Hell's highpoint began to tear itself apart. But there was no nervousness, for they were not sane, not alive, only unfeeling creatures tethered to the will of a dead man, their Lord of the Lost.

Flik knew he would die. And soon. He felt a preternatural calm, a peace born not at the surety of his own death, but that of every other creature here would die with him.

The impact of rocks and boulders could be heard aplenty as they bounded down the mountain now, some of them battering the keep, smashing its roofs and vacant wings. Flik thought of his own rooms, the library at the uppermost spire, and his shoulders sagged, a sadness at its loss, at its use.

The wall above Jesteel's chained body cracked open and lava burst forth in a small stream, spewing into the room. It flowed and dripped down the wall, burning into Jesteel's body. She screamed for mere seconds before it bore holes through her skull and extinguished her life.

The Lord of the Lost straightened and roared. 'What have you done?'

'I merely gave you the power to summon Hell's fury.'

'You will spend an eternity paying for this.'

'Maybe. But not at your hands, Lord of the Lost. Like me, you shall be irrevocably dead. And paying your own price.'

The creature roared, grabbing Flik by the throat. He lifted the little grey man to stare into empty eye sockets, a strange, rust red glow inundating the bony cavern of his skull.

A giant boulder crashed through the far end of the throne room, and another spout of lava opened up the wall. The outer hallway collapsed in on itself, and still the undead stood there in mangled consort, awaiting direction.

Part of the ceiling tore away and Flik saw spewing gouts of lava lashing the mountainside as rockslides tore at the keep. Then his consciousness left him.

***

Nobody knows how far away the death of the dark spire could be seen. But no one who saw it ever forgot the vision of Hell's Reach as it burned and crumbled, its fiery fingers grasping maybe for mercy, or salvation, for the unreachable sanctuary of Heaven as the dark spire destroyed itself.

Night of The Samhain Slaughter

Scott Harper

Sam Ravi gratefully locked the iron-screened door of his "mom and pop" liquor store on 47th Street, glad to finally be done after a long workday. His feet hurt from standing for ten hours, and his stomach ached from acid reflux. He was disheartened, knowing he would have to repeat the same drudgery in fourteen hours.

Sam yawned, keeping his hand over his mouth, an old habit his superstitious mother had instilled in him years past to keep his soul from escaping. He swept his grimy hair from his brow and doffed a beige cap as he stepped onto the uneven sidewalk. The autumn moon had crawled high in the night sky, a vibrant golden disk juxtaposed with the silky blackness surrounding it, bathing the city in brilliant amber rays. Sam took a deep breath of the cool air, letting it sift in his lungs and reinvigorate him for the walk home. He was surprised to see the sidewalks largely empty at this time of night; usually, by now, the pimps and perverts and gangsters that frequented the area were out and about.

It's Halloween, Sam thought. *Maybe they took all their shenanigans indoors.*

He looked forward to returning home and seeing pictures of his son in the Halloween costume he had worn to school that day. Little Sandip loved dressing up each year, and Sam loved seeing his son happy. His wife had already shared some of the adorable pictures with him via text: Sandip's sweet brown eyes beamed out from the openings of a latex werewolf mask; his small hands covered by oversized hairy claws as he posed for the shot.

Sam cut down an alley behind a biker bar on 49th street, taking a shortcut to his apartment complex. He normally took a longer route that avoided the alleyway and the ne'er-do-wells that made it their home, but tonight he was exhausted, his rickety knees hurt, and he just wanted to get home and sip a warm Nilgiri tea before going to bed. If some junkie or hoodlum made the mistake of bothering him, they would learn a quick lesson in manners. He kept a switchblade in his pants pocket for just such occasions.

The grime-caked walls were lined with garbage and abandoned furniture, and the ground was wet from earlier rain. Sam slipped in a dirty puddle, cursing as his knee hit the asphalt and got his pants wet. He stood and brushed off the filth from his leg, only to be greeted by a great exhaust of hot breath in his face.

He stumbled back, his head encircled by a miasmic cloud. Twin amber flames emerged from the shadows in front of him, a good foot above his eye level. The ambient moonlight allowed him to see the nightmare creature in front of him, an enormous, towering wolf that stood on two articulated legs.

Sam screamed as the creature opened its black-lipped maw

and exposed rows of yellowed razor fangs dripping saliva. The beast seemed to find his terror amusing, tilting its head slightly as if inspecting his horrified face at another angle. He fumbled with his pocket, drawing out the knife and activating the blade with a *Thwick* sound. There was a flash of black followed by the sound of ripping flesh, and then both his hand and the knife were suddenly gone. Hot blood jetted from the jagged stump of his forearm. Sam was too shocked to feel the pain of his amputated limb; he tried to run, but the wolf thing bit into his head, its teeth crushing his skull and puncturing his eyes. In his final, agonized moments, Sam thought about Sandip and his wife and how he would never see or hold them close again. He felt the profound loss as only a man who was both husband and father could. And then the monster severed his spinal cord and ate his brain.

***

Lars savoured the bloody flesh of his prey, gulping down large bites of meat and organ. The ravenous hunger that drove him was briefly tempered.

He was having more and more difficulty controlling the wolf demon that shared his body, particularly on nights of the full moon. The golden light provoked the beast within him, demanding freedom. The nights were getting longer as the winter solstice gradually approached, giving him more opportunities to unleash his animal side. Halloween was the perfect night for a being like himself, when the unnatural became ordinary. It was autumn, a time of transition in weather and nature, of impersonation and façade and faux devils and hobgoblins, when the unlikely became the inevitable. It was the season of the witch and the phase of the freak, the advent of mystery and ancient curses, the emergence of gibbous moons and murderous lycanthropes.

It was Lars' time.

It had not always been so. He'd inherited the curse from his father on his eighteenth birthday, a family secret, it turned out, going back several generations. The old man had tried to prepare his son for what was to come, offering a brief history of their legacy and the dark events that prompted an ancient sorceress to place a malison on their European ancestor many centuries past. Father had spoken of the Dark Side, a nightmare world existing parallel to our own populated by the Uncanny—supernatural creatures of all shapes, sizes, and temperaments.

The revelation had an unanticipated effect: Lars became terrified and panicked, triggering his first metamorphosis. After shredding his clothing and transforming into a gigantic two-legged wolf, he promptly thanked his father by disembowelling him. Lars had set out on his own, left the small Midwestern village where he'd grown up, and joined a traveling circus that toured the southwest. The owner, a Hungarian gypsy named Mithros, was a supernatural scholar familiar with his kind. He became a substitute father of sorts, explaining the lore of the Dark Side in greater detail to Lars. On nights of the full moon, Mithros would lock him away in an iron caravan constructed for the animals, preventing Lars from hunting. And, for a brief time, Lars had felt content among the other circus freaks.

But the young werewolf had soon tired of being confined. The urge to transform and kill had taken a life of its own. He'd broken free one moonlit night as the circus toured California, shredding the metal container before ripping the other freaks apart. He tore out Mithros' throat when the gypsy had tried to stop him. Fleeing, Lars had followed his nose to the nearest city and all the many soft targets it offered. The beast had been muzzled for too long and needed to feed.

The screams of his prey had not gone unnoticed. As Lars

took a bite of Sam's liver, angry patrons poured out of the rear door of the bar and into the alley, tattooed bikers with knives and clubs. Their eyes went wide in horror at the sight before them, a towering wolfman drenched in blood and gore, standing over the butchered remains of a human corpse. Their numbers gave the drunken louts the liquid courage to attack him.

In anticipation, Lars struck his claws off the ground, sending sparks flying in the darkness. The first biker, a muscular man in black leather with a red beard and skull tattoos on his arms, drove a knife into the werewolf's midsection, the blade sinking into the hilt. Lars felt no pain; the weapon was made of common steel and could not injure him. He retaliated, ripping out the man's throat and throwing his body across the alley like a child's toy.

Another biker slammed a metal crowbar across Lar's back, a blow that would have broken an ordinary man's spine. Lars shrugged off the strike and delivered a backslash that decapitated his attacker. The werewolf grabbed the headless torso and plunged his muzzle into the crimson fountain, battening on the hot blood and letting it flood down his throat.

Two more assailants slammed into him, attempting to restrain his arms. Lars pulled his head away from the headless corpse and drove his claws through the men's ribcages, smashing through bone and erupting out the back in a spray of gore and ruptured organs. He extracted the still-beating heart from one man and wolfed it down in a single bite.

The remaining bikers panicked and fled back into the bar. Savouring the bloodshed, Lars followed his terrified prey inside, gnashing his blood-stained teeth in anticipation.

***

Eliphas made his way into the alleyway, moving from shadow

to shadow, one with the darkness. The police had marked off the crime scene with yellow tape and were now conducting their investigation. The flashing red and blue lights of a radio car bathed the area in a luminous, surreal glow.

A stern-faced, short-haired female K9 officer stood guard with her animal at the entrance. The dog sensed Eliphas' presence, dropping its ears, and whimpering in fear. He reached out and easily calmed the creature's simple mind before moving unnoticed past the tape.

Officers and crime scene analysts moved throughout the area, documenting the atrocity. Eliphas walked amongst them unseen, stepping over sundry body parts and dismembered corpses. The remnants of the necrotic energy released at the moment of each death tickled his skin, glimmering embers of what had been a magnificent conflagration. He had not witnessed such carnage in years.

The bodies had been torn apart and, in some cases, fed upon. Eliphas inspected a disembodied hand that had been sheared off at the wrist. He ran a long finger over the bloody skin and inspected the blood transfer to his fingertip with dark eyes. The attacker was obviously a creature of superhuman strength that wielded claws and teeth sharper than honed steel.

Eliphas inhaled, not from an actual physical need for air but to sift through the alley scents. Beyond the refuse and blood and rotting organs, his keen nose detected the gamy, pungent scent of a wolf—or, rather, the unmistakable odour of a rampaging werewolf.

It all made sense, Eliphas realized. The body of the circus gypsy, Mithros, whose death had marked the beginning of this cycle of violence, had born a similar smell when he first inspected it. According to the employees, the missing caravan member was named Lars and had worked with the human oddities and cared for the animals before his disappearance. They maintained that a strange, almost father-son relationship had existed between Lars and Mithros, which had apparently soured at some point.

Lars had become the prime suspect in the investigation, which began when Eliphas had been assigned the case a few days ago by his employers. He'd been relaxing in his study, sitting in his charcoal Italian leather executive chair, and studying an incunabulum documenting the magic of Aztec blood sacrifices, when he received the assignment in the customary manner—via a note attached to the leg of a carrier avian, a sable-feathered raven that arrived at his downtown office with the setting sun and pecked incessantly at his window. The small vellum letter, written in ancient cuneiform in crimson ink and stamped with the seal of his patrons, contained information portending ill omens and required his immediate attention.

Eliphas drifted into the bar through the back door, where he encountered a similar scene of carnage. Ruptured bodies littered the ground, spilled blood collecting in vermilion pools on the wooden floor. A headless male corpse lay sprawled across an oak pool table, blood seeping into the green cloth fabric; nearby, a scruffy biker had been impaled to the wall by two pool sticks, hanging like a bug in a specimen display case. Another biker, a heavyset female in a leather jacket, had been stuffed face first through the front of a jukebox, her legs dangling above the ground. The front door to the establishment had been blown off its hinges and lay in pieces in the street.

Eliphas found the lone survivor of the carnage sitting in a booth off to the side of the kitchen, presumably waiting to be interviewed by detectives. The man was an older biker, grey-haired and craggy faced, wearing a sleeveless leather jacket that exposed his flabby, inked arms. He shivered, his hazel eyes wide with fear; he smelled of piss and cheap cologne. Eliphas was familiar with how traumatic events adversely affected people; he had seen the effects innumerable times throughout his long life.

Eliphas stepped from the shadows, allowing the frightened man to see him.

The biker flinched, taken aback. 'Who the fuck are you? You don't look like a cop,' he said, his voice quavering. 'You look like an undertaker.'

'I'm more of a private investigator,' Eliphas said in a soothing voice. 'I don't work for the city.' He pinioned the man with his intense gaze. 'You can tell me what happened here—you don't have to be afraid.'

The man lost himself in Eliphas' eyes. He opened up, and the words flowed out unfiltered, like water from a spigot. 'My name's Roy. I'm a coward, always have been and always will be. I've been picked on since I was a boy. I like to pretend I'm tough by dressing up as a biker and hanging out with them, but inside, I'm a scared little kid. I was just getting drunk tonight, hoping to score with one of the skanky bitches that hang out here. I have a little dick and need to take Viagra to get it up. I was talking to one of them, a big redhead with green eyes and tattooed tits, trying to get her interested enough to come back to my place, when all hell broke loose. A giant wolf that walked like a man tore in through the back door and started killing everybody, tearing them apart like they were made of paper. I saw strong men I know scream like children and beg for their lives. It didn't matter; the monster killed them all. It took the bitch I was talking to, picked her up like she weighed nothing and jammed her head through the jukebox. Her brains slid out the back of her skull and plopped on the floor. I pissed my pants and hid under a table like the coward I am. Somehow, it was too busy butchering other people to notice me. After everyone was dead, it tore out through the front door and ran away. Can I go home now? I don't like it here. I'm scared.' Tears dripped down his face, dampening his grey Mustache.

Eliphas released his hold on the man, who fell back, dazed, against the wood panel that separated the booths. Eliphas took pity on Roy, numbing his mind and allowing him to sleep until the real detectives arrived. He knew not all were born to be warriors and that humans capable of fighting monsters were few and far between. He moved through the bar and out the shattered front door. A trail of blood marked the creature's path, heading up the street toward the suburbs, where people went to avoid the city and its problems. Eliphas followed.

The luminescent spirit of one of the creature's victims, a middle-aged gentleman of Indian descent, stood in the road, invisible to all but Eliphas. Glowing with emerald light, the ghost gestured up the street, indicating the direction the werewolf had taken. The dead man's face was wan and desolate, bereft of hope. Eliphas sensed the disembodied soul's yearning for the peace of the grave, a peace which would only come with the severing of the wolf creature's bloodline. It was a longing Eliphas could appreciate.

'I will do what I can, spirit, to end your purgatory,' he told the ghost before rejoining the shadows.

***

Lars lifted his bloody muzzle from the ruptured torso of a young woman dressed in a witch's costume, chewing bone and organ. He'd come upon her as she approached a gated mansion on a cul-de-sac off Manchester Drive. The property was elaborately decorated in Halloween regalia, complete with strobing lights and pounding music and trees covered in cobwebs. Lars had snatched her up before she knew what was happening and whisked her across the street to a darker patch shielded by parked cars, where he could consume her at his leisure.

He'd left a trail of ruptured corpses as he made his way from the inner city to the suburbs: a homeless man rank with dirt and sweat begging for money; a personal trainer leaving the gym after training a client, his blood rich with amino acids and enervating caffeine; a female jogger in red sweats getting in an evening run after a long day at the brokerage firm. Lars sometimes could taste the memories of his victims with their blood, a talent not spoken of in the ancient texts. Perhaps, Lars thought, the sorceress' curse on his ancestor had created a unique werewolf bloodline, forever separate from their shifter kin, with special abilities beyond simple transformation.

He knew the police would surely follow him, but Lars was unconcerned. They could not harm him with their lead bullets; only silver represented a threat. They were weak. They were beneath him. And when it was all over, after he had killed them and bathed in their blood, he would return to his human form and blend back into society as if nothing had happened. He would lay low and bide his time until the wolf demanded release once more.

As he finished another bite of the faux witch, Lars raised his canine head and looked across the street toward the mansion. More costumed attendees arrived, a zombie here, a devil there, some escorted in limousines. The opulence enraged Lars: his family had been poor, and he resented ostentatious displays of wealth. He would enjoy killing the pompous pricks inside and guzzling their rich blood.

He dropped the butchered corpse in his claws and leaped across the road. The mansion was surrounded by a high stone wall with a metal gate barring the entrance. Lars tore through a man dressed as an alien waiting patiently to be admitted, sending blood flying into the air. He ripped the metal gates apart like tissue paper. Armed security guards in black uniforms awaited him, drawing their pistols and firing at him. Lars ignored the bullets peppering his body as he would a cloud of gnats, tearing through the frightened men like a freight train. They shrieked as he peeled the flesh from their bones and left them lying in bloody pieces as he made his way up the driveway to the lighted portico.

A couple dressed as caped superheroes screamed in terror before he ripped out their throats with his claws, splashing the doors and walls in crimson. Lars burst through the iron-reinforced oak doors and descended amongst a throng of bewildered partygoers. He had time to briefly admire the ornate furniture, the hanging crystal chandelier, the walls decorated with fine paintings and exquisite tapestries, and the magnificent twin staircases that led to the second story. Then he was amongst the attendees, smelling their colognes and perfumes and the alcohol reeking on their breaths, scattering them with swipes of his claws, crushing their fragile heads between his jaws. Antique vases and marble statues shattered beneath the weight of the bodies he tossed across the room. A mahogany chair smashed against him, desperately wielded by a partygoer dressed as Count Dracula, but he felt no pain. Lars tore the faux vampire's lower jaw off and disdainfully discarded it. He heard crying and violent retching coming from underneath an enormous dinner table that could seat a dozen diners. Lars tossed the heavy furniture aside, enjoying the thrill of his animal strength as the table shattered against the wall and became kindling. A faux Phantom of the Opera looked up at him, tears running down his puffy cheeks, leaving clear tracks in the ghostly makeup pancaked on his flabby face. Vomit covered the man's blubbering lips. Lars bit through his chest, through shiny fabric and loose skin and stubborn sternum bone, relishing the crunch of juicy organs in his razor teeth as he tore out the Phantom's innards and guzzled them down like hot spaghetti.

The screams of his victims became a tempestuous symphony, urging him to greater acts of violence. He could not resist and lost himself in the bloodshed.

***

It had been easy for Eliphas to follow the path of bodies from the biker bar to the gated mansion on suburban Manchester Drive. No particular detective skills required, simply follow the crimson piles of shredded flesh.

The pungent wolf scent increased as he walked up the driveway, avoiding the bodies of the security guards and broken metal gates, up onto the blood-stained portico and through the open doorway. The drawing room had been destroyed as thoroughly as if a hurricane had set down on it. Mounds of broken corpses littered the shattered furniture, with disembodied limbs and ropy entrails scattered amongst the ruins, soaked in pools of blood. In the centre of the carnage stood the culprit, a wolfman towering over seven feet in height, its coarse black fur slick with the blood of its prey. It gnawed on a skinless torso, stripping slabs of meat from the ribcage.

The creature paused when it noticed Eliphas, its nose twitching as it inhaled the newcomer's scent. The smell disconcerted the beast; it dropped its meal and growled menacingly.

Eliphas skimmed the surface of the young werewolf's mind and encountered only raging turmoil and hatred, a tempestuous fury far beyond his ability to control. Their encounter was destined for bloodshed. Eliphas had been in many battles throughout his existence and knew from painful experience that a confined space would work against him—he needed to take the fight outside to deal with a larger foe.

'Lars,' he said, hoping to disconcert the beast. The werewolf snarled, exposing its teeth and the bits of human flesh lodged between them. Eliphas vaulted across the room and past the werewolf, avoiding the debris (human and otherwise) on the ground as he exited the patio door.

Eliphas paused next to a marble fountain, water bubbling from the top of the male sculpture and flowing into a violet-coloured basin lit by bright lights. The wolfman followed, crashing through the door, and sending glass flying, reaching out to rend flesh with its long claws.

Eliphas acted with deadly precision, no movement wasted as he expertly bladed his body and seized the beast by its forearms. He pivoted and swung the creature into the fountain. It smashed through the marble sculpture and landed hard ten feet away in a field of cut grass.

Eliphas flanked the downed beast and moved to strike, but the werewolf quickly regained its feet and came at him in a deadly whirl of fang and claw he could not avoid.

***

Lars was enraged and unable to control his fury as he lunged desperately at the newcomer. He'd been caught off-guard in the middle of a grand feast when the strange man appeared, pale skinned and sharp featured. The newcomer was dressed from head to toe in black, with hair like melted tar and bright white teeth set in a cruel face.

The dark man gave off a strange scent unlike any he'd sampled before, an unsettling combination of rot laced with old magic. It struck a primal chord in the wolf demon, causing it to become enraged.

The dark man moved with more than human speed and grace, and his strength was formidable; he sent Lars crashing through the fountain seemingly without effort. But the man's actions had only served to incense the wolfman. Lars rebounded from the fall and launched himself at his opponent, smashing him off his feet.

The werewolf was amazed at the stranger's durability as they tumbled across the lawn. He slashed the dark man across his porcelain cheek, causing orange sparks to fly off, but the stranger's skin was otherwise unmarked. The man's Stygian eyes beamed at him with a cold intensity and grim resolution that withered his courage and cowed the demon. Lars was taken aback; he'd always felt invincible in his wolfman form. But now, a new sensation was crawling up his spine, one he hadn't felt since he was a small boy, causing him to panic: fear.

He redoubled his efforts, clawing the stranger's face with his other hand. This time he was rewarded—the resilient skin gave way. Lars' sharp nails opened bloodless furrows from cheek to chin. But the grooves rapidly filled with a flowing tar-like substance that became pristine porcelain skin; the wounds disappeared, leaving the dark man's face flawless and untouched.

The stranger head-butted him in the muzzle, breaking bone and sending some of his teeth flying. Lars reeled, staggered by the brutal blow. The dark man followed up with a right cross that caused stars to float in the werewolf's vision. The stranger was clearly inhuman; no mortal could stand toe to toe with a raging werewolf.

Lars allowed the wolf demon's rage to overtake him. He delivered a series of claw strikes that would cut an elephant to ribbons. But the dark man appeared unscathed as if Lars' blows passed harmlessly through a dark fog.

The man seemed alternately composed of mist or iron and was beyond the werewolf's ability to inflict lasting harm. Lars felt impossibly strong hands seize and raise him from his feet; he wondered briefly at the power necessary to lift a half-ton of raging werewolf before his opponent abruptly slammed him head-first into the ground.

Lars came to rest on his back, winded, the fight knocked out of him. He was trying to catch his breath when the stranger suddenly appeared over him, looming like an angel of death.

The dark man smiled, exposing long teeth. He reached down and grasped the werewolf's chin with a cold mitt before violently twisting Lars' head to the side. Lars felt his neck snap. Agony momentarily coursed through his body before giving way to numbness and cold. He knew such an injury could not kill him, but it would take minutes to heal, precious minutes he did not have.

Lars sensed the wolf demon cringe within him. He gradually reverted to his human form, shedding hair and mass. Even crippled as he was, he felt his body attempting to heal itself.

Grey bled out faces with haunted black eyes appeared in the night like dim, dead stars, staring at him with unbridled animosity. Lars recognized some of them as the partygoers he had just slaughtered, their souls caught between worlds, unable to move on.

'Go away,' Lars said in a low, weak voice. The store owner, who had become his first victim of the night leered at him, as if anticipating some upcoming, much anticipated event.

'They can't,' the dark man stated as if speaking on behalf of the ghosts. 'The nature of their deaths has left them stranded. They exist in a state of misery and despair and are visible only to the dead and dying.'

'You aren't human,' Lars said, his mouth bloody and missing teeth. 'You are cold, inhuman. You're from the Dark Side. A Nightstalker—a blood-eater.'

'Once, perhaps, but no longer. I'm something else now,' the stranger said, the moonlight reflecting off his predator's eyes. 'I am but a cog in a wheel, an instrument of stability. I've lived long enough to see what happens when the Uncanny are exposed. Fear forces humans to put aside their petty grievances and unite, joined in a fight against the Other by a primeval survival instinct. I've seen the purges, run from the mobs armed with lances and fire, seen those I love cut to pieces and burned to ash. The Uncanny can only survive in darkness; they wither and die when exposed to the light of truth. But the Uncanny Lords who command me are creatures of terrifying power far outstripping either of us.'

'Who are you?' Lars asked, sounding stronger. He sensed his neck healing rapidly. 'A lapdog running errands for his masters? An Undead bootlicker?'

The stranger smiled as if he found the question amusing. 'When you get as old as me, child, you owe others,' he answered. 'And sometimes you owe big. If the Uncanny Lords want something done, you do it quickly, with no questions asked.'

Angry black clouds formed in the sky, thick rumbling clouds that shook the ground, manipulated by the strings of a malevolent puppet master.

The dark man continued, his tone that of a stoic instructor lecturing a recalcitrant pupil. 'There's a fine line between the worlds, Lars, an order that needs to be maintained at all costs. Your killing spree threatens that fragile stability. The local police are on your tail. Soon, the FBI will be here. Even with all your power, you won't be able to avoid capture. They'll send you to their lab and dissect you. Your DNA will reveal secrets humans were never meant to know. I can't allow that.'

'You can't kill me,' Lars said, panic in his eyes. 'I can sense you don't have any silver on you.' He began to transform, his mouth jutting into a muzzle, his limbs lengthening. But his broken neck slowed the metamorphosis.

'I don't need silver to end you, *loup garou,*' the dark man intoned.

'I'm gonna hurt you, old man, make you scream,' Lars threatened. Panicked sweat glistened on his brow. 'Gonna cut you into little pieces and bury them all over the planet!'

Lightning struck, and thunder soon followed. The stranger raised a long-fingered hand to the heavens.

'Godspeed, Lars,' the dark man said. A look of terror

flashed across Lars' face, the incredulous expression of a man who couldn't believe the bitter fate that had befallen him. The stranger dropped his hand, and a lightning bolt hit Lars, obliterating him in a brilliant flash of coral light and leaving a scorched smoking hole in the ground. Waves of necrotic energy surged through the night, released by Lars' death.

***

'Sublime,' Eliphas commented as the dark energy buffeted his lithe frame, filling him with eldritch power that was a hunger itself. His form could barely contain all of it, his nerves seething with liquid fire, yet he wanted more; it was a heady sensation he never tired of experiencing.

When the necrotic barrage was over, Eliphas stood amidst the flaming mess that had been Lars, struck by a fleeting moment of regret. He felt sympathy for the young man, a boy who'd found himself forsaken in a cruel world where he didn't understand the rules. Eliphas recalled experiencing similar abandonment millennia ago when he became something other than mortal.

He remembered waking in darkness the first night of his new existence, his throat dry, like dust and his mouth aching. Filled with new strength, he'd dug his way out of a shallow grave, casting loamy soil aside in a grim parody of birth. An atavistic hunger had driven him as he staggered back to his ancestral home, where the occupants had cast caution aside to welcome home one they had given up as lost. They were unprepared for the ghastly apparition they had unwittingly allowed entrance and quickly regretted their decision. His parents and siblings begged Ashur and other ancient deities for intercession, but the Gods ignored their pleas. Their cries of pain and horror had echoed long into the night.

Eliphas looked at his fingers stained with the werewolf's blood and brought them to his mouth. He rubbed one finger across his lips and sampled the sanguine fluid. The sweet copper flavour brought back vivid memories of vibrant bloodlust, when he'd done far more than simply place a crimsoned finger in his mouth, when the icy lips and passionate kisses of an immortal woman had filled his nights. He recalled becoming enraptured listening to the sound of blood pumping through ripe webs of veins and arteries, begging to be liberated by his sharp teeth.

But those times were long gone. For a while, the sanguine liquid had granted him sanity in an insane world; or, at least, so he had believed until he finally realized no matter how much he took, it was never enough. There was not enough blood in the world to offset the misery of being unnatural…of being Uncanny.

He'd evolved over the centuries, the red thirst gradually disappearing along with his vulnerability to the old rituals and defences against his kind. A chance encounter one night with a scaly, reptile tailed demon in Greece, a female *empusae*, had led to a battle over hunting grounds. After a prolonged struggle, he overpowered the immortal creature and feasted on its unnatural blood. The next night he found his strength increased and his bloodlust mollified.

Buoyed by his victory and greedy for more power, Eliphas sought out more dangerous prey: goblins and ghouls, shape changers and fey. He'd nearly lost his head in a prolonged battle with a fearsome troll underneath a French bridge—no matter how many limbs he tore off, the stubborn creature kept regenerating and refused to die. Finally, he'd been forced to tear out and eat its heart. The more supernatural blood he consumed, the less the red thirst dogged him, to the point where he stopped feeding off mortals altogether.

Eventually, he found he was strengthened by the never-ending supply of negative energy spawned from human misery and suffering and could live off the necrotic energy released at the moment of death. He wallowed in the wretchedness and despair of two world wars in the 20th century, so replete he could barely move. Eliphas had become truly immortal and discovered the curse of immortality was boredom.

Fortunately for him, the Uncanny Lords had needed hired muscle, someone to keep order amongst the unruly. It turned out that even the mightiest of the Uncanny were still required to feed on the misery and suffering of others. Eliphas had accepted the offer and gladly spilled blood for them ever since. There was great power in blood sacrifice; the agony and despair unleashed when Eliphas shed the *loup garou's* blood would satiate the Lords for months.

Still, deep down within what passed for Eliphas' soul, he realized that monster hunting was just a bandage on the seeping wound of boredom that plagued him, a rationalization for his continued anomalous existence. Yet, at some point, an immortal had metaphorically seen and done it all—the endless bloodshed became dull and derivative.

The blaring of police sirens brought him back to the matters at hand. Eliphas harnessed the potent energy inside him and summoned more lightning, striking the mansion and setting it ablaze. The less evidence left, the better.

Eliphas knew that humans were generally a gullible lot. There would be a short flurry of outrage, with wild stories in the press about a rash of serial killings that culminated in a Halloween massacre. But the passionate indignation would dissipate with time; with no trace of the murderer remaining, the police would move on to other crimes. Things would go back to normal, and normal was the ultimate goal. If the mortals ever discovered the truth about the Uncanny, they would rise up; with their superior numbers, they would soon overwhelm and destroy the supernatural races.

And so Eliphas departed as the first patrol cars arrived. He became a sentient fog that rose into the sky and disappeared in the deep shadows of night, floating weightless on the chill wind, only to reform within the comfortable confines of his coffin in the stone crypt of a nearby cemetery, nestled in the portable grave dirt of the Mesopotamian locality he had died in scores of centuries before. As Halloween night gave way to the Day of the Dead, he slept the sleep of the damned, content with his lot in an inconstant world.

Godhead

Rachel Searcey

The Night symphony grew still as the bounty hunter bled out on the forest floor. His body shuddered with a final gasp at Nomi's feet. She wiped her blade on the wet grass and sheathed it. Searching through his clothes, she found a pouch of coins with her father's royal seal. This man wasn't the first to come after her since she fled the castle, but he'd been the closest to fulfilling his duty. The money was useless to a fugitive like herself, but she tucked it into her jacket pocket, nevertheless. In the hunter's wallet, Nomi found the assassination warrant.

Nomi Varyaen, Seventh Daughter of the King, and Captain of His Majesty's Armed Forces. Wanted for regicide and illicit relations with a duke's son. Anwell. Dear, sweet Anwell. Who was pretty enough but dumb as a brick. He couldn't keep his damn mouth shut about their affair and his loose lips set off a chain of events that damned Nomi to a life on the run. Bitterness was a serpent coiled around her heart.

Wanted dead or alive.

She laughed. She would never be taken alive. The reward was the same either way.

Nomi's portrait had been reproduced in miniature for the warrant: her broken nose, the pale scar running down the length of her profile. Her one asset, luxurious black hair lay coiled and styled under a military cap, tucked behind elegant, pointed ears. It held no resemblance to Nomi's current appearance.

She'd been hiding in the Northern territories on the Harash border, after fleeing with nothing but her military uniform— traded for coin in a back alley. She cropped her waist-length hair short to keep down the lice to no avail. To blend in with the natives, she dyed her skin green with plant dye and kept her ears under a turban. Most days, she slunk along dark country roads, stealing when the opportunity arose, killing when forced. The Harashians were a suspicious, ugly people and she didn't trust them to help. But she had nowhere else to go.

Nomi, arms shaking, dragged the man into the bushes. Her sore body had reached its limits and she needed to rest. She decided to sleep and resume travel in the morning. But the snap of branches set her nerves on fire. A dagger slammed into a tree trunk, inches from where she was standing. Poison oozed from the blade, turning the tree's flesh black where it struck. Nomi ducked and hid behind the tree, eyes scanning the thick foliage. The bounty hunter wasn't alone, and his colleagues had caught up. A black shadow detached from the darkness, then another one. Two slight figures, their eyes shining in the dark, darted towards her position. Scouts, with poisoned daggers drawn.

A third joined, a brute of a warrior, sliding through the night with hardly a sound despite his hulking size. He was a head taller than Nomi and twice as broad. She recognized him and shuddered. Vasher, the head of father's Night Guard. And the rest of them would be along soon. Outnumbered and exhausted, Nomi slunk into the underbrush and fled. Vasher was a mighty foe even during training when they fought for her father's entertainment. His ugly face inches from her own, spittle dripping from his lips while he bore down on her with his girth. Nomi had surrendered to him one too many times. Vasher would relish the challenge of capturing and subduing Nomi. To lay her corpse before King Varyaen guaranteed Vasher a Medal of Honor, all the women he could stand, and a significant chunk of property. He would crush Nomi like she was nothing. She wouldn't give him the satisfaction.

Fear drove her on and on, through tangles of forest and insect-infested swamps. She lost sensation in her feet, in her hands, but still she pressed on. They wouldn't take her. When she stopped to rest, she didn't know if the sounds she heard were animals, or Vasher and his guard on her heels. In their eyes, Nomi was no better than an animal to be routed out. Low hanging branches whipped her tired body, and she stumbled over tree logs, scraping her hands and knees bloody on the unforgiving earth. Blisters broke on her heels, and she suffered lancing wounds on her arms and legs, shredding the thin fabric. All the while, she cursed her father for his close-mindedness. She cursed her mother for not protecting her, for being weak. Her selfish siblings, watching Nomi's downfall and allowing it to happen. For it meant they were one step closer to the throne with their eldest sister out of the way.

She didn't see the wall until she crashed into it. It rose out of the underbrush as if it had grown from the forest floor itself, circling a stately manor engulfed in greenery. An eerie feeling swept over her. The black and foreboding peak hit the canopy where carrion birds were circling as the sun rose. Vines wove between crumbled masonry and invaded dark windows, unhindered by broken glass. Rotted shutters lay buried under dense plant growth. The sounds of the forest were dampened by the building's looming presence.

Nomi, half blind with fatigue and fear and rage, felt along the wall for a way around. But it was an endless length of vine covered stone. She whipped around to look at the forest, as if Vasher were upon her. But there was no one there.

Her hands found a seam in the wall, a different texture than all that came before. A door, dense with moss and swollen shut with dark wood. She jiggled the massive doorknob, but it was tight. She threw her shoulder into the wood with a rabid fury. On her third attempt, the door gave, and she almost fell on top of a young Harashian girl who had opened the door from the inside.

Nomi's mud-caked hand clamped over the girl's mouth before she could scream, and she kicked the door shut behind them. They were in a well-stocked kitchen with a fire in the oven. Nomi listened—surely someone inside this house had heard the commotion. The girl's over-sized teeth dug into Nomi's palm, breaking the flesh. Nomi lost her grip and the girl backed away, snatching a butcher's knife from the table.

'I won't harm you,' Nomi said, and perhaps meant it. Her voice came out in a croak from her parched throat. She hadn't stopped for more than a handful of water from whatever puddles she came across. Her stomach spasmed with hunger in the aromatic kitchen and her eyes fell on the counter, where uncooked bacon and sausage lined a plate, next to a dozen boiled eggs.

The girl's face was smeared with Nomi's blood, and she wiped it away with her apron, revealing a swollen belly. The girl was pregnant, several months along. Typical of her race, she was short, stocky, and her skin was dark green. The antithesis of elegant Ellysian breeding. She levelled the knife at Nomi.

Mud mixed with blood and pus from Nomi's open wounds

dripped to the floor. The girl put a hand to her mouth and nose, and Nomi could see she was disgusted by the feral creature leering towards her.

'I need a place to hide, that's all,' Nomi said. She raised her hands in supplication, a move so foreign to her that she shivered with repulsion. She had never surrendered in her life, let alone to a pregnant female Harashian. The girl shook her head at Nomi, mouth hanging open as if she were going to speak again. But a clatter of footsteps on the stairwell into the kitchen took them both by surprise. A middle-aged man entered and looked between them. He was human—rounded ears, smartly trimmed beard—and wore an elegant housecoat over silk pyjamas. Nomi hadn't seen his kind in a decade since the Border Wars when she was a mere squire.

'Lord Sai, thank the gods you're here.' The Harashian girl kept her eyes on Nomi and backed towards the man. He snaked an arm around her and stroked her neck.

'Cassandra, who is this person?' The man's voice was velvety smooth, the cultured timbre of a noble.

'An Ellysian, I think,' Cassandra said. Her voice carried the familiar hitch and accent of a Harashian trying to form Ellysian words with their ill-formed mouths.

Nomi noted the way the man's hand laid against the girl's neck—protective, possessive. The thought disturbed her: a high-bred human male with a common Harashian girl. Mating with her. She'd heard of such pairings, but they were often routed out and publicly humiliated before the woman was so far along. If Nomi played her cards right, she could leverage something from this situation.

The girl wore the clothes of a servant but there was a thin gold chain around her neck, glittering with enchantment. A protection spell? Nomi decided they must be in hiding. She didn't want to be found out and neither did they. A plan began to form that would benefit them all.

'I need a place to stay until the danger has passed. Then I'll be away from here.' Nomi said.

The lord smiled. 'Danger?' He laughed, arching an eyebrow at Nomi. 'You may stay, of course. Please, make yourself at home. Cassandra, ready a bath for our guest.'

His invitation took Nomi off guard. She expected a fight, for the lord's men to appear and throw her from the house. Suspicion whined in her bowels but perhaps it was the hunger pangs. The rich, homey scent of bread baking in the oven made her nose twitch.

'Lord, are you certain?'

The lord whispered inaudibly to Cassandra and her face relaxed. His fat fingers twitched on the gold chain. 'You may join me for breakfast.' He bowed as if they were in court and swept back up the stairs. Nomi stood frozen for a moment; sure she was walking into a trap. She considered running. But she was exhausted, and the kitchen smells were tantalizing.

'Come on, then,' the girl said. She left the butcher's knife on the kitchen table.

Cassandra led the way through the manor. Little golden trinkets lay out on regal, hand-carved furniture. The house smelled of wood oil and floor polish, reminding her of the castle. Nomi's father flashed before her eyes, mouth open in a soundless scream. Regret flooded through her. If she'd left before he struck her across the face like a commoner, before he insulted her womanhood, her loyalty to the throne... Before she returned the blow with the blunt of her knife and his skull folded in like an eggshell. Her military training ensured the blow had been true and deadly. Blood spurting across the court floor. Her mother shrieking like a wounded animal. Nomi shook away the images.

Lord Sai was wealthy. He could send Nomi on her way with heavy pockets and enough food to last through the winter. If she kept their secret.

'Where's the rest of the staff?' Nomi asked.

'Only Lord Sai and I live here,' Cassandra said, not bothering to turn around. She led Nomi upstairs through the servants' passage.

'No guests? Family?'

'No,' she said. Cassandra opened the door on the third floor to an empty servant's bedroom. Dust eddied in the corners as the open door brought in a draft from the passage. The window was boarded up, but dawn's light streamed through the planks. 'I'll bring you some fresh water and clothing.'

Nomi thanked her and threw herself into a chair draped in oil cloth. Mud flaked from her body, and she had left a dirty trail into the room. After a few moments, Cassandra brought a painted ceramic bowl filled with steaming water, a towel, a simple tunic, and a pair of house slippers. Once she'd left, Nomi bathed and dressed. She looked around the room, opening the drawers and examining the furniture under the cloths. All hand-crafted furniture. Whoever this Lord Sai was, he came from a good family. Perhaps disgraced by scandal or fallen into disrepute. What other reason would a man of his bearing be shacking up with a Harashian girl in the middle of nowhere? Nomi found a jade figurine inside the nightstand, shoved in the back, and wrapped in tissue paper. A hunched being with wings and a monstrous face. It was heavy, worth something. She tucked it into the tunic pocket, still wrapped in paper.

On the other hand, there was no one to interfere with Nomi's plan. In fact, what stopped Nomi from taking her plans a step further? Keep the manor for herself, packed as it was with riches.

Nomi strapped her belt and sword sheath around her waist. She used the towel to wipe the blade clean. In the fading light, she examined it for damage and was happy to find it in good shape despite her struggles through the damp countryside.

Cassandra knocked on the door, swaddled in scents from the kitchen. Nomi hurried after her down the passage, eager for her first real meal in days. She kept her face relaxed, fighting the twisted smile threatening to rise to her face like a knife edge. Soon, it would all be hers.

***

Plates of rich food lay decimated across the vast dining room table. Cassandra had served Lord Sai and Nomi an extensive breakfast of sausage, omelettes, fresh squeezed juice, and tiny pastries. Lord Sai ate like a pig, shovelling food into his mouth with no regard for decency. He wore a bib, as if he were a child, and it was smeared with bacon grease and jam. Beneath the slovenly bib, he wore a silk embroidered purple jacket over an azure blouse with a flamboyant stylized collar. His hands were heavy with gold rings, each dotted with exotic gemstones. A corpulent gold pendant hung from his neck. The lord could have been mistaken for someone in the king's court.

Nomi watched him with disgust, having eaten her fill early on, unwilling to stuff herself if there was a change of plans and she had to make a run for it after all. She still feared Vasher showing up at any moment. The lord's casual behaviour did nothing to abate the wariness that held her like a vice.

'Nomi, my dear, relax. You're stiff as a board and barely ate anything,' Lord Sai said, pushing a plate of jellied persimmon closer to her.

'I never told you my name,' Nomi said. Her hand was resting on her sword pommel during the meal, but shifted to the grip and tensed, ready to draw.

The lord smiled; his teeth filthy with bits of meat.

'Did you think I wouldn't recognize you? The news of your

betrayal spread like wildfire across the four kingdoms.' He took a sloppy gulp of pomegranate juice. It spilled like blood down his chin, absorbed by the bib.

'News travels, even amongst the crude Harashians.' His eyes flashed at Cassandra who stood meek in the doorway. Lord Sai plucked a steaming sausage from a saucer. 'Your mother must be at a loss after your father's death.' Lord Sai bit into the sausage, chewing it with relish, closing his eyes as if in pleasure. 'Who do you think sent the Night Guard after you? My bet's on your siblings.'

Nomi clenched her jaw. 'You mean to collect the bounty?' She stood; sword unsheathed. 'It must be a pittance to a man like you. Your wealth is apparent. Besides, give me up and you reveal yourselves.' She looked pointedly at Cassandra's swollen belly. The girl kept her eyes on the floor. 'A human laying with a Harashian. What abomination will come from her womb, Lord Sai? They'll hang you and worse for the girl.' Nomi's threat carried weight; she was sure of it.

Lord Sai laughed. 'Nomi, nothing is as it appears.'

Nomi lunged and pressed the sharp edge of her sword across Lord Sai's throat. Blood thumped in her temples. His carrion reek filled her nostrils, and she held her breath. Cassandra screamed and ran downstairs to the kitchen.

'Explain yourself,' Nomi said.

Sai seemed amused by the blade at his throat. 'I'm well acquainted with your family. Your father will be missed. He was always one to keep me well supplied, shall we say? I've had news that your brother Jeremiah has ascended the throne. What a fine monarch he will make. I hope he will be as generous as your father.' He gasped as the blade drew blood, Nomi's body bearing down on him and pinning him to his chair.

'I don't know who you are, or what your arrangement is with my family, but I will not go back there. I will kill you first.'

His laughter erupted, distorted and guttural. Bits of food splattered from his mouth. 'You think I would give up a tender morsel such as yourself? They said I could do as I wished.' He smiled at Nomi's confusion. 'You are mine now.'

Nomi's stomach flipped. He meant to keep her like he had the Harashian girl. Pregnant and barefoot, nowhere to run, no one to help. A slave. No better than the ill-treated whores who followed Nomi's garrison around and gave birth to their bastard children.

Nomi severed his windpipe and jugular vein in one swift draw of the blade. Blood spurted across the table in a great fount before slowing. Lord Sai slumped in his seat, his neck gaping open like a second mouth. Blood dripped into the carpet and oozed beneath her boots. Nomi remembered Cassandra and charged down the kitchen steps. She could easily track the pregnant girl through the forest before she ran for help, if she did indeed run. Instead, Nomi found her pacing the kitchen with the butcher knife in hand.

Her words were clumsy and jumbled, hysterical.

'Thank the gods, you're alive! Did you sever his head from his body? It's the only way. We need to leave.' She turned towards the kitchen door and tugged at the door handle. Nomi took her by the shoulder and spun her around, sword at the girl's throat.

'Take me to where he hides his riches. This manor is mine now, and you'll do as I say.'

'No, it's not worth it! You don't understand. Let us get away from here!' Cassandra said.

Nomi shook her until she stilled. 'You're going to show me what I want and then I'll decide what to do with you.'

Cassandra began to cry. 'It's not what you think! He's not dead. Please, this chain around my neck, I can't take it off myself. You can do it, please.' Her hands shook as she clung to Nomi's collar. 'Please. He wants my baby. Lord Sai killed the father and took me. Do you understand?'

Nomi was fed up with Cassandra's blubbering.

'Show me, now. Or I kill you both.' Nomi brought the sword up against Cassandra's navel. She wailed and almost collapsed, but Nomi forced her to her feet against the wall.

Cassandra sobbed but Nomi was sure she would obey. 'I will do it, but you'll regret this moment. I'll see that you will.'

Cassandra pointed across the room. 'That door there leads to the cellar.'

'This better not be a trick. I'll gut you here and find it myself if I need to.'

Cassandra, head lowered, shuffled over to a small door that opened off the kitchen. She lit a torch found on the wall. Stone steps, rotted with mildew led down into a dank cellar. Nomi pushed Cassandra ahead of her and they descended.

***

Nomi's boots slipped on the damp steps, but she kept her balance by bracing one hand on Cassandra's sturdy shoulder. In the other hand she wielded the sword inches from the girl's spine.

With Lord Sai's wealth, Nomi could stay on the run for a lifetime. A few forged documents and a loyal servant went a long way. She could weave a web of deception and protect herself. In her mind, she built a life for herself, free of family and obligation. A life of luxury after a lifetime of endless struggle.

They passed through a larder, stacked high with preserves and dried meat. Then a wine cellar lined with barrels. Stone walls gave way to packed earth and the roar of running water in the distance. Black lichen crawled along crevices, spreading across the steps until they became a black mass as if a blanket had been thrown over the earth. The pressure in Nomi's ears built until her head throbbed. Moisture seeped through the thin house slippers and cave born insects with too many legs scuttled across her feet.

Cassandra wept, a constant stream of tears to match the growing dampness. She clutched at her belly, claiming cramps, but Nomi ignored her. Finally, they came to the last few steps. The sound of rushing water echoed off the walls and brought a chill breeze with it.

There was a clatter on the steps above them. Nomi took the torch from Cassandra to look but saw nothing. Nomi shook Cassandra by the shoulder. 'Who else is here?'

Cassandra cringed and whimpered; eyes wide with fear. 'No one, I swear it! But Lord Sai,' she whispered.

He can't die.

Nomi gave Cassandra another shove to break the spell. The girl was out of her mind. Who knows what terrors she suffered living alone in this house with Lord Sai. The nobles always had the most disgusting sexual appetites. And Lord Sai was a pig of a man, like all the others, nothing more. 'Come on,' Nomi said, fed up with it all.

The narrow cellar passageway opened into a larger cavern. A dragon's hoard of treasures glittered in the torchlight. Gold coins piled high, crystal bowls filled with gems, exotic jewellery laid out in velvet boxes. Nomi took the torch and left Cassandra in the dark by the stairs to run her fingers over her newfound wealth. Beneath the tinkle of coins and rustle of piles of bills, there was a slithering, sucking sound, like water going down a drain. Nomi walked across the cave to find an underground river, rushing away into the darkness. She raised the torch. The water was black as pitch and there was no way to tell how deep or wide it was.

Then Cassandra shrieked.

Nomi turned to find Cassandra running towards her, away from the narrow tunnel. The girl stopped at the water's edge. Her eyes were trained on the dark space behind Nomi. The torch light revealed Lord Sai's body crumpled in a heap. Nomi approached with caution. A trail of fresh blood soaked into the black lichen and disappeared as if it had never been there. His head lay almost detached from the body at an unnatural angle and dirt was ground under his fingernails, as if his corpse had crawled down the stairs on its own.

'Who else is here?' Nomi thrust the torch before her as she climbed a few slippery steps upwards. 'Who moved the body?' Nomi asked Cassandra.

'Please, we're alone. Take off this chain and let me go, for both our sakes.' Cassandra backed into the river.

Something stiff and wet slid along Nomi's leg in the dark. She swiped blindly and stepped back. Her blade hit flesh and slid across bone, flinging whatever it was away from her against the damp wall. Lord Sai's twitching hand. Cassandra ran into the water, splashing away into the dark.

Nomi's breath hitched in her throat as she watched Lord Sai's body twist, almost boneless, like an otter turning over in the water. A gurgling, throaty noise rose from the quivering mass. Spasms wracked the body, thumping up and down as if in seizure. The head came loose and rolled away towards the pile of treasure where it came to rest with eyes glazed open, staring.

The carrion reek she smelled earlier came on ten-fold as the corpse's stump of a neck bulged and twisted. Nomi overcame the nausea roiling in her gut, the disgust threatening to drown her senses, and forced herself to watch. The lord's chest expanded beyond the confines of his house coat, ripping the fine cloth to shreds. His torso ballooned, throbbing with blue veins stretched beyond all reason. The headless corpse spasmed once more before a tear opened, a gash beginning at the navel and ending at the clavicle.

Nomi had seen horrors on the battlefield, been the cause of them herself. She had tortured, skewered, and dismembered her share of the enemy. She had fought rotting, undead soldiers, brought to uncanny animation by necromancers. She had hidden beneath a pile of swollen dead to sneak out of enemy territory, digging herself out of a mass grave to slaughter the guards. But nothing had prepared her for the violence of a man torn apart from the inside by a creeping abomination.

Black tipped claws reached through the gash and tore the skin like paper. Nomi's vision blurred as she forced herself to focus, unable to comprehend what she was seeing. Bile crept up the back of her throat at the slew of awful smells. A gush of intestines slithered onto the floor as a misshapen head pushed forth. Nomi's stomach lurched at the reek of split intestines. The beast's skin was leathery and grey, grub-like, long hidden from the sun and more comfortable in the dirt than open air. Nomi readied her sword, bracing against the stairs to launch herself against the monster that crawled from Lord Sai's bowels.

A swollen head, cradled by rolls of flesh, sat atop a gelatinous, asymmetrical torso, and branched into wriggling appendages, tipped with onyx talons. Each one probed the air like a blind man until the wrinkles shifted and opened. Sweat broke out on Nomi's brow and threatened to blind her. The sword shook in her hands. Now, do it now, she told herself, but she couldn't move. The face before her was the same as the weighted jade statue, still in her pocket. The one she'd taken from the servant's quarters, the monstrous face in miniature now a grotesque reality.

Innumerable eyes slit open, each one a black orb ringed with red. They swivelled and focused on her, shaking on the stairs. It slid free of the corpse and beneath the undulating arms, a wet mouth opened, layers of teeth as thick as her thumb. A roar erupted from its gaping maw and the stench of rotting corpses filled the underground cavern.

Fear and adrenaline, such as Nomi had not felt since her first battle at sixteen, rose within her. A thick arm whipped against the side of her head and sent her to the floor, but she rolled, sliding behind the odious creature. She dug her knees into its back; the skin was damp and cold, sticky with corpse fluids. Nomi went for its eyes, slashing the sword in diagonal movements across its hideous face while it screeched.

An arm wrapped around her neck and yanked, hurling her against the cavern wall. Winded and dizzy, she staggered to her feet when the thing's drooling mouth closed on her thigh. They fell together on the floor as its tentacles wrapped around her body, threatening to crush her in its coils. Nomi's hips shifted and popped, grinding in their sockets. She screamed, flailing with the sword to gouge deep slashes in the tentacles. The blade slipped, slicing into her own leg.

Its mouth found her wrist and almost severed her hand from her arm. The blade was lost along with her sanity. She tore with her fingers on her good hand, digging deep into the eye sockets until they popped like jelly from the pressure. Deeper, deeper, deeper—her fingers slipped into its skull, past ridged bone. She cocked her elbows back and with every ounce of strength left, she bashed its head against the floor until it was a pulpy mass. her biceps burned with the effort.

Nomi extricated her hands from its ruined skull and collapsed on the cavern floor. The monster's grotesque body rolled and spasmed until it stilled, pinning her with dead weight. She let out a gasp when the tentacles released their hold and fell lifeless. But its jaws were still deep in her thigh muscle and seared her skin when she tried to move.

Blood and mucus seeped from the wound until her leg went numb. Feverish and shaky, her hands scrabbled around the creature's mouth, trying to find leverage, a release. The corpse grew cold, but its jaws remained tight around her thigh with no give.

Nomi panicked, screaming for help, and knowing there was no one who cared if she died in this hole. Her family would extend the warrant for a year at most and then she would be forgotten. Her name scrubbed from the family's records; her military awards had already been stripped. And sweet, stupid Anwell... damn him! Nomi cried with great hitching sobs. Her nails scraped against the packed earth in a futile attempt to crawl with the abomination trailing behind her. 'Cassandra! Help me!'

Water splashed and thank the Gods, Cassandra came back. Her green skin was shiny with moisture, almost glowing in the dark.

'Cassandra!' Nomi pleaded, reaching for the girl's dripping skirt.

Cassandra watched Nomi for a moment, taking in the carnage. A smile played on her lips. She nudged the abomination with her foot. She knelt and bared her neck to Nomi. 'Take off the chain first.' With her good hand, Nomi scrabbled at the necklace until it snapped. Her fingers left smears of black flecked blood on the girl's skin. Cassandra caught the necklace as it fell. Her fingers moved deftly, and Nomi realized too late what the girl meant to do. The necklace snapped closed around Nomi's neck. A burning sensation cut through her and then it was gone. Nomi tugged at the thin metal with bloody, clumsy fingers.

'No, no you can't do this to me!' Nomi's whimpers turned into howls.

Cassandra moved around Nomi and took the guttering torch with her. She disappeared up the stairs and the cellar was plunged into darkness. Nomi screamed like a primal beast, clawing her way towards the stairs, dragging the beast with her. Cassandra had damned her to oblivion.

The hideous dark closed in and the only sound was rushing water and the beat of her slowing heart. The beast broke the quiet, sighing like a bear waking from hibernation.

He can't die.

Rippling heat from the monster's breath engulfed her trapped leg. Its head shifted side to side, the teeth burying deeper into her thigh. Its warm tongue lapped against the slow drip of blood from a rent open vein. Wet, smacking sounds of a tongue against teeth, raking against thigh. Nomi lost control of her body and the acrid stench of her own urine and shit flooded her nostrils, mixing with rot.

Wet tentacles slapped against the damp earth as it shuffled towards the river with her in its jaws. Her scrabbling fingers left routs in the mud and her raw screams echoed off the cavern walls, only silenced by the river's dark current.

Sandman's Loam

K. A. Tutin

Fourteen nights after my mother was presumed dead, Sandman showed himself to me. Before then, he'd appeared as eyes knuckled from dust – a sore, raw-thick grit that crusted beneath my lids.

Streetlight glowing through the window sharpened his stark outline from where he perched on my bed, gangly and thin, shadowed against midnight. There was nothing more, until he smiled. The sudden glint threw me off, his jaw set into a twitching grin. I'd seen creepy smiles before, like the boys who had stared at me across math's class or the monster in a horror film before devouring the victim. Sandman's was something else, because the discomfort that gnawed at my stomach disappeared as soon as his smile did.

Must have been the wine, I thought. I'd consumed the bottle over the previous evening as I packed my mother's belongings into boxes to be stored in the loft, the only things I could stand to face; newspaper scrapbooks, stained coasters, recipes shorn from magazines as old as the 70s, or stale polo mints and boiled sweets; that and the fact I'd had to sign for my inheritance. The one I'd tried to avoid because it felt like surrendering to an unfathomable truth, but there was no other choice lest I wanted the council to take everything instead. As if I'd give them the last traces of my mother.

Oh, Anne, little one, Sandman said. I frowned at this. I'd long peaked into my forties. *You look tired.*

I sat up against the headboard, scrubbing my grimacing face, and said, *burying your mother without knowing if she's dead will do that to you.*

He leant forward until his cool breath ghosted over my cheeks. Had he always been that close? *Do you want to sleep?*

Sleep is the last thing I want, I said. The sheets bunched around my hips as I shifted, scrunching in my fists. *I want her back.*

She was everywhere already. From the creaking wood that sounded too similar to her slippered foot on the staircase, to the lavender bags she'd hung on the rails of my wardrobe to hide the damp smell. Things you couldn't get away from; an inescapable intimacy that marked you like fingernails digging into skin, bloodied crescent moons and bruised flesh. But that was her ghost, not her.

Sandman razored another smile, letting out a stuttering breath from pale lips. A hand appeared in front of me, palm open. Gnarled, his nails filed to a fine point, beckoning. *Let me that dream and have her you shall.*

I eyed him. *I thought the Sandman was supposed to be the one to give dreams.*

One must feel the soul from whence the dream was born before its awakening. My nerves slackened when his smile eased again, his fingers curling on themselves ever so slightly. *Do you not believe me?*

There was a distinctness between believing him and believing in him, and it felt as though he meant one despite saying the other.

I'd have thought both were true as a child, when the nightmares came for my mind, festering and choking. And when they were swept away by the taste of strawberry popping sweets or the warmth of summer sun, within the dreamworld, my mother told me that was because of Sandman. The one who came to gift you with what you wished – whatever that may be.

An illusion, a figment, couldn't give me what I wanted. I'd not slept for days, my head aching from dehydration, from the drink and the crying.

Those same tears stung my eyes, and Sandman must have noticed, because he reached over and laid his cool hand over mine. My hand twitched before something washed over me.

My mother was here. A faint presence, caressing the air like the refreshing breeze on an early spring morning. The shadow who I could almost touch if I pressed down hard enough. But then the moment was gone, replaced with the feeling of our hands still overlapping. He pulled back, until only our fingertips brushed. I shook my head (because she was gone. Not dead but gone anyhow – but couldn't gone be found?) but the surreality remained planted in the nook of my skull.

I let my head drop to my chest, breathing deep and heavy. *How can you bring her back?* I muttered; my voice lilted like a wilting dandelion.

You will have to see for yourself, Sandman said, and he waited. Waited, and waited.

The exhaustion that had been sinking into me intensified, enough to curl my fingers into his for a moment. I wanted to feel something other than agony, than grief. Than the feeling that felt like swallowing glass, tearing me apart from the inside.

As I laced our hands together in agreement, Sandman smiled. My gut twisted as he said, *I will give you your dream and take you as mine.*

***

Morning streamed over me with a sense of confusion and scepticism. Once Sandman had come, if he had at all, I'd dreamt about laughing and citrus – the scene after an hourly winter walk down the abandoned railway line. My mother and I sat at a bench to rest our twinging knees. We ate apples and peanut butter, scooped from the Tupperware boxes she'd insisted on preparing. Our cold fingers touched each time we reached in for a slice. *Here you go, darling,* she would say as she gave me the last one, like she always had when I was a child.

I pulled myself out of bed and headed downstairs, the bottom of my dressing gown dragging on the carpet. I turned on the gas stove for the kettle and the heater to warm the chilly living room, because she hated to evolve with the times, hated the thought of change. She might have been right about that, as I stood in her home, struggling to breathe with her absence.

I'd conceded to sorting out most of her things because I'd nagged her about the cramped and suffocating feeling, and this was the chance to tidy that away, a fresh start for us both. But others, what was too sentimental to even glance at, I'd shoved into the corner, concealed by shadows. Because they were something else. They were peeling open ribs and cupping a dead heart in your hands, even though my mother's was still beating.

Instead, I went to the box that I couldn't stop returning to, stamped from when the police were still bothered about investigating.

I peered inside to find the usual things: a leathery handbag cracked and worn, house keys, two packs of tissues. They had all been on the kitchen table when she went missing. Nothing untoward, until I'd seen her purse opened to the plastic sleeve, where my photo stared back.

A tense, lung-clenching moment slid over me, until I forced the sadness aside to focus on what mattered. Finding her. Several hours followed with rifling through trivial items, drinking more tea, scrubbing the tiredness from my eyes, before coming across something unknown. A journal. It had a cracked spine and flimsy cover, knotted shut with fraying string. My mother never used diaries as a child, let alone as an adult or near pensioner. Yet I was still surprised when I looked inside, expecting her handwriting – messy, scrawled, barely skimming the paper – and finding it empty. Not a single splatter of ink, despite the worn and wrinkled feel to the thing, like my mother had thumbed through each page to the end.

Something crawled over me. Dread, unshakeable and fierce. Enough to make me drop what I was doing and sit outside on the porch.

Dusk coloured the sky orange mellow and dragged the moon up high. People still wandered by. An old lady shuffled back from the shop, her elbows weighted down with plastic bags; a few joggers waved and smiled and huffed. I sipped at another cup of tea, though cold and bland. My eyes felt gritty and sore. But as I sighed and rose to head back inside, a soft voice interrupted me.

It's Anne, right? the woman asked. I recognised her as Margaret, the freelance gardener who had knocked on doors around the street, offering to uproot weeds or cut grass. Her hands were grimy, the same as her dungarees. *I'm sorry about your mum.*

I paused before answering. Her apologies sounded like condolences. Thank you, I said, continuing forward, heading for bed.

Saw her eulogy in the paper. She was a lovely lady. Always wanted tulips planted each spring.

I turned back. *You knew her?*

Margaret nodded, smiling sadly. *We'd have a cuppa and biscuits afterwards.* A light, humourless laugh. *She insisted on me taking home the rest.*

Typical of Mum. *Did you see her before she went missing?* I asked, desperate even to my own ears. *See or hear anything? Anything at all?*

Weeks before, my mother would still do the same, sitting at the kitchen table with the radio blaring the classics; though, she barely seemed to listen. I'd brush her arm and she would flinch away from the blank and deadened stare she had pinned to the wall. At my touch, her look shifted. Bleaker, wet with tears, and, worst of all, afraid. I'd asked her what was wrong, but she told me nothing. She was gone before I could ask her again.

Margaret looked at me with sympathy and concern now as she shrugged, an answer unwanted. *Losing your mother's hard. I'd know.*

I bit down on my lip to hold back the urge to say my mother was not dead. My mother was alive, but Margaret's was not.

Sorry to hear that, I said, deflating in a way that I might sink into the ground.

Her mouth turned down, wavering. She sniffed hard and cleared her throat, as though to make herself move on from the subject. *I'm next door but one, if you ever want anyone to talk to.* She waved over to the house with all the flowers on the front garden. I'd never even noticed she was the one who lived there, but then not much else had held my attention. Not much else besides watching my mother become unrecognisable. Watching who she was disappear before my very eyes.

***

Sandman returned that night with something unexpected about him: a misted aura rippling around his body, grey tendrils slithering between his fingers as he reached out to me again.

My mother appeared in my mind, a version of when it felt like a similar darkness infected our lives. I'd been selfish and angry; she'd been stubborn and overbearing. We'd fought over something that would seem trivial now, faded like an overexposed photograph. At the time my life felt stretched thin and leaving meant not speaking with her for nearly five years. Until, without warning or reason, I was drowned with the need to see her.

We'd embraced on the front doorstep once I came back. Said nothing because we didn't need to. Her hand leafed through my hair, with mine stroking over her upper arm as though a child again, when I'd be comforted by the cold feeling of it.

The moment did not last long as those days went by. Soon the blank stares came, the uneasy muttering, as though she was somewhere else.

When she thought I couldn't hear, she would say to herself, *He's coming. Don't let him take me.*

Doctors couldn't find or diagnose anything despite numerous tests and medication and therapy. The only thing left was to stay with her.

Let me that dream, Sandman said to me now, *and have her you shall.*

I hesitated, inching away from him. *Nothing has happened since the last time you asked.*

Those who dream nourish those who fulfil them — and them both. A break, that splitting smile. *And that takes time, little one.*

Despite the tension wringing me taut, telling me to get away, the hope pulled me forward, offering my hand. Except, Sandman moved past me, and I watched as his own hand disappeared into my chest.

As he eased out, clutched within his fist, was my heart. Beating, blood dripping onto the bed, still attached to my insides with thick vessels. His aura webbed over it until the thing seized and shrivelled. He tore it from my ribcage with a sharp and searing yank. My scream stuck in my throat as I crashed into darkness, his gaping grin being the last thing I saw.

***

In my nightmare, my mother and I sat on the bench again. We ate our apple slices. Only when I bit into mine, the taste was sour. The crevice where I'd sunk my teeth into was grey and rotten, and my hand seemed to undulate, like the hazy and darkened aura around Sandman.

To my unease, I woke slow and steady, peeling my eyelids apart from the crust that clung to my lashes. No flinch, no sweat or laboured breathing. Any remnants of the dream manifesting as the familiar nerves pinching at my stomach and my head swimming like I'd been held underwater. That seemed worse, like when something was wrong, but you didn't understand why. Couldn't find the reason that felt within your reach.

I sat up and stared down at my hands. Thin, pale, but as normal as ever. I clenched them into fists, then dragged myself out from bed.

As soon as I entered the living room, my gaze fell on the journal, left on the coffee table from when I'd looked at it last.

An inexplicable sensation overwhelmed me, shoving me forward. A calling that rung out across the distance. My name shaped by my mother's voice.

The journal felt heavy on my palms, sweeping it open with an arch of paper. Nothing, like the previous time. And then, something. Her handwriting veering across the page, looking even shakier and cramped than usual, written with grey ink. There was only one line, which appeared to ripple the same way Sandman had; like my hand had. *He calls it Sandman's Loam. His loam.*

I brushed over the letters and found that they felt strange – a cold and fine wetness beneath my fingertips. Before I could investigate further, the doorbell rang. I pushed aside the net curtains to see Margaret outside.

As I turned back to the journal, the page was empty, as though the words had never existed. The doorbell rang again.

The breeze that filtered through the open door was warm with its spring evening. A sky brandished pink and orange softened the air around Margaret.

Hey, uh, she started, rubbing at the back of her neck. *I just finished work and thought I'd pop by to see how you were doing.*

I said nothing for a long moment because my breath refused to even, until I manage to force out: *I'm fine.*

Margaret glanced past me, to what I knew was the contents of my mother's things spilling out into the hallway, piling up against the walls. *Need any help with that?*

Irritation dissolved into sadness and then empathy. Even though my guard tried to shutter close, my gut told me she only wanted to extend a hand. Sandman had done that too, and now everything felt shifted, tilting enough to make me feel as though I'd plummet and keep falling. Margaret was just as unfamiliar, but, unlike him, the discomfort gnawing at my stomach disappeared when she smiled.

She eased past me as I stepped aside, leading her to the living room where most of the chaos laid. *I'm packing everything away for the loft.*

You could always donate some things to charity—
Margaret cut off when she saw my face, which was stretched taut with a frown. *No, no. I don't want to do that.*

Right, of course, she said, and sat on the sofa, looking over the various items as I returned to my usual schedule of placing, sealing, and taping.

We worked in silence for several minutes, filled with clinking porcelain from the trinkets; the flicking pages between magazines. I startled at the third noise. An unmistakable crackling plastic from a photo album being opened, loud and teeth-grating. My neck made the same sound from how fast I looked up, reaching out to yank the book from Margaret's hands. I should have hidden it away, from her eyes. From my own.

My hand froze when Margaret gently laughed, not even noticing my panic. At her speaking, my hand dropped back to my side.

You look lovely together here, she said. Her smile widened as she turned the next page. *Oh, this one especially. Who took it for you?*

I shuffled forward, the carpet burning my knees. The gasp fluttered up my throat when I look at the photograph. Rather, what shouldn't have been one at all. It was of my dream, where my mother and I were at the bench with our apple slices, heads tilted back whenever sunlight broke through the dull clouds. We'd never documented the moment. Kept it for ourselves.

That wasn't the only giveaway. The image seemed smudged, streaking our faces grey; our smiles warped into a too-white stain. Hazy and rippling the same way that everything else seemed to be doing. The photograph was not real, but the dream from where it had come was. Margaret didn't seem to notice the wrongness of it.

My hand shook as I reached over again and laid my fingers

over the photo. Despite expecting the cold damp, I still flinched.

Sandman had done something to my mother, as he was doing the same to me. Never just the gravelly eyes or hallucination. Never just the myth.

The tear slipped from the corner of my eye, scrubbed away, turning away. Margaret's gaze was burning on the crown of my head. *Tea, tea. We need some tea,* she said, matter of fact, standing and brushing herself down. She vanished into the kitchen, clattering around with the kettle and sugar tin. She returned with two mugs held in one hand, a plate of biscuits in the other. *Might be a bit stale.*

Her look was encouraging enough for me to nibble on a bourbon. I collapsed back against the sofa. I swallowed, inhaled, and said, *you think she's dead.*

Margaret paused, then she shrugged. *Doesn't matter what I think, but what you think.*

I know what I should think, I said. *Except I don't. I can't.*

That's what I thought too, until I didn't. She sighed, soft and sad. *It gets better, Anne. Don't have to believe me – shit, I didn't believe it either. But it does.*

They said that after a certain number of days the chance of my mother being alive were less than. She had been gone for months. Even though I knew Sandman was involved, the suspicion still brought me no closer to an actual answer. Except for the unavoidable feeling that something bad had happened to her; the fleeting possibility breaking through that unfathomable truth. From the suggestion of cruelty in his smile to the thickening grey fog around me. Despite being against my own stubborn belief, even I couldn't ignore those thin and gnarled fingers as they choked the life from my world.

But the crack in that door suddenly slammed shut and locked. I closed my eyes, shook my head, setting down my mug none too gently. *It's getting late.* I kept my eyes down so not to see what I knew would be a reflected sorrow. *You should leave.*

Right, sure. But Margaret hovered at the front door, smiled at me. She squeezed my shoulder, warm through my cardigan. *See you soon.*

My skin tingled from where she'd touched me, a feeling that lingered throughout the evening. And, strangely, a welcome one.

***

Evening drifted into night, but sleep evaded me, rooting me to the floor where dozens of photos were scattered around me.

As soon as I clicked the door shut behind Margaret, I'd found myself itching toward the corner, reaching for the things that had been untouched for months. The knife sliced through the duct tape, the cardboard cracking along the edges. Mould had dampened the leatherette, slicking my fingertips with residue, which it seemed was nothing compared to the inside.

The photos I'd remembered whenever I'd been a young child wanting a peek or as an adult feeling nostalgic: that of grandmothers and cousins, ancestry that spanned three generations; long forgotten holidays to the coast or unsmiling strangers that not even my mother could recall the identity of. They were gone, replaced by my dreams. Dreams of us on that bench eating apples. Our faces smudged, the wet touch. The sensation of another world not my own.

I moved onto the VHS tapes after, sliding them in and hearing the familiar whirring noise. I hoped for the usual static and shuddering picture when the video caught, but only greyed smeared faces of my mother and I stared back at me.

My name being spoken tore apart my smothering thoughts – as soft as a falling feather, its force as devastating as a hurricane.

Something between horror and confusion sunk into me as I watched my mother's journal open. Slowly, deliberately. As I neared, the room seemed to darken and thicken like midnight. I followed each word that appeared on the fluttering page.

He asked me for my dream, the sentence begun, growing more jagged with every letter. *My dream to see my girl again.*

The gasps wrung my lungs wrought, forcing them out until they were short and strained. Sandman had visited her, just as suspected. Sweat gathered at my spine, a cold marsh that slithered up around my throat. Around the borders of my vision the haze pressed in. Furniture disappeared, the walls rotting away, dulling the sharpness to the flat grey. To his plane of existence, damp and frozen and detached.

He reached into my chest and took away my heart. But she came. She came to me. Just like he said.

My dreams are changing.

What's my name? Who am I? What's happening to me?

He's coming for me.

Help me.

He's taking me—

Then, with words that were smoother and almost forced with clarity: *Do not trust Sandman.*

As soon as I touched her handwriting, the rest of my world disappeared with a loud whoosh of warping and dense fog.

My hair whipped over my face, and once I shoved the knotted strands behind my ears, there she was. My mother. Sitting right in front of me, the journal opened up across the floor. Her whole person was smeared grey, like a streak of charcoal across a canvas. As though sensing me, she turned toward me. I choked as her mouth trembled around my name.

Within a blink, she was gone, and I was back in my dimly lit and cluttered living room. The photos, the videos, all were as they once were. No mist or rippling atmosphere. I might've been none the wiser weeks ago, but the underlying unease latched onto me now. A lingering dread that seemed like termites crawling behind the walls, unseen but gnawing away until only dust remained.

Sleep avoided me, not that I wanted it, propped against the sofa still, surrounded by scattered memories and full of inescapable scattered thoughts. (Like my mother. She was scattered too – how much of her was around me?) Sandman would come to me; that I knew from his ever-looming presence. Like when the cold still sunk its teeth into your skin long after you step into warmth.

As expected, he came as dark shadow and pale flesh. The aura around him pulsed as thickly and as intensely as ever.

I staggered to my feet and got as close as I could to him. *Give me back my mother.*

You have her, he said, his inflection snarky and mocking. His breath was like frost over my cheeks. *She's right here with you.*

She was and she was not. A ghost without death.

What matters how you have her, as long as you have her at all? Sandman chuckled, an almost dream-like sigh. *Have her you must – well, what better to give her to you than to take you to her instead?*

His hand slammed into my chest, pulling me forward with an agonising yank of my heart. It pattered in his open palm, like the first time.

My breath hitched along with three beats, weak and sluggish, until the beating stopped, and I passed out with my mother's voice washing over me.

***

Sandman's Loam greeted me with its empty world, a void and infinite stretch of grey. As though trapped within the eye of a storm.

To my horror, neither me nor my mother were the other ones. They crowded around me – at least, what appeared to be, their forms smudged and blending into the backdrop. People who swayed and whispered like the fog submerging them.

The air was stale and chokingly thick, making me cover my mouth with the crook of my elbow. I kept walking, and walking, until time morphed as one long moment. Longer than when I'd stay awake wondering where my mother was, staring out the window at the empty night, waiting for the sleeping pills to kick in. Each step felt like pushing against a wall, the pressure weighing on my chest, intensifying the hollow gaping under my ribcage from my missing heart.

She was even thinner and gaunter than before when I saw her. The ghost, like the rest. But alive. Right here, with me.

Mum! I yelled, because the months of questions and no answers; because she had been with me this whole time, burst out from me. My voice sounded muffled, as though screaming under water. *Mum, it's me! It's Anne!*

The way she moved reminded me of the way netting did when caressed with a breeze, floating and fragile. At me, her face twisted and collapsed.

When she tried to stand, and failed, knees buckling beneath her, I hurried over. Her hand was cold in mine. With a dry hitch in her breath, she asked, *where are we?*

I frowned, suddenly unable to say. The word was on the tip of my tongue. I shook my head. *I don't know.*

You shouldn't be here. My mother studied me. An expression torn, wavering with wretched sadness. *What's your name?* She asked me, stroking my hand.

A long exhale rattled within my chest as I tried to reach out and grab the answer. I'd spoken it only seconds before. (Or was it minutes, hours? My name. What was my name?)

Fear strangled the remaining steady breaths in my throat, feeling my eyes bugging out from their sockets. My hand trembled.

We've been here too long. My mother shook her head, to herself, a correction; *You've been here too long.*

Anne. That was it. My name was Anne. I'd heard someone say it. Saw them. A woman with a soft smile and mud-crusted hands. I told my mother my name.

She broke into a smile, watery and frozen. It then fell. *You need to go, while you still can,* my mother continued. She stood, fast enough to make me flinch. Her hands gripped my shoulders. *You know who you are.* Desperate, gasping. *You have a chance. Please, go.*

I dug my heels into the floor, which felt as though it sunk under me, as she tried to drag me away. *Not without you.*

My mother made a noise between a cry and a sigh. *Darling,* she said, her hand cupping my cheek; it disappeared through me. *He's taken too much of me.*

You're here, I said, desperate and raw and sputtering. *You're right here.*

But I won't be there.

We can make it out. We can go back. I tried to grasp her hand to no avail. *Mum, please.*

She only shook her head and hurried me along. I let her, because the numbing sensation prickling over my body stopped me from doing anything else. We waded through the fog, seemingly with no destination, the stifling grey stretching on and on. Walking, and walking, until finally we grounded to a stop. My mother crouched down and waved her hand through the mist, batting it away to reveal something buried beneath. A photograph, the one that wasn't real, a dream: us, sitting on the bench, eating apples.

How do you have this? It doesn't exist. My fingers dragged through the wet smudging, with they themselves turning faded and faint.

She sighed again. *There was always one thing; there was always this. It takes everything to hold it in my hands. For a small moment like this. For you.* She then placed the photograph into mine, moulding to her movements without protest, scrunching my fingers around the crinkled material. Cold, damp, as much as the air around me, sinking to bone. *You believe gone does not mean dead. Believe now that dead does not mean gone.*

Colour bled into the edges of the photograph, the memory awakening as citrus and sweetness. A sob choked my throat.

And then it all vanished as a pale and gnarled hand folded over mine. Sandman, his breath cold on my neck.

You'll never see your mother again, he whispered, a forked tongue flicking across my ear. *You don't want that, do you, little one?*

I twitched, easing back the slightest inch. My mother's hand overlapped both of ours, and she spoke only to me. *Look at me, darling. Just at me.*

We held gazes, even as an icy feeling sunk into me; even as Sandman pressed in as close as he could go, feeling that razored grin against my cheek, the aura around my shaking body. I closed my eyes to concentrate on what was good, as muted as they were: our laughter that echoed around the park and earned amused looks, the tang-crunch of an apple slice with peanut butter. Our hands linking over the park bench, just because we could. An ease filtered into my once staggered breathing. I finally rested my other hand on top of my mother's.

Sandman growled, an inhuman sound that vibrated over my skull. My answering flinch whipped up my spine, painful and cold.

I gave you your dream, little one, he hissed, harsh with spittle, burning like acid on flesh, *and I took you as mine.*

My chest started to hurt, a breath-stealing feeling as the hollow cavern throbbed with its void. I'd known no agony like it.

He yelled as something else happened. Hands reached through the mist, smudged, and trembling but belonging to many. They laid over Sandman's body, curling around his arms, pressing against his back. Each spot they touched changed, the dull grey brightening to shades of the real world. The warm glow from the sun as it slipped through the curtains, a green that could be from summer grass or waves of an ocean.

Sandman thrashed as his aura diminished, like water dampening smoke to weak and pathetic wisps seeking out the embers.

The rage that came over me scorched away the ache within. I reached out, into Sandman's chest, closing my fist around the heart nestled below his ribs. My heart, wet and beating. As thunderous as a storm ravaging the dead of night.

I yanked it from his being and pushed it into mine. The noise he made was small, a whimper. The air burnt white, and the last thing I felt before being torn away from Sandman's Loam was the faint sensation of my mother kissing my cheek.

***

Dawn settled over me as sombre overcast on waking, bleeding like when the rain would hang on the air during a light shower.

My belongings were still scattered around me: photo albums fanned open; video tapes piled on top of one another by the television. On the mantelpiece the clock ticked. I'd been gone almost thirteen hours. My aching bones and creaky neck made it feel like far longer. As I straightened, my eyes stung – that raw, gritty thickness crusting my lids. Except, once I scrubbed them with my knuckles, the feeling lessened to a bearable itch. I looked down at my mother's journal, still where I'd left it. Her handwriting was gone, the pages blank. The outcome of returning to our own existence. There were handprints indenting the leather from where she'd held it, the paper diverted with her fingertips. An object that caused sadness to catch my breath, the reminder of where she was (was she still within Sandman's Loam, were they all? Could they be elsewhere, where the air was clear?) but also that she had once been with me. In a way still was.

A gentle knocking on the front door eased me from my thoughts. I peeled the netting back again to see Margaret on the doorstep.

Fatigued, I stood and opened the door. She looked at me through matted hair, flattened from the sheeted rain. The sky seemed to strain with sunlight.

Oh, she said, but then she paused, studying me. *You look like you've been—*

I brushed the tears away, shook with an unsteady laugh. I sniffed and asked, *how did your mother die?*

Margaret said nothing. A pause, pensive. *Heart attack.*

I nod, at the ground, to myself. *I don't know how my mother died.*

Anne, she said, all soft and comforting. *Are you okay?* At my gentle shake of my head, she added, *do you want to talk about it?*

Neither of us said anything more, because neither of us needed to. My stepping aside, and her brushing past me, was enough.

Before Nightfall

James Austin McCormick

Fire burnt its way down Anna's flesh, waking her. She sat up, staring at the wards glowing on her arm. Another summons, but to where exactly? In answer to her question an image flashed inside her head, an old, dilapidated church.

She reached for the quarter full bottle of whisky and swigged down the remaining contents. Her flesh continued to burn, as she suspected it might, until she was out the door. She ignored the discomfort, waiting for the alcohol to do its work. She wasn't going anywhere until then.

She watched the wind rattle her run-down apartment's window. Raindrops sparkled briefly in the moonlight, then vanished. Finally, with a great sigh, she flung her legs over the side of the bed and tied back her dark hair. She threw on a t-shirt, jeans, boots, and a long coat and made her way to the door. It was time to find out what the Magus wanted.

***

Anna halted her Oldsmobile Rocket outside the church and made her way through rusted iron gates. She hurried through the numerous puddles of a narrow, cobbled path. Copper plate doors parted as she reached them.

She slipped inside. Rows of candles cast a soft haze over the interior, just enough to make out the outline of someone stood before the alter. Anna made her way down the aisle, shadows sliding by on either side. Whether they were phantoms or just a trick of the light, she had no idea.

'Magus?' she hissed.

The figure turned a fraction. 'Anna.' The voice was male, and sounded as if it came through dry reeds. 'Good of you to come.'

The woman rubbed her arm. 'Yeah, right.'

The figure raised a bony hand. 'Assist me if you would.'

Anna laid a hand under an emaciated arm and helped him towards the pews. They took slow, deliberate steps, sitting themselves on the front benches.

She noticed the open casket just in front of a Corinthian pillar. It was empty. 'Who was he?'

Impossibly blue eyes looked at her.

'A rich man who believed his money could buy his way into heaven.

'And could it?'

A twitch at the corner of the cracked lips suggested amusement. 'I have no idea. I'm merely borrowing the body.'

'Why did you summon me?' Anna asked.

The blue eyes went to the crucified figure of Jesus. 'Tell me, what does that image mean to you?' He snapped his fingers. In response, the candles around the altar flared, lighting up the figure.

The woman shrugged, regarding the tortured form.

'Sacrifice,' she said at last.

Her companion nodded. 'The lamb of God, laying down his life to save humankind.'

Anna shrugged. 'Never quite bought that story.'

'Nevertheless, one can appreciate the selfless act. Something happened four nights ago that reminded me of this. A young man burst past reception at the Plantagenet Club and slit his throat in front of Lord Simmons and his friends in the reading room. He told them he was dying to save them.'

'I'm guessing he knew Simmons.'

The corpse nodded. 'The man was Sam Jacobs, a former barman at the club. Simmons paid him to take part in one of the occult ceremonies they hold from time to time. Paid him quite handsomely it seems. Jacobs is a devout Catholic and has a rule against such things, but, well, he needed the money. He was to act as an avatar allowing Simmons and three of his associates to talk to the deceased.' He gave a stiff wave of an arm. 'A primitive, naive ritual based on the misguided scribblings of that charlatan Crowley.' The sapphire eyes flitted across Christ's tortured form. 'It failed of course, but it did something to Jacobs. Witnesses said he became 'unhinged.'

'Let me guess, Lord shithead and his cronies threw him out onto the streets.'

'They sent him to a sanitorium. But what these esteemed gentlemen didn't know was that Jacobs had been possessed.'

Anna let out a whistle. 'You mean, like with a demon?'

'A very dangerous one. It used him to anchor itself to this realm.'

The woman frowned. 'But didn't Jacobs kill himself?'

'Medics started his heart again in the ambulance. By the time they got him to hospital he was in a coma, but alive. That evening he went missing from the hospital.' The corpse seemed to sigh, but there was little more than a dry rattle in the throat. 'Then the killings began. That same night one of Simmons' associates was found withered and desiccated in his bed. The night after a second. The same again this night.'

'So, just his Lordship left,' Anna quipped. 'I do hope he'll be okay.' The words dripped with sarcasm.

'If the demon does take Simmons, it will have succeeded in destroying all its summoners. It will then gain purchase in this realm, consuming Jacob's innocent soul in the process. It was a noble thing the boy tried to do. In a world of selfishness and cruelty, his actions were pure. I would save him if I could.'

'And you want me to find him?'

'Before nightfall.' He stretched out a withered hand. 'Give me your card, would you?'

Anna did as asked, handing him her private investigator's card. The figure took it, turning it over in bone white fingers, muttering arcane words Anna could not understand. 'Here.'

He handed it back. It was now black, her name and details gone. In their place was a gold symbol which looked very much to Anna like several ornate T's in a ring, their stems all pointing outwards.

'This will serve you in your search.'

He looked upwards, making a motion with a finger, drawing a golden circle in an area of the ceiling above them. Within it, stone and brick vanished, leaving them looking out into the cloudless, early morning sky.

'Almost dawn. The priest will be here soon, nursing a hangover and desperate for a bottle of communion wine.'

Anna stood up. 'I'd best be off, then.'

'I will be with you when you need me.'

The woman gave a grunt and turned to leave.

'One more thing.'

She turned; a quizzical eyebrow raised.

The corpse held out an arm. 'Help me back to the casket, would you?'

***

She didn't get far with the surly, blotchy faced receptionist, nor with the half dozen nurses she harangued. As soon as she mentioned Jacob's name, no-one seemed to want to know. Out of ideas, she started flashing the black card at everyone, including a portly doctor whose breath smelt like battery acid. He pushed her aside, but Anna grabbed his sleeve.

The man scowled at her through thick glasses.

'Security,' he yelled.

A moment later, she felt a powerful hand on her shoulder. She turned to look at a huge, bullet-headed man glaring down at her.

'Get rid of her,' the doctor growled, striding away.

The guard gave a grunt and took her arm. Surprisingly, he didn't lead her towards the exit but rather in the opposite direction, through a private security access door and along a long white corridor.

'Hey, bozo,' Anna demanded, 'where are we going?'

The man didn't answer.

She turned and sent a fist at the man's oversized jaw. To her surprise, the blow actually felled him. She looked at her hand in disbelief. It could only be the Magus' doing. Whatever magic the markings on her flesh were working, one of the side effects was apparently to make her stronger.

The big man gazed up at her, rubbing the side of his face.

'Where the hell did you learn how to punch like that?'

Anna glowered. 'If you don't want another one, tell me where you were taking me.'

The man reached into a pocket and pulled out a black card with gold engraving. It was identical to hers.

'The Magus told me to watch for you. I'm trying to help.'

Anna regarded him. 'So, help. Do you know where Jacobs went?'

The man shook his head, getting warily to his feet. 'No, but I got some footage you're going to want to look at.'

The woman regarded him closely. 'Show me.'

The big man led them to an office with a glass frosted door in a sub-basement. It was a smallish room, an entire wall filled with monitors, each one recording a specific location inside the building.

He snatched a coke can from his desk and took a gulp.

'From here, you can see everything.' He slumped into a high-backed leather chair, leaning forward to hit a couple of controls. 'All kinds of weird shit. This was three days ago.' A recording of a sleeping patient appeared on one of the screens. The guard leaned back, as if about to enjoy a good movie. 'Jacobs was brought in in a coma,' he speeded through some minutes, 'then this happened.'

The patient sat up and very stiffy got off the bed. A nurse sat writing at a nearby desk looked up and started to rise. The patient's eyes opened, revealing crimson fires burning within them. The nurse fell back in her seat, dazed, and confused. She didn't even look up as the patient exited the room.

The guard cut to footage outside. The patient now made his shambling way down the hall. Clad in a surgical gown and trailing tubes from his arm, no-one paid him the least attention.

'It's like he's invisible,' Anna muttered.

'Crazy, right? No-one saw a thing. The suits freaked and told me to wipe the tape.'

'Any idea where he went?'

The guard switched the picture. The screen now showed Jacobs exit the hospital and begin to shamble way down the street.

'That's the last of it.'

'Great,' Anna muttered, 'and I have to find this guy by evening.' She turned to leave.

'So,' the guard asked, 'why are you doing this?'

The woman arched a questioning eyebrow.

'Working for the magician? Me, well I'd be rotting in a prison in Columbia if it wasn't for that guy. What's your reason?'

Anna opened the door. 'Me?' she said, stopping at the doorway. 'I'd be dead.'

***

As she made her way along the street, the wards down her arm begin to itch. The sensation grew stronger the further she went, and she began to suspect she might actually be able to locate the demon in this manner. Yet as she felt herself drawing close, the trail suddenly went cold. The creature someone had sensed her, burying deeper inside its human host, hiding. It knew it was being hunted.

Anna stopped. Her detective instincts, much more than any unnatural sense, told her this was the area. Any further and she'd be moving into more affluent areas. But Jacobs, or rather the creature he was now bonded with, would be wanting to lay low. It was time to ask some questions.

She found just the kind of pub she needed, run down, carpet ruined by cigarette butts and beer foam. A smattering of lost souls, numbing another day's existence, glanced up as she entered. A red-faced barman, no stranger to the optics behind him, leaned against the bar, cleaning a glass.

'Double whisky,' Anna told him.

The barman poured out the drink and handed it to her.

'Is there any kind of shelter around here?' She asked, throwing the drink down in one go.

The man regarded her, a puzzled look on his ruined face.

'You know,' Anna went on, 'like a hostel for homeless, a soup kitchen maybe. Something like that.'

The barman grimaced. 'Hope you can pay for that drink you just threw down your neck.'

'Relax,' his customer told him, laying a twenty down. 'I'm looking for someone. Someone in trouble.

The barman sniffed. 'There's a half-way house just around the corner. Salvation Army started it up, but the council runs it now.'

'That sounds like the place my friend would be. Thanks.' She slid the note across the bar and left.

It took no more than a couple of minutes to find the place. The door was locked, bolted as she'd expected. She hammered on the entrance but saw no movement through the translucent glass. She went round the back, slamming a shoulder against the gate to force her way into the yard. There were scattered chairs and a couple of log tables where residents could meet and eat their meals. It was a bare, grim, desperate little place.

A damaged, useless alarm hung off the wall. Anna slipped a metal pick from her pocket and went to work on the door. It took only moments to work the cylinder lock. As soon as she stepped into the building, she felt it, a cold that didn't quite register on the skin and the faint, unpleasant smell which tainted the mind rather than the nose.

A hallway brought her out to the front of the building, into a reception area. A heavy, leather-bound storregistry lay open on the desk, names scribbled on the pages in various inks. Anna looked a couple of pages over but there was nothing there.

A flicker from an adjoining room caught her eye. She moved towards the open door and peered inside. A TV dominated one wall of a social room. It was on, but the screen showed little more than distorted, writhing figures half glimpsed behind a blizzard of electronic snow.

Two men sat in front of it.

'Hi,' Anna greeted them.

Neither moved. She went closer. Both looked half-starved and severely dehydrated, as if they'd been there for some time.

'I'm looking for Sam Jacobs,' she went on. 'Blond, mid-twenties. You know where he is?'

The two men were like statues, paralysed by an unseen power. Anna crouched down in front of one of them, a younger man with matted red hair straggly beard.

'Can you talk?'

Muscles danced at the sides his jaw. A faint moan escaped his throat as his eyes rolled upwards.

'Upstairs?'

Again, the same moan.

'Thanks.' She went over to a jug of water by the window and brought it back to them. 'Here.' She gave a little to each man in turn, as much as she could without choking them. 'I'll be back to help, I promise.'

She headed upstairs. The stairwell was old, each step creaking as she ascended. The upper floor was in equally poor condition, a frayed and threadbare carpet revealing rotten floorboards. There were three doors ahead of her and as she entered the first, she realised that all the rooms had been knocked into one to form a dormitory. Bunkbeds dominated the walls. Desiccated, withered bodies lay everywhere. Some stared at her with glassy eyes, mouths opened in silent, frozen screams. The demon had drained them, feeding on them as it grew more powerful.

The creature itself was nowhere to be seen. Nevertheless, she could sense its presence. She took a couple of steps forwards, towards the centre of the room. Immediately, the markings on her body began to itch. It couldn't hide itself any longer. It was here, right in front of her. She reached out a hand and felt the force pushing her. She pushed back. The air rippled, disturbing shards of energy which played in the currents.

A sphere revealed itself. Jacobs floated inside like some bizarre foetus. Luminous veins stood out at his temples and ran down the face and neck. His whole body trembled at some impossible frequency.

Anna slammed a palm against the sphere, shouting the man's name.

Eyes opened; luminous red eyes slit down the middle like a serpent.

She reached inside, seizing Jacobs. Burning cold tore through her body, overwhelming her senses. She refused to let go, dragging the man free of the magical cocoon. Jacobs collapsed but she caught him, laying him on one of the bunks.

'Sam,' she said to him, 'can you hear me?'

The eyes turned to her, the crimson fading slightly. Lips parted but he was too weak to talk. Already he seemed to be drifting once more into an unnatural slumber.

'Okay Magus,' Anna muttered. 'I have him.'

Moments later she felt eyes open behind her own as the magician's consciousness flooded into her own.

'See as I see,' a voice told her.

Suddenly, Anna was able to witness the entity inhabiting the man, a writhing mass of tentacles and claws. Slowly, it was kitting itself into Jacob's mortal form.

'Bring him back to himself,' the Magus told her. 'You cannot let him sleep.'

Anna grabbed the man by the shoulders, shaking him. 'Sam,' she yelled. 'You have to fight this thing.'

Drooping eyelids opened. Anna pulled him up into a sitting position.

Jacobs looked around, seeing the corpses. 'I did this?'

'No,' she told him, 'not you. That thing inside you.'

'I didn't mean to hurt anyone.'

'I know. That's why you tried to take your own life. You wanted to stop it. You're a good man, Sam.'

He took her hand. 'What do we do?'

Anna knew that the Magus would be coming, how soon before nightfall, and in what actual form, she had no idea. She squeezed Jacobs' hand. 'We wait,' she told him.

***

She managed to keep him awake and calm. Yet she was also able to witness the demon inside stirring as the autumn sky began to grow darker. Soon, it would leave its host to seek out and consume Summers, before returning to claim Jacobs' flesh as its own. If the Magus was planning to do something, it needed to be very soon.

'Anna.'

Thunder rumbled in the distance. Wind rattled the doors and windows.

'Turn your head,' she warned the man.

No sooner had she uttered the warning than the panes shattered, sending shards of glass flying through the dormitory. Vines dragging moss and stones slithered inside, twisting, moving in accordance with a single will. The mass came together, forming itself into a humanoid form that continually moved and undulated, the vines slithering across it like serpents. A swirling oculus opened in the chest, revealing a sapphire light within. It turned its attention on Jacobs, reaching out an arm. Tendrils extended from the fingers, weaving their way towards him.

'Help me,' Jacobs pleaded.

'It's okay,' Anna reassured him.

The vines wrapped around the terrified man. Anna saw pulses of energy travelling through them, passing through the man himself and attacking the demon within. The Magus was seeking to destroy it like the parasite it was.

The creature thrashed and writhed in protest as its form

began to dissipate and for some moments it seemed as if it would be destroyed. Yet then it began to fight back. Tentacles shot out, ripping into its host's cells, flooding them with its own demonic energy. Jacobs' form began to grow and swell. He rose up, ripping the vines free. Bones cracked, limbs broke and reformed themselves into elongated insectoid appendages. A second pair of arms broke through his ribs. The mouth too shattered, forming into bony mandibles. The transformation took only a moment, but in that short time, Anna realised they'd lost any hope of saving the unfortunate Jacobs.

The demon made flesh, gave a cry of defiance, and leapt towards the intruder. The Magus caught it, throwing it down with such force it crashed through the boards beneath. Anna was knocked off her feet. The demon scrambled back through and swung out at its enemy, sending it crashing against a far wall. Wood and plaster fell from above.

The Magus reached out, shooting veins from its arms, and smothering his enemy. The demon cut through them with its razor fingers and came charging at its enemy. The two opponents engaged in a frenzied exchange of blows, yet the demon was quicker and with its additional limbs began to tear the Magus' avatar to pieces. Anna watched in horror as the form fell in shreds to the ground.

The demon turned fiery eyes on the woman. It took a couple of steps towards her with its segmented, insectoid legs.

She raised a hand. 'Jacobs, you have to fight this thing.'

Yet the creature continued to advance, trapping her into a corner. Mandibles snapped inches from her head.

'Fight it,' she yelled. 'If you don't, it'll take your soul.'

The snapping suddenly ceased. The red eyes faded just a fraction as her words seemed to reach the man inside. Then they flared once more, and the terrible jaws closed on her throat. Anna turned her head to one side, hoping it would be quick.

Yet the attack never came. Instead, a fist of writhing vines exploded out of the top of the skull. Yellow ichor poured from the mouth as the mandibles quivered feebly. The fist withdrew and the demon collapsed in front of her. The physical form destroyed; the demon lost its purchase in the physical world. With her enhanced sight, Anna was able to witness the mass of tentacles and claws seep away, dragged back screaming into the hellish void from whence it came.

Close by, the Magus' form of vines and roots was already re-assembling itself, the arm which had destroyed the demon crawling up the side of the body and re-attaching itself.

'That was close,' Anna sighed.

Then the floor gave way, pulling part of the wall and ceiling beams with it. She felt herself fall. And then there was simply darkness.

***

She awoke to a barren, mountainous landscape, high above the clouds. Before her was an ornate ziggurat-style temple, carved partially into the rock. A biting wind drove her towards it.

'Okay then,' she muttered to herself, moving towards it.

The gilded archway opened as she approached, and as she stepped through, she found herself inside a circular chamber. A huge mosaic pentacle dominated the area. In the centre a robed figure lay atop a platform. Flaming eyes floated above his form, circling slowly.

'Anna.'

She felt a familiar consciousness reaching out to her.

'Magus?' She regarded the form before her. 'Is that you?'

'It is.'

'Where am I?'

'Your body is in hospital. What you're seeing here is my sanctum.

Anna came closer. The lined face was partly hidden by a long beard. 'Are you ... you know?'

'A sleep hex, to keep me from my mortal death, but from this place I can send my spirit anywhere I wish.'

She sensed a presence behind her and turned. She found herself facing the ephemeral form of the Magus. He was younger, the hair and beard still long but now dark. Impossibly blue eyes regarded her.

He smiled. 'I wanted to say goodbye.'

Anna regarded him in surprise. 'I'm free?'

'To live your own life, our deal is done.' The Magus took her hand. 'And now Anna, you have to wake up.'

***

'Remarkable,' a male, authoritative voice cut through the darkness. 'The fall should have been fatal.'

Another voice joined in, a female one. 'X rays showed multiple fractures. But now...well, it's like magic.'

Anna opened an eye a fraction, just enough to see the two speakers, a pretty blond nurse and a white coated doctor who looked like he spent a lot of time on tropical beaches.

'The police are on their way. They want to question her the moment she wakes up.'

The two chatted for some moments, then left to continue their rounds.

Anna sat up. Her body ached, but otherwise she seemed fine. She grabbed her clothes piled up on a wall shelf close by, threw them on and hurried out of the room.

No-one paid her much attention as she made her way down the steps and out through the hospital's exit. As she did so, she began to reflect on the Magus' words, to "live your own life." Yet, she wasn't really sure what that would be. For so long her purpose had been to track down her father's killer. Cancer would have stopped her if the Magus hadn't saved her, placing the markings on her body which drew the mystical energy necessary to fight the disease. After she'd put that piece of dirt away for life, she'd been an agent of the Magus', neglecting almost entirely her own PI business.

Yet now, she was "free." But to do what? Get a mortgage, get married, have kids? She realised only now that none of that interested her. It sounded more like a cage than a life. Even much of her own PI work bored her. Her accountant mother always told her she and her father were alike, hard wired to seek out danger and take risks.

She noticed a pub at the corner and decided she needed a drink. The place was busier than she'd have liked and after fighting her way to the bar, retired to brood in a quiet corner with a double whisky already warming her insides and a pint of lager in her hand.

'You drink because of boredom, don't you?' a voice asked her.

Anna looked up to see an overweight man in a business suit standing by her table. She was about to ask him what the hell it was to him when she noticed the impossibly blue eyes.

'Well, this is a new look for you.' She gestured to the chair opposite.

'A heart attack, I'm afraid,' the man said as he took a seat. 'Finance is a high stress, lonely occupation. No-one will notice for some time.'

'What is it with you and dead bodies?' the woman asked.

'Would you prefer I possessed the living?' He threw a newspaper onto the table. A headline told of the death of Lord Summers from a heart attack.

Anna took a drink of her beer. 'He had it easier than the others.'

The man leaned across the table. 'I heard your thoughts, Anna.'

The woman was silent for some moments. 'How about we make another deal?' she suddenly announced.

Her companion nodded he was listening.

'I continue to work for you.'

'And in return?'

'Magic,' Anna told him. 'I want you to teach me magic. Think how useful I could be to you then.'

The blue eyes widened incredulously. 'Do you have any idea how dangerous that would be?'

'Not really,' she answered. 'But you know what it won't be?'

Her companion shook his head. 'Enlighten me.'

Anna leaned forward, a gleam in her eyes.

'Boring, Magus, it won't be boring.'

Hunger

James Hancock

With penne pasta and tomato chunk vomit flushed away, Chester reached for the mouthwash. After a quick swish, gargle, and spit, he stared at himself in the bathroom mirror: ashen pale, with clammy skin and sunken eyes. He'd always wanted to lose a few stone in weight, but not like this. He looked unwell and he knew it.

'You been sick again?' Came the feeble voice of an old lady from a nearby room. Chester's mother, Patricia, didn't miss a thing.

Chester stuck out a grey tongue. 'Aaaaaah!'

'Chester? Are you...' Patricia's words were cut short as a dry cough took over.

'Coming, Mother!'

Chester rushed from the bathroom and into his mother's bedroom. Patricia was propped up in bed. Thin, liver-spotted skin hugged her hunched skeleton, and long white hair draped over the shoulders of a faded pink nightie. She was a frail stick of a woman: brittle and ready to snap.

Patricia hacked into her hanky, struggling to breathe as she coughed, until Chester eased a glass of water to her lips and doused the tickling fire in her throat. He gently rubbed her back as she relaxed.

'Thank you,' Patricia wheezed and slowly eased back against her pillows.

Chester's eyes fixed on red spots as Patricia folded the hanky and tucked it under the duvet. 'You okay, Mother?'

'I warned you. But did you listen? And now this...' Patricia ran bony fingers across her scalp and pulled away a fistful of white hair. 'See? Not long now.'

Chester shook his head.

'Denial. You stupid boy. When are you going to realise, I'm dying?'

'Don't say that.' Tears welled in Chester's eyes as he sat on the bed and placed a hand on his mother's. 'What can I do?'

'For starters, you can pull yourself together.'

Chester nodded and forced a smile.

'We can't go on like this.' Patricia tapped Chester's hand and looked him in the eyes. 'We need meat. Without it, we're both going to die. Do you understand?'

'Yes, Mother. I understand, Mother.' Chester fought back the tears.

'Good. Because it has been ten weeks. Ten long weeks, and if we carry on the way we are, I won't see eleven. Am I getting through to you, Chester?' Patricia held open the blood-specked hanky. 'We must have protein. I don't care where you get it, but we must have it. Now...' Patricia's words were interrupted by another coughing attack, and as she brought the hanky back to her lips, Chester rubbed her back and reached for her glass of water.

'Yes, Mother.

***

Like most nights, Chester was tormented with vivid dreams of flashing lights and ambulance crews. His mother was a rag doll, thrown from gurney to hospital bed, taken from him by men in uniforms. He screamed for them to let him see her, but whenever he pulled back the curtain, there were always more men standing in his way. Then he heard her coughing, and he felt his throat tighten and breathing became a struggle.

They had found themselves in the lion's den, in the heart of the virus, terrified and alone.

His nightmare always ended with death rolling in like a shadowy fog, separating him from his mother.

***

Chester stared at the kitchen worktop. Four tins of tomatoes and the last two packets of spaghetti. The cupboards were bare, the fridge and freezer were empty, and the remaining dry goods and canned food were polished off weeks ago.

When the pandemic hit, Chester took lockdown seriously. He stocked up and locked up. Quarantine was the only way to stay safe. The only way to ensure survival. Leaving home and risking a visit to the shops was out of the question. Unfortunately, most of the food was consumed within the first four weeks, and no matter how hard he tried, Chester couldn't secure a delivery of fresh supplies. Even with his elderly mother in the high-risk category, he found the home delivery slots were always unavailable. Supermarkets, farms, and other online grocery suppliers were constantly booked up.

They had been eating canned tomatoes and pasta for breakfast, lunch, and dinner for weeks.

***

The cramps had become unbearable, and Chester was dry vomiting now. His mother was worse; her gums had started to bleed, and she had spells of unconsciousness. Chester prayed for help, but his pleas fell unanswered. He fought against it, but his mother's words interrupted every thought, sending shooting pains through his skull... *'We must have meat! We must have meat! We must have meat!'*

Mrs Finnegan, the old lady next door, was the obvious choice. Chester didn't have to travel far. Covering his mouth with a scarf, he popped around to her back garden and tapped on the door with a claw hammer. She was a friendly, less cautious soul, and opened the door without question. The incident was quick but brutal. A full force blow to the forehead, her eyes rolled, and she collapsed. As she lay twitching, Chester stepped over her and cracked two more strikes to her temple. The ordeal was over.

Chester lifted Mrs Finnegan onto his shoulders, propped her against the garden fence, and rolled her over into his back garden. Dragging her to his patio, he stripped her naked, poured two bottles of antiseptic liquid over her leathery skin, and washed her down with a hose.

The log saw in Chester's shed had hardly seen action over the years but was proving invaluable. He'd never had the need for a power saw but regretted not owning one now. Doing it by hand was hard work. He cut through fat and muscle and used the claw hammer to snap stubborn bone. The head was awkward; the saw's silver teeth moved with long and slow precision until Chester was able to twist and pull it free. When he'd finished, Chester burnt Mrs Finnegan's clothes in his garden chiminea and hosed the evidence off the patio slabs and onto the pea shingle border.

Chester reminisced about the days of his mother's mincer. A

metal beast that would bolt onto the worktop and operate with a handle. He had no such device now and was forced to cut fist-sized pieces of flesh, and using the cheese grater, apply elbow grease until the task was complete. Grating chunks of meat was slow and painful. Blister-inducing.

Most of Mrs Finnegan was worked, bagged, and in the fridge or freezer by the time the cheese grater broke. A week's worth of meat broth, steak, and proper bolognaise.

***

Chester placed a plate of fried liver on Patricia's lap, and cutting bite-sized pieces, forked some into his mother's mouth. She chewed and swallowed.

'Did Doctor Richardson send any bacon or onions?'

'No, Mother. He just got a butcher he knows to give us some pork and liver.'

'Pity. Liver tastes much better with bacon and onions.' Patricia took another mouthful.

'I'll see what I can do, Mother.' Chester gave her a reassuring smile.

'And see if he can deliver fresh meat. The first few steaks were lovely, but this tastes like that frozen packet stuff.'

Chester gently eased another small piece of liver into his mother's mouth. 'It's definitely not packet meat, Mother. I had to freeze some to keep it good…'

'Well, see if this butcher will send half as much but twice as often, so it is fresh.' Patricia scowled as she reluctantly chewed another mouthful.

'Yes, Mother.'

***

Excluding nuts and berries, the caveman diet was giving

Chester a newfound strength. To please his mother, he'd prepared meals in a variety of ways, but was still limited in what he could do. At the end of the day, meat was meat. Thinly sliced tongue and kidney, sautéed in belly fat and drizzled with a heart and eyeball broth. The foods which couldn't be disguised weren't going to waste. He had defrosted a leg, slow roasted it all morning, and was now frying it in a pan to give it the crisp edge his mother loved, when there was a knock at the front door.

Chester peeked through the curtains. Rachel, Mrs Finnegan's daughter, was peering through his letterbox. 'Patricia! Chester! Can you hear me?' She knocked again.

Chester considered ignoring her until she went, but part of him needed the interaction. He'd always liked Rachel. His mother had said she'd be a good match for him. She was late forties now, so only a few years younger than Chester. She'd been divorced for five years, no kids, and Chester always did like a shapely brunette. Wrapping a scarf around his nose and mouth, he answered the door.

'Oh, Chester. Thank God.' Rachel pulled a mask from her coat pocket. 'May I come in?' There was concern in her tone. Chester knew why.

'Err, Mum's not well, so I...' Chester looked over his shoulder, fishing for an excuse. Why did she need to come in? He was sweating, twitching, and needed to calm down.

'I just need five minutes. Please, Chester.' Rachel's face was hidden behind the mask, but Chester could see the desperation in her eyes.

'Okay.' Chester stepped back and Rachel shut the front door behind her.

Rachel removed her coat and Chester stared at her; aside from his mother and Mrs Finnegan, she was the first person he'd seen up close in months. Naturally tanned skin, enhanced by a white blouse and thin silver necklace. The blouse was low cut and Chester found his gaze fixed to her cleavage. Had she dressed this way for him? Did she think the same thoughts?

'Chester?' Rachel awaited a reply to something.

'I'm sorry.' Chester forced a nervous smile. Thanks to the scarf, she couldn't see it. 'Mother's not been well. I'm terribly worried.'

'My mother, Chester. I was asking about my mother. Have you seen her?'

Chester shook his head. He dare not speak. Rachel was intelligent. She would hear something in the tone of his voice. She would tell there was something… *Beep! Beep! Beep!* The kitchen smoke alarm interrupted Chester's thoughts.

'One moment. Sorry!' He dashed into the kitchen and turned off the gas hob. The hunk of Mrs Finnegan's thigh spat fat as Chester lifted the pan onto the draining board.

'What is that?' Rachel stood in the kitchen doorway.

'Oh, err, a leg of lamb.' Chester couldn't help himself. He glanced at the very thing he didn't want to draw attention to. Knee, lower leg, shin and foot, all recently separated from the "leg of lamb" and sat to defrost on the worktop. Rachel followed his eyes and looked straight at it.

As her expression changed from curiosity to realisation, Chester reached for the nearest thing to hand. 'It's not what it looks like,' he said, and slammed the frying pan into the side of Rachel's head.

***

Three days ago, Chester's Amazon order had arrived and was now being used for the first time. 50cm cable ties had bound Rachel's hands and feet, gaffer tape wrapped around her mouth and back of head, and the living room carpet had been covered with a clear polythene sheet. Rachel was on her belly when she came around and immediately started to moan and wriggle, sliding across the polythene inch by inch, screaming a muffled groan which Chester droned out, turning up the TV's news channel.

'Keep still!' Chester straddled Rachel, untucked the blouse from her skirt, and lined up the tip of a butcher's knife against the skin of her lower back. Rachel tried to jerk her body free from Chester, but his weight held her fast.

'I need to get this right. Please, Rachel.' Chester put the knife's tip to Rachel's spine, and timing it with her left to right wriggling, he thumped the flat of his hand onto the knife's handle. The point cracked into the spine. Rachel's eyes went wide with terror, and she muffle-screamed into her gag.

'No, the legs are still moving.' Chester moved the knife's tip and felt the vertebrae with his fingers. 'The spine is a wonderful thing, and if I can hit the lumber region just right...' Chester thumped down again, and Rachel went silent. 'Perfect!'

***

'You missed the PM's speech. Percentages have gone right down. Things are finally on the up,' Chester whispered into Rachel's ear.

She was on her back, skirt removed, legs wiped with disinfectant, and cable ties pulled tight around the lower thighs and below the knees. Rachel took deep breaths through flared nostrils and stared up at the ceiling as tears dropped on the polythene sheet.

'I don't have any anaesthetic, but you shouldn't need it. You won't feel a thing.' Placing his saw over the line he'd marked out with a blue sharpie; Chester pulled the saw's teeth back across the flesh of Rachel's upper shin. Blood flowed, her legs didn't move, but she screamed. The TV showed vaccine stations in full swing and a queue of people being interviewed as Chester pulled and pushed the saw back and forth through bone. Rachel couldn't feel a thing, but she screamed anyway. She knew what was happening. Even the TV couldn't drown out the sound of her leg being amputated.

***

'What was all the banging about?' Patricia asked, as Chester brought her a plate of medium rare steak.

'I was just doing a bit of DIY, Mother.'

'Don't waste your time. Your father was never any good at that sort of thing, and I expect you're the same.'

'Yes, Mother.'

'You were in the garden, using that hose again. And you left the television on. It was too loud. I called out, but you couldn't hear me.'

'Sorry, Mother.' Chester cut the steak into small pieces.

'It took all my strength to get to the window, but you couldn't hear me banging on it.' Patricia chewed some meat and Chester wiped bloody juice from the corners of her mouth.

'It won't happen again, Mother.'

'Good. And get some vegetables. I've eaten nothing but pork for two weeks.'

'Yes, Mother.'

***

'We could have been great together, you know?' Chester leaned against the kitchen worktop.

Rachel was sitting on a dining room chair, cable tied in place, and tape covering her mouth. Pieces of torn bed sheet were wrapped around stumps below her knees, dried with browny-red and yellowing stains. The wounds were raw. The wounds were angry.

'We still could.' Chester smiled. 'It's up to you.'

Rachel stared through vacant eyes. Trauma had taken over and she had dissociated herself from the here and now.

'Something to think about.' Chester opened the oven door and pulled out a baking tray. As the foil was carefully unwrapped, Rachel's eyes turned to the freshly cooked meat.

***

The latest Amazon order was unboxed and ready for close inspection: Teppanyaki grill, glass lid wok, 7-inch meat cleaver, boning knife, meat tenderiser hammer, six cans of oil spray, and a case of 18 herbs and spices for seasoning meat. And then came a knock on the door.

With his mind set in the world of culinary experimentation, Chester answered the front door without thought.

'Good evening, sir. I'm PC McCammon, and this is PC Garret.' The male policeman held his ID card out from a chain around his neck, with his female colleague stepping up beside him and holding hers out for Chester to see.

PC Garret talked into her shoulder walkie-talkie, 'We're at the neighbour's house now.'

Chester remained silent, his mind racing.

'May we come inside, sir? We'd like to ask you a few questions.' PC McCammon tucked his ID back under his shirt.

'Err, the virus. We're in isolation, and my mother isn't well. She's on the vulnerable...'

'That's okay, sir, we have masks.' PC McCammon pulled a black cloth mask from his pocket. 'We'll be as quick as we can and let you get back to your evening.' He placed the mask's elastic over his ears and covered his nose and mouth. PC Garret followed suit.

'Yes, okay. The place is a bit of a mess at the moment.' Chester moved aside and the two police constables walked past him. He took a deep breath and shut his front door.

'We just need to ask a few questions about your neighbour, sir. Have you seen or heard from her recently?' PC Garret's eyes fixed firmly on Chester's.

PC McCammon had walked over to get a better look at the line of recently unpacked Amazon goods. Chester shook his head.

'When was the last time you spoke?' PC Garret's questions had knocked the air out of Chester. All he could think about was his kitchen and the things that might be found if his new guests decided to open a few doors and drawers.

'I stay indoors. Keep myself to myself.' Chester watched PC Garret's attention turn to his hands. He was nervously wringing them together. He stopped and put them by his side.

'Quite a selection of cookware you've got here.' PC McCammon looked at Chester. His eyes burnt into him. He knew something. He had to know something. Chester just nodded. He was aware that he'd started sweating again and didn't know where to look. Was his breathing right? Was there a smell coming from the kitchen?

'Are you alone in the house, sir?' PC Garret brought Chester back to reality.

'Err, yes. I mean, no. My mother is upstairs.' Chester nodded and smiled, trying to make himself look relaxed but was aware he was making things worse.

'Oh, good. Would you mind if we had a quick word with her?' PC McCammon walked past Chester, towards the stairs.

Chester held up a hand to object, but PC Garret interrupted, 'Our records have you as Mr Chester Maddox, is that correct, sir?'

Chester nodded, about to speak...

'And your mother is Patricia Maddox. Am I correct?'

Chester nodded, watching PC McCammon walk out of view, heading upstairs to question his mother. He could feel the air become hot and thick, the room beginning to move, and he sat down on the sofa.

'Are you feeling okay, sir?' PC Garret stepped closer to Chester and crouched to his level.

Chester shook his head, grabbed the nearby meat cleaver, and brought it down onto PC Garret's head. A swift and unexpected attack had taken her off guard, the hatchet was buried deep, and PC Garret collapsed onto the living room floor.

Chester stood up, ripped the cleaver free with a forceful tug, and quickly followed after PC McCammon.

'Excuse me, Mr Policeman!' Chester picked up the pace and caught up with PC McCammon at the top of the stairs.

***

'What was all that thumping and banging?' Patricia was out of bed and trying to steady herself when Chester entered the bedroom.

'It's okay, Mother. We had a couple of visitors, but they've gone now.' Chester took his mother by the arm and steadied her back onto the bed.

'It sounded like someone had fallen down the stairs. Is everything okay?'

'Yes, Mother.' Chester helped her back into bed. 'Everything is just fine.'

***

The boning knife and cleaver proved useful tools, and great hunks of flesh were wrapped in cling film and jammed into Chester's fridge and freezer. Uniforms burnt, patio hosed clean, and Chester's mother convinced the noise was the continued effort of his DIY project, Chester set three large plates on the kitchen worktop. They would be perfect for displaying a surprise for any future guests. Chester knew they'd be coming soon.

***

'These chunks are too big,' Patricia snapped. 'And there are hairs on the plate.'

Chester stood by his mother's bedroom window, looking at their street and waiting.

'And still no vegetables. We need vegetables, Chester. Do you know how difficult it is to have a bowel movement when all you eat is meat?' Patricia scowled and dropped the fork onto her plate. 'Are you listening to me?'

'Sorry, Mother.' Chester watched as three police cars turned into his street, lights flashing.

'Sorry, Mother,' Patricia mocked. 'Sorry isn't good enough.'

Chester smiled. 'Some people are here, Mother.'

'What do you mean, "people"?'

Chester drew the boning knife from the belt behind his back. 'People who want to take you from me.'

'What are you talking about? And what are you doing with that?'

The police lights flickered across the window behind Chester, and car doors slammed. Chester looked at the blade of his knife and then at his mother's throat.

'They won't take you from me, Mother.'

***

Rachel, PC McCammon, and PC Garret were discovered in the kitchen. Three severed heads lined up on plates, and a bloody saw and meat cleaver on the worktop beside them. Meat and wrapped organs were packed into the fridge, freezer, and scattered in scraps across the sink and draining board. Chester and Patricia were found in bed, locked in each other's arms, with their bloody throats cut from ear to ear.

The police report kept the gruesome details to a minimum, and the death toll was recorded.

Six more virus-related deaths.

The Dream Dealer's Cigarette and the Stars

Phoebe Barr

He moves like a ghost. Slipping through the steaming, rain-slick streets, he makes no noise; too light, maybe, with his wasted limbs, the bones of his ribs and hips and elbows sticking far out from his skin. Although, to him each footfall feels like an avalanche. This body made of burning clay, its constant, vicious contact with the ground, feels like it should echo through the whole city.

Yet it's silent. He's silent, hands shoved in his pockets, wet, rough-cut hair clinging to his hollow cheeks, teeth gritted against a cold no one else can feel, a cold that emanates from his starving body. No one sees him, or cares to.

***

'Here,' he calls through the dream dealer's window.

The word comes out hoarse, like fabric worn threadbare, but he doesn't doubt the dealer will hear. He climbs over the sill onto the kitchen counter, splattering mud around the sink before he kicks his boots off, wincing at the mess – filthy, why is he always getting everything filthy? Then he drops down and shoves the window shut behind him. It's warmer in here, and light, and dry (a cheap space heater is still better than the unallayed wind of late October, flickering fluorescents on peeling wallpaper are better than burned-out streetlights, the leaky drip-drip of the faucet is better than the buckets pouring from the sky outside).

'Up front,' the dealer calls back, words slurred – no surprise in them, despite the late hour.

He pads in ragged socks from the kitchen to a larger room, one with a battered table and a mould-smelling sofa unfolded into a bed. The dream dealer is sprawled against a pillow in a haze of bluish smoke, a multi-coloured cigarette at their lips. Its bright orange end contrasts with the rest of them, grey sweater over white button-up, pale khaki pants, rumpled black curls.

Outside smells like gasoline and piss. By contrast, the smell of the cigarette is heavenly – like a full moon on a forest, burning.

The dream dealer grins up at him, slow and devilish. Their grey eyes gleam like sharpened blades. They take a last drag, blow out a blue-green-purple stream of smoke, swing their legs over the side of the bed, and saunter toward the table.

The way they move shouldn't be possible. Legs too elastic, arms lengthening and shortening, as they wobble in and out of existence. They shouldn't be able to make the movement look so elegant, either. He pushes that thought away.

'Think I've almost got it right this time,' they say.

The dealer opens a box full of crushed leaves, fine iridescent powders, liquids in tiny jars. They cut paper from a roll and pinch each ingredient onto it, obeying a calculus only they understand. Their hands are swift, deft, gentle, the pads of their fingers caressing the paper, their knuckles crooked at precise angles which he has long since memorized. Traces of glowing dust cling to their cuticles, the creases between finger and thumb. Is it obvious he's staring?

They use the end of their own cigarette to light his, then stroll back to offer it to him.

He snatches at it, clumsy, greedy. Shouldn't be greedy – it's beyond generous of the dream dealer to give him anything, seeing as he can't pay. The dealer only lets him keep slinking back here for free dreams because his request is like a challenge to them. The dream dealer bills themself as an expert on sensations – sunlight on skin, snow on eyelashes, money piled on palms. Flesh on flesh (the absolute last thing he wants, hell, it makes his skin crawl to think about it). But how can they make someone feel like a God?

He breathes the dream-smoke in. At first, it's just warm, his first real warmth in days. Fire in his mouth, his lungs, the shivering empty cavern of the rest of him. He doesn't want to exhale. But when he does, the smoke crowds and solidifies around him, onto his eyes, into his ears, and it transports him.

Weightlessness first. The real kind, which he can't achieve outside this room no matter how little he eats – dissolving the hellish pressure of sheet and sofa and floor and earth. He shuts his eyes. He's expanding, ascending, and this dingy room doesn't contain him, he's here and outside and underground and in the sky all at once.

He opens his eyes and through the smoke he sees the world spread beneath him. The city from a bird's eye, stinking streets resolved into coloured-pencil strokes, fickle streetlights like scattered stars. Then real stars around him, ones invisible from the ground. Pinpricks, then constellations, then vast brilliant swaths of them that sweep out the darkness, open up all of space and time for him again.

'This is good,' he croaks. 'This is – yeah, it's the best one yet. Hell, how do you do this?'

The dream dealer's not impressed. 'But?'

But. He drags again, longer, tries to fill his lungs even more. 'Well, the sense of space, it's there. And time. But not the sense of power. The feeling like you could create a world in a second.' Or destroy one, he doesn't say, not wanting to frighten the dream dealer. Though destruction was always at his fingertips, too.

'Shit,' says the dream dealer. 'Man, how am I supposed to do formless but omnipotent?'

'Omnipotent's going a little far.'

'You're impossible.' But excitement warms their voice. He hears them scribble something on their rolling paper. 'All right, tell me more about the power. Is it a desire to create? To make things happen?'

'Not a desire.' He shakes his head. The dream is strengthening around him, colour bursting through the starscape. 'You don't want anything when you're a God. You don't need to.'

'I'll think about it. Maybe modify what I give for physical strength...'

He leans his head back and exhales a nebula. It sings as it swirls around him. He abandons his hunched perch on the bed and lies down, splayed over the rough cotton blanket, arms spread wide.

He hears the precise way the dream dealer sucks in air through their teeth. He tenses again. This position, he realizes, has spread his jacket too, exposing the undershirt that clings half-heartedly to his torso.

'Hey,' says the dream dealer, voice gone quiet. 'Listen, man –'

'I'm fine,' he says, too quick, and sits up again.

'I have food here – if you're hungry –'

'I'm not hungry.' He tries to laugh; one dry ha is all he manages. 'Please. Just because I fell doesn't mean I'm all human now. I don't need – I'm fine.'

They want to say something else. He tastes the unsaid words on the other side of the stars. They're spoiling his trip – making him remember his body, collapsing him back into this claustrophobic form, and didn't he come here to forget that?

'How about I fix that faucet leak for you?' he says, to change the subject. 'When I come down. I bet it's eating up your water bill, right?'

The silence drags on a second longer. The dream dealer's deciding whether to take the bait. Sometimes they get it into their head to push harder, interrogate his constant claim that he doesn't need food when his body is thinning before their eyes.

But not tonight. They sigh instead. 'Yeah, that would be nice.'

'Least I can do in exchange for this.' He knows the dream dealer can't fix the faucet themself – not corporeal enough to push pipes around. Crushed leaves and paper are all they can manage most of the time. And a being that gains life from other people's desires doesn't have the bandwidth to manipulate things that they're the only one to use. Still, everyone needs water. Even he hasn't had the strength to deny himself water.

'Thanks, man,' says the dream dealer, still quiet. He hears them take a final drag on their cigarette, a sound he could place from the other end of the universe.

***

Faucet fixed, he's out on the streets again. The rain has faded to mist. It's four in the morning, and he wonders about finding somewhere to sleep. There are some dive bars around here that might turn a blind eye to him ordering a drink or three and then hunkering down at a back table until sunrise. But they'll give him a bill first.

There's a shelter somewhere in this maze of blocks, but if he goes there, they'll feed him. They'll force him to eat before anything else, worried otherwise he'll die in their care. He passed by the place once, weeks ago now, and he still remembers smelling their mass-produced chicken noodle soup and ham sandwiches. Revolting, the stench of salty broth, chunks of hot snow-white meat, squishy bread slimed with mustard. He almost threw up, passing by it then, had to rush to an alleyway and lean against a stone wall and breathe hard through his mouth to let it pass. Not least because a part of his weak-willed stomach still begged him for it then.

He walks until his knees ache. That's been happening faster these days, too, and he's noticed bruises blooming below his kneecaps on the rare occasions he has to check. Finally, he wanders into a city block-sized park where a few scraggly trees poke apologetically up from the ground. A bone-dry fountain hunkers in the centre of the meagre green. He collapses on the ground with his back to it, stretches out his legs, and stares at the inky sky. No stars.

Despite the cold setting in – real cold this time – he slips toward sleep. He's exhausted; last night he didn't stop to rest at all, just wove relentlessly through the streets, trying to calm his shuddering limbs and outpace his racing thoughts. He's a little calmer after visiting the dream dealer. If he sleeps now, he'll dream of what the dealer gave him. He relaxes as dark folds over him.

Then, what feels like seconds later, he blinks; the horizon is paling, and someone's beside him.

A woman. Coat, duffel bag, ripped cardboard sign clutched in wind-chapped fingers. Mother of two, anything helps. And a plastic coffee cup with a faded fast-food label.

'Have you been here long?' she asks him.

'On the streets?' His voice rasps: he needs to drink something soon. 'Three months.'

'What happened?'

What should he tell her? All sorts of beings inhabit this city, but a fallen God is still something rare. What are the chances she'll believe this scrawny, sunken-eyed thing could ever have wielded power over the universe? He grimaces and chooses a vague version of the truth. 'Criminal background.'

'Oh.' The mother of two fidgets. He looks young enough, with his oversized jacket, that maybe she thought his parents threw him out or something.

'What about you?' he says, before she can ask what he did.

She rubs her hands together and blows on them.

'My husband got us into some bad debt. Children went into foster care.'

'Where's he now?'

'Prison.' The corners of her mouth turn down. 'On domestic violence charges.'

'Oh, shit – I'm so sorry.'

'It happens.' She looks down and away.

And it does happen, he knows. He's seen it in bars, through windows at night, the white-hot violent streak that runs through the human bloodstream. He considers feeling a savage gladness that the man who hurt her is in jail. But that's no good either; he's spent his share of nights in jail for public drunkenness, and he knows what happens there. Guards get to take their own violent streak out on the prisoners. Cruelty for cruelty, abuse for abuse.

He doesn't want to sleep anymore. His nerves buzz and he needs to move, though his legs still ache. But before he rises, he pulls his gloves off. She'll make better use of them.

'Here,' he mutters. 'Try and stay warm.'

Before the mother of two can say anything, he's dropped the gloves in her lap, jumped to his feet, and sped away.

Once a dried-out desperate town sent a prayer up to him for rain, and he spent a week fashioning them a thunderstorm. They sang his praises for generations after that. Sent acolytes streaming to his temples.

Where are those temples now? Have they been smashed, his name erased from the stone walls, when the temple-keepers learned what he did? Did they ever learn? Or are the temples still full even now, acolytes still burning incense and singing, chanting, praying to a God they don't know can't hear them anymore?

***

He spends the day slipping between bars, drinking, and sneaking out before the bill. By his third stop, he's resolved for the hundredth time not to go back to the dream dealer. All he does is take from them. Use them to grasp at what he's deservedly lost. And aside from his addiction to that torturous memory, there's a new desire growing in him – he's known it for weeks now, though he won't say it aloud. It's obscene. Has he really not learned his lesson? The memory of skin on skin, flushed, hot, flashes through him with the force of a blow. Was his first crime really not enough to kill that savage human hunger?

The sun sets. Tonight, he tries a low-traffic subway stop, but staff kick him out at midnight. They try sympathetic words first, then, when they realize he's drunk, haul him up by his armpits and support him up the stairs and out the door.

He finds his fourth bar and nurses a brandy for as long as he can stay unnoticed. At three in the morning, he's back on the streets, forcing down the urge to throw up until it's background noise again, and he walks, walks, walks until sunrise.

Hell. He used to go from one end of the galaxy to the other in the time it took to blink. He used to jump from star to star like a grasshopper. He used to make a game of being in as many places at once as he could think of.

Four days pass before he goes to see the dream dealer again.

**

He's just coming down from his high, working to unclog the dream dealer's toilet, half-hidden by the bathroom door as the dream dealer rolls a pack of cigarettes from another customer. She's an athlete, clad in leggings and sporting a severe buzz cut, and she wants to dream of winning a marathon. On her first puff, her face breaks into a dazzling smile.

'Gods, you're good,' she says to the dealer. 'I can feel my shoes on the track.'

The dealer smiles back. They look a little more substantial as they hand her the pack, as she pays and leaves, still smoking; a wish granted, a purpose fulfilled.

'Regular of yours?' he asks, leaning away from the toilet.

'Oh, yeah.' The dealer's already rolling a cigarette for themself; they don't smoke around their other customers, but with him, they hardly stop. 'I get a lot of that kind. Athletes, theatrical types, people who compete.'

'What if they never get their dream? When does it stop working?'

'Never, if I'm doing my job right.'

He raises his eyebrows. 'What, so if that woman never gets first place in a marathon, will she still be here in twenty years, buying these cigarettes off you?'

'Why not?' The dealer shrugs. 'If she keeps wanting them.'

'But it's just a delusion.'

'No, no, there's a difference between dreams and delusions.' This is an old line of conversation between them, and the dealer loves to philosophize about it. 'These people know what I'm selling them isn't real life. It's not about deluding yourself, it's about the act of imagination. You have to be able to imagine things.'

He turns and sits on the bathroom floor, leans for a moment against the toilet seat. He sees the dream dealer in profile from here; the sunlight catches and combs through their curls from behind, but their face is in mild shadow, their eyelashes thin threads of darkness against their skin. Then from below comes the bright point of light that's the end of their cigarette. It illuminates their jaw, throwing a harsher shadow of their nose onto their forehead. Their eyes glow orange with the cigarette, then crimson, then indigo.

'Is that what it's like, to be made of desires?' he asks. 'Desire being the only thing that keeps you alive, and the only thing you can offer people. The only thing that makes you real?'

They turn to look at him. Their eyes bore past the haze. 'Is that so bad?'

He remembers what it was to have infinite power at his fingertips. The power to give people dreams would still be better than the nothingness he is now, but what can it mean in the long run? The dreams the dealer has given him, aren't they only a temporary comfort, a glimpse of the past, during his long run down toward worm food?

'Well,' he says, 'I guess you don't mind it.'

And the dream dealer laughs. Their face tilts back just a little, and the sun melds with the cigarette, bathing their face in light for a moment. 'No, yeah, I don't mind it. There's lots of bright spots.'

***

But there are worse customers. There's a sobbing man who's there on his next visit, asking for visions of the wife who left him. At the first puff, he stops crying and starts screaming, calling whatever vision he sees a traitor and a slut and promising to punish her.

The dream dealer patiently rolls out the entire pack of cigarettes, one by one, ignoring the shouts. They're audible for a long time descending down the stairs.

'Hell,' he says, when the husband is gone. 'How often do you get that type?'

'Often enough.' The dealer scowls as they sweep their leavings off the table, then goes right to mixing a blend for themself.

'Why do you let people buy that shit off you?'

'What can I do? It's what they want.'

'Don't you have the option to refuse?'

'I…' They sigh. 'It's not that simple. Any person I refuse, I get a little less real. I need to save my refusals for when it counts.' They roll the cigarette tight. 'I save them for the ones who come in here to dream about peeling people's skin off or setting them on fire.'

'Fucking hell.' He tries to imagine running on people's dreams and being face-to-face with someone, having your space crowded up by someone who dreams like that.

'It comes with the territory.'

'Why are humans so terrible?'

They take a long drag of their cigarette, and after a moment their shoulders relax. 'Oh well, they're not all bad. Plenty of them, you know, come in here wanting to dream about their friends, or watch their kids be born a second time, or just imagine someone they used to know being happy. It's sweet.'

- 252 -

'Sure, maybe they can be sweet. But then in the next second they're terrible again.'

'So they're not all one or the other. Isn't that true for Gods too?'

'No, it isn't.' He scowls. 'We choose the way we want to be and stay that way.' He has no right to use the word we.

They shrug. 'I know I'm biased. If it weren't for humans and their desires, I wouldn't exist at all. If it weren't for them all being packed into this city, kicking up the dust of all their needs and wants and fantasies, I'd just be a glimmer in a field somewhere. So, I could be biased – but I think I know them better than you do.'

The objection he's going to make dies on his tongue. It's too close to the unspoken pain. He turns his attention back to his high, and the dream dealer, seeing he's not interested in talking further, returns to their work.

In fact, he's known humanity more intimately than the dream dealer guesses. He used to take on human form when he was still a God. He used to be fascinated by it, the constant movement of atoms and breathing of cells and crawling of bacteria that makes up a living thing. The burning ferocity of human desire, whether for colossal banquets of food or barrels of aged wine or for the sweat and spit and lips and flesh of another body.

But he can't talk about any of that. Those are nightmares, now, not dreams.

***

Sometimes the dream dealer is sly.

'I've got something new,' they say as they light his cigarette. 'For power, like you said. But with a blend like this I recommend people eat something alongside it.'

He avoids their eyes. 'No, thanks.'

'It isn't personal, man, I'm trying to get the blend right.' As though they're worried he's declining to be polite.

'I'm not hungry. I trust your blend – give it to me without food.'

There's a beat of silence. They waver in front of him, a beam of grubby sunlight shining through their chest, turning their sweater cloudily transparent.

'I really,' they say, 'I really think it would be better.'

He presses his lips together. He folds his arms over his chest and looks away.

'Man, we don't have to talk about it, but you look like –'

'I know what I look like,' he snaps. 'You don't have to remind me.'

'Well, I'm worried about you, all right.'

'Well, you're not pretty enough to be anyone's mother, let alone mine.'

They huff. 'Fuck you, dude.'

'Fuck yourself.' He knows he's being cruel, and he knows why, and that knowledge hurts in the deep space within him where hunger should be. He's snapping at the dream dealer, his only friend in this Gods-forsaken city, because his head feels like it's being struck with mallets, because that weak sunbeam is burning his eyes like a brand, because his insides are writhing and rioting, because he's starving, starving, starving. And he, everything that he is, or everything that's left of him, anyway, is at the mercy of this pathetic body.

He needs to get hold of himself.

'I'm sorry,' he forces out, after a long silence.

The dream dealer just stands there, wavering.

For a split second, in his guilt, he considers placating the dream dealer. One token bite of food, and that'll prove they don't need to worry about him. Then they can have an easy conversation about divinity or philosophy or maybe he can just take the dream dealer's laundry downstairs and laze around until it's done. For a second it sounds easy. How bad could a bite be? The thought is dizzying in the way it refigures everything in his mind.

But that lasts only a second before the real prospect of eating lands hard on his tongue, and he has to press his hands together over his mouth to keep from retching. He passes the movement off as a gesture of frustration, and sighs.

'No,' says the dream dealer at last. 'You're right. You don't have to justify yourself to me – I'm just a dream anyway. Here, smoke.'

He takes the cigarette and smokes. The weightlessness sets in at once, hunger fading to nothing.

'Thank you,' he whispers. 'Thank you for this. It's all I have.'

'No problem.' Their eyes are black with the light of the cigarette taken away.

***

Then there's the night he goes to sleep and doesn't wake up.

He managed to find a good spot, for once. A sturdy old bus shelter with a long, unbroken bench. He's exhausted, sober but shaking uncontrollably, feet swollen and blistered, eyes unable to focus on anything more than thirty feet away.

He doesn't dream, except of a vague sinking, black water closing over his head. Like he's breaching the depths of the ocean. He's aware of a long time passing, aware of the world lightening around him, of noise in his ears, but the water muffles it all. He feels impervious. This is the opposite of being a God, really – falling instead of rising, feeling the ever-exponential increase of his own helplessness. But it's the same tranquillity, and he welcomes it.

Many cycles of light and dark pass before something cracks through his sleep that he can't ignore.

'Fuck!'

A fist strikes his jaw. First the bright burst of pain, then the jerk as his head snaps back, and his eyes burst open.

He's upright on swaying feet. Noonday sun glares into his eyes. There's a hand gripping his arm, stopping him from tipping over. The buzz-cut woman's face is inches away.

He sees movement from the corner of his eye. At first, he thinks he's really going blind, the other person beside the athlete looks so faint, but no – he recognizes this figure, though he's never seen it outside in direct sunlight, though it looks more like the memory of a ghost than a person.

'Are you awake?' demands the dream dealer.

'I...' his tongue feels like wool in his mouth, sticking to the roof and the sides. 'I'm, mmm...'

The athlete pulls out a water bottle and squeezes water into his mouth. It soaks his tongue and trickles down his throat, healing for a moment, then choking. He coughs.

'Come on,' the dream dealer snaps. 'My place isn't far.'

He's hazily aware of the athlete dragging him down the street, of the dream dealer hovering beside him, sidestepping toward their destination, their eyes never leaving him. They seem like a half-erased spray painting on the walls of the buildings they pass, or an impression of the light of passing cars, thrown around in the exhaust fumes.

Somehow, he's pulled inside, pulled up the stairs, deposited on the dream dealer's couch. Somehow the athlete is dismissed. And then the silence sets in, as the dream dealer stands above him, eyes gouging into his, arms folded over an insubstantial chest.

He fixes his gaze down at his knees, which show, bruised and swollen, through his torn jeans.

'What the hell,' says the dream dealer at last.

He breathes deep. It hurts. 'What the hell what?'

'Don't give me that shit. You need to eat something, right

now.'

'I don't want to.'

'You're dying!' They swing their fist down on the table. It passes straight through. With a cry of frustration, they drag their fingers through their hair. 'Gods, have you looked at yourself? Your lips are blue, you've got bruises under your eyes, your hair's falling out – I don't know what kind of God shit you think you're on, but if you want to stay the fuck alive then you need to –'

'I don't want to!'

There. It's out in the open now, the thing they've been dancing around since the day the dream dealer first noticed his body was thinning.

'I know what's happening to me, all right,' he says. 'I'm not an idiot. I know what I'm doing.'

The dream dealer's fists don't unclench. But when they speak again, their voice is changed; it's small, broken. 'Why –'

'I can't live like this.' He looks back down. He can't look into those bottomless eyes while he says these things. But what's the use in hiding them now? He knows he's on the brink. He knows if the dream dealer will leave him alone, it'll be over soon.

'I can't live like this,' he continues. 'Being made of dirt. It's all just – just hunger and pain. I don't want –'

'For fuck's sake.' The dream dealer sits beside them on the couch; the cushion doesn't depress beneath them. 'Of course, being human is all hunger and pain for you. You aren't eating. If you'd just –'

'No, no, you don't get it.' He pressed his palms over his eyes. 'Eating doesn't help. This body, it's always decaying. I can feel it happening, every hour and minute, every time my heart beats, it's always just demanding more and more. It's violence. Every day a human body lives is earned with

- 257 -

violence. Consuming and burning. It's not worth it.'

The dream dealer exhales.

'You're too hard on them,' they say at last. 'You always have been. I don't understand why you can't see any of the good in them.'

He raises his eyes to the ceiling. This argument never gets them anywhere.

'You could be happy as a human, if you let yourself,' the dream dealer continues. 'You could find other things to dream about. Ask me, man, I could show you what it feels like to win a race – or to swim in a hot spring on a mountain – or to make a sculpture, a painting – or to make love, like humans do –'

'I know what that feels like already.'

The dream dealer opens their mouth, then shuts it again.

Oh, that was far too close. With his mind already swimming, those words, make love like humans do, bring the picture back to him far too clearly – flesh beneath his hands, between his lips and teeth, the dip of a neck, the curve of an earlobe – bright against his eyelids, throbbing on his skin like he's feeling it all over again –

He clenches his teeth and waits for the urge to retch to pass.

'I don't need you to try and show me the pleasures of the world,' he says. 'They're worse than the pain. I don't want them.'

'And you want…'

'You know what I want.'

That silence descends on them again. What more is there to say? There's nothing the dream dealer can offer him. They did their best to replicate the feeling of being a God, but they never quite managed it. They're too bound to humanity. In the end, they can't help him any more than anyone else in this world.

Then the dream dealer speaks. 'Do you want to know what I want?'

The question startles him. He takes his hands from his eyes. The dream dealer looks terribly vulnerable, for a moment – knees folded awkwardly on the sofa's edge, hands still in fists, but trembling, eyes in their lap. The greasy light shining through them seems cruel, suddenly.

'I make dreams for myself, too,' they say. 'Do you want to see one?'

'You…' He swallows. 'You want to show me?'

The dream dealer stands, their limbs wavering as they always do, and crosses to the table. They mix slowly, carefully, pausing to flex their fingers whenever something falls through them.

The cigarette flares red and green when it's ready. The dream dealer's eyes ignite like fire from coals. They take a long drag. They blow out smoke that sparks and glitters in the low light.

Then they come to him and press the cigarette into his hand.

He squeezes it tight. That the dream dealer is trusting him with such a thing feels momentous. He feels unworthy of it – who is he, after all, but another human who takes up the dream dealer's time with demands? But he can't refuse. He can't deny the dream dealer, whose hands are deft and tender and fragile and so beautiful, who knows nothing but giving, day in and day out. How can he deny them anything?

He smokes.

It doesn't feel like any of his own dreams. There's no weightlessness, no expansion. He shuts his eyes and, rather than sensation slipping away, it floods toward him – and at first he wants to flinch, wants to throw the cigarette away, but he manages to keep it still. He can endure it, this once.

The first familiar thing he feels is warmth.

His body has been burning since the beginning, but this isn't the same. It's a softer warmth in his veins, less like an inferno and more like a spring bubbling from deep underground. His blood rivers through him bright and clear. His heart drums instead of throbbing as it pushes those rivers along their course. He itches to move. His legs, which don't ache at the knees and calves and heels, beg him to walk or run or dance. He's full. And this sensation is new too, though he remembers eating, vaguely, from the other times he took human shape. The fire in him then was insatiable. He thought he could have eaten a continent, drunk an ocean. Now the fullness stretches at his stomach a little, discovering his edges, his limits. It's human fullness.

Sight is next. The red and green of the smoke clarifies into a bright image. It's the city, the streets he knows, but the dingy buildings are changed – hung with string lights and streamers, the sills and the patches of grass around the sidewalk dusted with snow. The sky is black, but the street is so bright that the snow still gleams. And people are everywhere – bundled up in hats and gloves, carrying steaming drinks, cheeks red, calling out greetings to each other. A holiday festival.

Then scent. The street is closed to traffic, and the stink of gas fumes has given way to aromas floating from dozens of little vendor tents crowded everywhere. Aromas of hot food and drink. Instead of sickening, they're enticing, spinning pleasantly through his brain like the fumes of a dream.

The dream dealer stands beside him. He expected to be seeing through the dealer's eyes, but instead he's still himself – almost unrecognizable, though, when he looks down at his hands and chest. His jeans and shirt and jacket are freshly laundered and smell clean. And they're snug around his waist, his limbs, not hanging off jutting bones. He's himself, only fed.

The dream dealer isn't unchanged either. They're solid against the street, limbs not wobbling, and their shadow is stark on the ground. Their sweater is maroon instead of grey, their coat and hat a pale blue.

In the dream there's no explanation. The dream dealer smiles at him. They join hands, their fingers intertwine – his warm, theirs solid – and they walk down the street together.

Sound. The street is full of laughter and music. A guitarist seated on a stool in the snow waves him and the dream dealer over, and she coaxes them to let her teach them a few chords each. The dream dealer can only manage two; he manages none. They laugh at their own and each other's attempts. Eventually the guitarist offers them a hot, spicy drink spiked with rum, saying they're good sports.

Taste. Taste. The drink is unlike any alcohol he's ever had. He thought at least he knew what being drunk felt like, but when he's full like this, it's freer, lighter, less like numbness and more like euphoria. Floating on the feeling, he and the dream dealer drift toward another tent and buy little fried arepas, hot sweet cheese and crispy dough, and share them both. It's only a few bites, but he's already full anyway, he knows that he's eaten well for days and weeks.

The dream dealer's lips taste like rum and arepas and snow and dreaming smoke. They kiss him, he kisses them, as naturally as if they've done it a thousand times. It's easy.

Then, little by little, the sensations dull. This part does feel familiar – collapsing back into his ruined body, after having been larger. He feels how the hunger seeps back into him. The weariness. He feels how the thought of food, which for one shining moment felt warm and bright and natural, sours again.

He sits on the couch, eyes on the dream dealer. As the butt of the cigarette falls from his lips, he's aware that his mouth is hanging open.

The dream dealer has rolled their own cigarette. They were dreaming along with him. Now, staring at him, their eyes still glow red and green, that whole festival street still shining there. The banks of snow are just visible, sparkling, a couple of unshed tears.

He can't find names for any of the emotions swirling within him – because there's something that wants to cry out with joy, the part of him that's been staring at the dream dealer's hands and wanting, and how can that be? How can he let any part of him consider this a good thing? Oh, he has to run, he has to cut his way out of this apartment and never return, he's brought destruction upon someone else, and he's liable to pursue something he can never have if he stays here longer.

'You,' says the dream dealer. 'I want –'

'No,' he says, panicking. 'No, no.' He stumbles up from the couch.

Overtop of the terror, rage coalesces like a storm cloud. The dream dealer doesn't know him, damn it. How can they make themself a dream like this? What are they trying to do, showing it to him? They haven't even bothered to ask why he was cast out. Not once. How can they be so stupid?

'I need to go,' he says. He bolts for the door. Doesn't look back for a last glance at the dream dealer's face. He knows the tears will still be in their eyes.

Why did he accept that dream? He was so close to the end, to acceptance, and now everything's been stirred up again, the dream dealer is trying to keep him trapped in hell here, for a minute he was actually drawn to the idea, what is wrong with him?

He stumbles out into the street. No festival here, but night has fallen; rush hour has passed, there's no crowd to struggle through.

By instinct his legs carry him toward the nearest bar. His worn-through boots crack against the pavement like thunder as he half-runs down the street. He has to stop almost immediately, a stitch deep in his side – too weak to run. He coughs as he limps toward his destination. He shivers, and he has no idea anymore if it's really cold or if it's only him.

But when he reaches the bar's flickering neon sign, when he

crawls in and sits at a corner of the bar like he's used to doing, suddenly the idea of drinking turns his stomach too. If he drinks now, he'll remember what drinking felt like in the dream. What it felt like when he was healthy. This feels like ingesting poison by comparison.

He needs to drink something, though. He needs to knock the anger and the fear and the shame out of his mind. He needs to black out instead of sleep – because if he sleeps, he knows he'll dream of that festival again, knows that festival will haunt every minute of any sleep he gets for the rest of his life.

'Scotch,' he mutters to the bartender.

The same phrases and images keep flashing back through his mind, like bits of debris in a tornado, a little more torn apart each time. The dream dealer wants him. He should have gone through with it one of the hundred times he resolved to leave them alone forever, and he didn't, and now he's found one more person to hurt before his death. Why is he so selfish? Why is he such a curse?

A glass of scotch appears in front of him. He looks at it and his stomach rebels. But he forces his hand around it anyway, tips it back like it's fighting him, and chokes down a sip, then a second, before he has to shove it away again. (With that much effort he could have choked down a piece of food. In fact, he could choke down a hundred pieces of food that way, and stop starving, and sleep a full night in the dream dealer's bed and feel the way he did in that dream. He could go back right now and do it, the dream dealer would welcome him, they'd offer everything they have to him, little as it is.)

Except he doesn't want that, damn it. That's nothing but a foreign dream the dealer has implanted into his mind. Shuddering, he pitches from his seat and staggers toward the bathroom. He pulls on the door – locked.

'There's a line,' grunts someone on the other side of the door. 'I'm already waiting.'

He looks up with the fury already funnelling, hands already in useless fists. The man is a full three inches taller than him, broad-shouldered, bearded. He doesn't care; if he can't itch to dance or to laugh, he itches to fight instead. 'Fuck you.'

The giant raises his eyebrows. 'Hell's wrong with you?'

'You have no idea who you're talking to.' Stupid, empty thing to say, but heedless human instinct guides him. 'You're a baby. Fucking baby. I could have fucked your great-great-grandfather. I could have stopped you ever being born.'

'You're drunk.' The giant turns his eyes back toward the bathroom door.

'You think I'm kidding?' Fuck it, fuck it. He'll be cruel. He's already eyes-deep in filth – why not sink even lower? 'You think your miserable little life means anything to me? You think any of your lives mean anything?'

The giant's eyes snap back to him when he lurches forward and shoves him. He hardly expected to be able to move the giant, but with this boiling hot rage inside him he's found some reserve of force. The giant reels and catches himself. He pulls back his fist.

The giant holds still and catches his punch. Large fingers close around his wrist so tight he wonders if it's going to snap.

But when he raises his eyes to the giant's, expecting fury that mirrors his own, it's absent. The giant's brows are drawn together, but they're concerned, not angry.

'You don't look so good,' he says. 'What's the matter with you?'

He tugs on his arm. The giant releases him, and he stumbles backward, panting.

The giant's eyes flick down over him, then widen.

'Gods, what happened to you?'

No, this isn't right. This is supposed to be a fight. He feels the urge to kick and pound and battle in his own blood, why is the giant trying to talk to him? Why is he holding up his hands now, palms out, half a surrender and half a plea?

The bathroom door opens. Someone else peers around the door. 'What's going on out here?'

'Nothing,' says the giant. 'Except this guy needs help.'

He has no words. The swirling in his gut has only one potential outlet, and he knows what's coming as the two sips of scotch come crawling back up his throat. He bolts past the man who was in the bathroom before, slams the door behind him, sinks to his knees by the toilet, and vomits.

At first it's the scotch. Soon after that, bile. But he doesn't stop vomiting until well after it's all transformed into blood.

When his insides at last let him rest, he kneels on the tile floor and stares blankly at the crimson water.

A knock on the door. 'Hey, uh – can I come in?'

It's the giant's voice. He's too exhausted to keep trying to be angry, so he lets out an affirmative grunt instead. It comes out more like a groan.

The door eases open. The giant's eyes slide from him to the bloody toilet. His brows draw together again, like before.

'Sorry,' he says. 'Look, I don't know you, at all, and I don't make a habit of getting in other people's business. But I –' his voice cracks; he clears his throat. 'I get the feeling you might be trying to kill yourself.'

Silence. He doesn't deny it.

'And you don't know me,' the giant continues. 'So this doesn't matter, whatever, but I ought to tell you that I lost my best friend that way.' His head bows, his eyes on the floor. 'I think he did the same thing you're doing. Stopped eating and just drank. I watched it happen, and I didn't know what to do.'

He stares at the giant. He just stares because he has no way to respond. He's had no preparation for this kind of interaction.

The Gods choose what they are, and their moods, their emotions, can't sway them. Everything a God does is well-thought-out and rational. He can't imagine a God responding to an insult and a thrown punch with this much fumbling kindness, this laying himself bare to try and stop the downward spiral of a single mortal he doesn't even know.

If the dream dealer were here – and his eyes start to burn, because he knows just what the dream dealer would say.

'Anyway,' the giant mutters. 'If you need help, I'm here, that's all. If there's anything I can do, if you need somewhere to stay…'

'I killed one of my acolytes.'

The words are out of his mouth before he realizes what he's saying. He feels so wrung-out, so weak, that he can't help what spills out of him now. Scotch, then bile, then blood, then truth.

The giant looks at him with troubled eyes. When he offers nothing else, the giant retreats, mumbling that his offer stands, then returning him to privacy.

He rises unsteadily to his feet. His eyes still burn. He totters through the door, back into the bar, then out onto the street. He starts down the sidewalk, tracing the only route he knows better than the route to the bar.

It's so quiet. Too late for cars. The streetlights flicker: one goes out, leaving a puddle of shadow in its wake. He walks through it without stopping. This whole street is full of darkened minds, each one dreaming something – maybe terrible or maybe beautiful, but certainly impossible.

And then he screams. 'I killed one of my acolytes!'

The call echoes, bounces from building to building, reverberates down the street and up it, acolytes, acolytes, acolytes. He stops and waits while the street vibrates around him like the inside of a drum.

'I killed one of my acolytes!' This time louder. His lungs burn with the strain of screaming. 'I killed one of my acolytes!'

A third-story window cracks open. A woman in pyjamas leans out. 'Will you shut up down there? Some of us are trying to sleep!'

That's all, and then the window shuts again.

He starts to laugh. All of this, for a moment, strikes him as so absurd that he can't believe he hasn't been laughing this whole time. He stops, leans heavy against the side of a building, holds his stomach as laughter steals his breath.

Then the burning in his eyes intensifies, and the laughter turns to sobs – sobs that wrack his whole ruined body, so he thinks they'll split his brittle ribs open.

Oh, Gods, he still remembers seeing the acolyte's corpse. The flesh cold and stiffening. Mouth lolling open. Blood pooling into his eyes, dripping from one nostril, flecking on his lips. Bare chest stained blue and purple, just beneath the skin, evidence of sudden haemorrhage.

He weeps for a long, long time.

***

The sky is going pale in the east when he approaches the dream dealer's apartment. They yank open the door just seconds after he rings. They're framed in weak light, a silhouette against his fading vision.

'I'm hungry,' he says, and collapses.

***

Chicken fried rice is what the dream dealer has in their little refrigerator. They heat it up in a battered microwave, and the box burns his fingers when he wraps his hands around it. The first greasy bite burns his tongue. He swallows without chewing. As it scalds his chest on the way down, he starts to cough. He forces himself to breathe in around the burning, around his hammering heart. He counts the seconds. After fifteen, it's gone down.

'All right?' says the dream dealer tentatively, hovering above.

He nods and takes another bite onto the flimsy plastic fork. Sweat breaks out on his skin. He shudders as he swallows, coughs again, lets it burn, breathes deeply when it settles into him. He lets the nausea roll over him like a tide and just tries to hold himself still, to keep it all inside him.

'If it'll help,' says the dream dealer, 'I can make you a dream.'

He shuts his eyes. His first thought is the weightlessness he's been chasing for months, the shadow of divine recollection. He can hardly believe how unappealing it suddenly sounds. It was never more than the crudest approximation, after all. His second thought is the festival – the fullness, the warmth, the music.

He looks at the dream dealer, but his eyes slide away again before he can speak. 'Can I... can I have one of yours?'

The dream dealer releases a heavy, staccato breath, as though they've been hit in the stomach. They're silent for a long time. Then comes the sound of a box opening, and seconds later, a hand that has rarely ever felt so substantial presses a cigarette into his fingers. The hand even contains traces of warmth, like the shadow of blood pumping under the skin, evidence of a heartbeat.

'You can have as many as you want,' the dream dealer says. 'You can have them all.'

This time the dream is daylight, it's spring, the city's meagre trees are bursting into limited but enthusiastic bloom and a crowd is forming around an ice-cream vendor. The dream dealer gets chocolate soft-serve, and he gets an ice cream sandwich. The ice cream melts all over both their hands. The dream dealer takes him by the wrist and, grinning, licks a line of sticky white drip from his thumb. He grins back.

Then he takes advantage of his hand's position to stroke their cheek, brush his fingertips along the underside of their jaw. They shut their eyes. It's so easy.

***

The process is messy. At first, he can't eat more than a few bites of anything at a time. The dream dealer brings him simple food – bread and butter, apple slices, eggs, cheese, grapes. He discharges a hot, foul-smelling slurry every few hours for the first several days. He feels like someone's taking steel wool to his rusted insides, flushing, and rinsing him out with acid.

The dealer is patient. They hurry their customers in and out, they delay appointments, and they stay with him. They wrap their arm around his shoulders as he sits clutching his stomach and groaning. They roll him cigarette after cigarette; they give him dozens of dreams, all in dazzling detail. Movies they watch together in packed theatres, their hands brushing over popcorn bowls. Amusement parks, Ferris wheel rides that fling them high into the sky. Bars that host drag performances at two in the morning, where he and the dream dealer, drunk and roaring with laughter, toast the queens and toast each other over and over again.

He never really understood the dream dealer's love of humanity before. It's overpowering in these dreams. It's so strong that, despite himself, despite how this city has always been grey streets and cold benches and dirt and darkness to him, he finds himself falling in love with it.

Despite their loss of business, the dream dealer grows more substantial every day. Every day the grocery bags they bring back from the store are heavier. By the time a week's gone by, their shadow is as dark as his. By the second week they're helping him up, holding him, when he feels too weak to stand on his own.

***

The day they venture out of the apartment together is the day he tells the dream dealer the truth.

Walking isn't as painful anymore. He's been off his feet for a month, and the bruises on his knees have receded, the blisters on his heels and soles faded away. The sunlight hurts his eyes, but it's a good kind of ache. He's aware that he's been in dimness too long. He shuts his eyes and tilts his head up toward it, letting it warm his eyelids.

The dream dealer tugs him along. Incredible, how real they look even out here in the sun, how easily they pull him forward. He understands why, by now, though they haven't spoken about it. That's why he has to tell the truth.

Fifteen minutes later they're seated in a secluded corner of a little café, by a window where the sun streams in. They both have steaming mugs of tea, and a plate of dates stuffed with almond paste and pistachios sits between them. He nibbles at a date, cataloguing the tastes: sweet, rich, nutty. The tea is a blend of cream and spice.

'Listen,' he says.

The dream dealer's eyes stay on him. Their grey has started to deepen into hazel. Through the steam from the mug at their lips, those eyes are warm.

He lays his hands on the table.

'Listen,' he says. 'I need to tell you why I fell.'

The dream dealer nods. They set the tea down. They've been waiting for this, he knows; never pushing him into anything, but waiting, still, to be trusted.

He pitches sideways into the explanation. 'I need to tell you because I know you want... something physical. I know you have those dreams too.' He looks down at his hands, examining his cuticles. 'And I – I would. With you.'

The dream dealer's exhale is just audible. They reach forward.

He flinches. 'Wait.'

They pull away again.

'There was an acolyte. One of the ones who lit candles and chanted prayers for me at night, while the rest of the temple was asleep.' He gnaws his lip. 'I... got to like him. So one night I took a human form and came down to talk to him.'

The dream dealer nods. Everyone's heard, in a vague way, that sometimes the Gods take human form. The temple-keepers were ecstatic when they learned their temple had been blessed with such a visitation – they all stayed up every night for the next week, trying to catch a glimpse of him too. But he would only appear when the acolyte came alone.

'He was nice to talk to,' he says. 'Funny, and clever, and not intimidated the way mortals sometimes are. He taught me so much.' He takes a breath, working to dispel the lump in his throat. 'About being human. He's how I learned why humans shave their faces, and put metal in their ears, and why they need shoes.'

He clenches his fists. 'We were friends. It wasn't even like we were in love. He dreamed of falling in love one day, you know. I didn't fuck him because I loved him – we did it for fun, because I'd never tried it, because he thought it'd be funny to show me how. And –' he presses his fists to his forehead. He's shaking again. 'I didn't know I still had divine power in that form. That it would have the same effect on mortals if I got too close to them. And – and he didn't realize what was happening until it was already –' His words speed up. 'And then I tried to lose my body, I tried to get back into my divine state so I could heal him, but I was panicking, all right, I'd never seen someone dying in front of me, and then it was over so fast –'

He cuts himself off, teeth gritted, breath shallow.

The dream dealer is still. For the briefest space of time, he's terrified that they'll push back their chair in disgust and flee when they realize what he's just confessed.

The killing of a mortal is the highest divine crime. What he did disqualifies him from ever having charge over another temple, ever commanding another acolyte's respect. He was cast down not twelve hours after he confessed. He never even saw what happened to the acolyte, what the other temple-keepers did when they found his body.

But the dream dealer doesn't turn away. They sigh, and then they reach out a second time, hand on his arm.

He flinches again, but not as badly. He doesn't draw away from the touch. He accepts the warm pressure of their hand, which he wants so desperately, which he would never have had the audacity to ask for, but which the dream dealer has always been offering. For a moment he lets himself forget how little he deserves it.

'Drink your tea,' the dream dealer says, and there's heartbreaking compassion in their voice. 'And eat. You need it.'

***

'What if I hurt you?'

The dream dealer draws him down onto the unfolded bed. The red-orange light of the setting sun drapes over them, turning their skin to glowing gold. Their lips are a gravity well, pulling him in toward them over and over. He can't get enough of the feel of them. They taste just like they do in dreams, the lingering smoke of their last cigarette mixed with what they've eaten, and no combination has ever been more intoxicating.

'You won't hurt me,' they breathe, between kisses.

They're unafraid, but anxiety still buzzes over him despite the eager heat rising from within. 'I wasn't trying to hurt him, either.'

The dream dealer shakes their head. Their fingers are at his belt buckle. 'You were a God then.'

'I know.'

'Man, how many times do you have to almost die before you realize what being human means?' They pull his belt open, his jeans open, they grin their devilish grin when he moans above them. 'You're human now. And you can do this, like humans do, and it won't hurt.'

'How do you –'

'I know you.' They reach one hand up to run through his hair, and then their fingers tighten, pulling him down again, dragging their lips back together. 'I know you, man.'

He grabs the hand in his hair and pulls it to his lips. He kisses the dream dealer's knuckles hard. They're so warm, so real, so alive. They've become that way because of him – he understands that now, he's starting to understand the whole strange shape of human desire, so much more complex than he thought. The dream dealer gives people their desires for a fee, and that sustains them. But they come alive when they're desired themself. When the transactions, the business of paper cigarettes and paper bills, concludes, and all that's left is this trembling, glowing thing that's held between his lips and theirs, held in the tight space where they end, and he begins.

He thinks he could make them real for a thousand years with how he hungers for them.

***

Hot lips, heavy kisses, fluttering eyelashes, bodies that push and pull. He remembers the sensation well enough. But with the acolyte he felt powerful, divine – felt the capacity, at any moment, to create a world or destroy one. He felt the whole universe spinning around his sweat-damp frame, surrounding them. Now, even as he pushes inside the dream dealer, he feels utterly defenceless. This petty thumping heart nearly gave out a month ago. His hair falls into his eyes, and he remembers nearly going blind. The dream dealer's hands stroke the skin over his ribs, and as he shudders, he remembers how they've seen these ribs stark and exposed, a testament to his starvation.

He knows how fragile this body is, and he feels inclined to beg the dream dealer to be gentle with it. He lets them set the pace, in the end. He's carried along on their tide.

There is no power here, either terrible or beautiful. The stars are far, far away, and they're silent, cold, unmoved. It's only in a tiny, dim, dingy apartment in the midst of a dreaming city where two feeble human beings can taste the beginning of joy.

Authors Biographies

J.M. Faulkner
J.M. Faulkner teaches English in the Czech Republic, the perfect place to steep himself in a tumultuous history that fuels his curiosity. His darker writings have appeared in venues such Cosmic Horror Monthly, Eerie River and Nosetouch Press; his sunnier work has appeared in Solarpunk Magazine.

His debut novella, Her Being Toward Death, is forthcoming from Grendel Press. Find out more on jmfaulkner.com.

Caleb James K.
Caleb James K. hails from Washington, Pennsylvania. When he's not lifting heavy things or drinking mid-shelf whiskey, he's talking to other creatives as the host of the Drunken Pen Writing Podcast. You can find some of his forthcoming and recent works in The Sirens Call, PA Bards, Strange Days Zine, miniMAG, Diabolic Press Issue One, and HorrorScope Volumes 3 & 4.

R.P. Serin

R.P. Serin was born in 1981. He lives in Shropshire, UK with his wife and two children and has worked in the NHS as an Operating Department Practitioner for over 15 years. In 2018, he graduated from the Open University with a 1st class Honours Degree in History and is an Affiliate Writer with the Horror Writers Association.

His work has previously been published in Nightmares of Strangers Vol II, Dream of Shadows Anthology, Paranormal Magazine, Horrified Ezine, and elsewhere. He was diagnosed with Autism in 2019.

Brett O'Reilly

Roulette Croupier. Carny. Professional Fundraiser. These are a few of the titles Brett O'Reilly has held before adding Author to the list.

Brett lives in Surrey, British Columbia, Canada, with his wife, children, and feline Lord of the House, Joey Bojangles. Brett's hobbies include golf, pickleball, paddleboarding, boardgames, and watching horror movies, none of which he seems to ever have time for. Writing. Always writing.

Karen Heuler

Karen Heuler's stories have appeared in over 120 literary and speculative magazines and anthologies, from Asimov's to Conjunctions to Fantasy & Science Fiction. Her most recent novel is The Splendid City (Angry Robot Books), a political satire about a state that secedes from the U.S. and a cat with a gun, and her latest short-story collection is A Slice of the Dark from Fairwood Press. Find her on Facebook, at what we used to call Twitter, and at www.karenheuler.com.

Gregory Glanz

Greg has spent a lifetime pursuing creative writing and

storytelling. He has a passion for the hidden tale, the ignored subject, the absurd. He has had a number of short stories published in genres from realism to fantasy and science fiction, as well as cross genres such as magical realism. He is a homebrewer and biking enthusiast. Surprisingly, they go exceedingly well together as more and more microbrews chase thirsty bicyclists across city trails. In his spare time, he loves to travel through the villages of Ireland and document rural, generational Irish pubs in the series, 'A Proper Pint' (https://www.aproperpintfilm.com/). His book, 'In Human Shadow,' was released last fall by Nordic Press.

Scott Harper
Scott Harper is the author of numerous speculative fiction collections, including Anton the Undying and Lethal Lords and Ladies of the Night. His fantastic tales have appeared in Space and Time Magazine, Weirdbook, and Best New Vampire Tales. He lives in Southern California with his wife and son. You can follow him on social media and his website Scottharpermacabremaestro.com.

Rachel Searcey
Rachel lives in the Florida panhandle with her husband, two children, and two cats (1 black, 1 torti). She's bi-racial— Indian and white— and grew up in Texas. She has recently ventured into prose after over two decades of producing indie horror films. Her work has been published in Cosmic Horror Monthly, Diet Milk Magazine, Flash Point SF, Aphotic Realm, Pyre Magazine, and various anthologies. To view Rachel's films and news on published works, visit www.agirlandhergoldfish.com.

K.A. Tutin
K. A. Tutin resides in Surrey, England, where she writes dark

and strange speculative fiction. Her work can be found in Kaleidotrope, Lamplight, and elsewhere. Find her at mskatutin.com.

James Austin McCormick
James is a college lecturer from Manchester, England and has been writing speculative fiction (science fiction, horror and fantasy) for almost three decades. The biggest influences on James as a writer, he would say, are H. P. Lovecraft, Robert E. Howard, Frank Herbert and Clive Barker.

To date James has been fortunate enough to have had several short stories and novellas included in various anthologies as well as some short novels published by Class Act Books. For James writing is all about escapism; the more he can create his world, the more he enjoys it.

You can find most of James's published work on ISFB at: https://www.isfdb.org/cgi-bin/ea.cgi?195589

James Hancock
James Hancock is a writer/screenwriter who specialises in bizarre comedy, thriller, horror, sci-fi and twisted fairy tales. He takes readers down strange and seldom trodden paths, often dark, and always with a twist or two along the way. A few of his short screenplays have been made into films, his stories read on podcasts, and he has been published in several print magazines, online, and in anthology books. He lives in England with his wife, two daughters, and a bunch of pets he insisted his girls could NOT have.
Website: jameshancockauthor.com

Phoebe Barr
Phoebe Barr is a young queer writer focusing on character-driven narratives and exploring surreal, dark, and supernatural themes in her work. Her short fiction has previously appeared

in The Spectre Review, a magazine focused on horror and ghost stories.

Printed in Great Britain
by Amazon

50262227R00158